ChangelingPress.com

Arcane Kiss (Arcane Talents)
An Arcane Talents Novel
Angela Knight

Arcane Kiss (Arcane Talents)
An Arcane Talents Novel
Angela Knight

ISBN: 978-1-60521-811-3

Publisher:
Changeling Press LLC
315 N. Centre St.
Martinsburg, WV 25404
ChangelingPress.com

Printed in the U.S.A.

Editor: Margaret Riley
Cover Artist: Angela Knight

The individual stories in this anthology have been previously released in E-Book format.

Table of Contents

Chapter One

The tiger bounded toward him in a blur of striped fur and powerful muscle. Kurt Briggs braced himself as the big cat reared to thump huge paws down on his shoulders. Somehow he managed not to fall on his ass, though eight feet of cat made an awkward dance partner. Rumbling, the beast touched a cool, damp nose to Kurt's.

"Hi to you, too, Stoli." Kurt dug his fingers in thick reddish gold fur to give his Familiar a scratch.

Golden eyes narrowed in feline ecstasy and Stoli chuffed a greeting. The tiger dropped to all fours again, and turned toward the lake with a flick of his striped tail. Kurt strolled after him across the thick grass.

Through the trees ahead Kurt spotted the flickering glint of afternoon sunlight on water -- the spring-fed lake that lay at the heart of Briggs Feral Sanctuary. Another tiger lounged in the shallows, six hundred pounds of stripes, attitude and luminous golden eyes.

Dave gave them a lazy blink, indolent as a pasha. And like a pasha, he apparently had a harem -- or at least a gang of devoted fans. Ten female volunteers clustered just outside the enclosure fence as close as they dared get. Dressed in shorts, hats and T-shirts with the BFS lion logo, they all wore grins of anticipation as they waited for him to do something amazing. *Or, knowing Dave, inappropriate.*

Stoli catapulted off the bank, sailed through the air, and landed on the other cat with a huge splash. The volunteers fled the arcing water, yelping and laughing.

Dave roared, batting at Stoli's nose with

sheathed claws. "Back off, Tigger! Do I look like fuckin' Pooh Bear to you?"

Stoli raced off, chuffing like a giggling ten-year-old who'd pranked his brother. Which was exactly what he was. The two cats had been littermates before they'd melded with their human partners. Otherwise they couldn't have shared an enclosure. Their fights would have been real.

"You'd better run, asshole! I'll turn you into a rug!" Dave flopped back down in the water with a huff of feline disdain. "The crap I put up with."

Kurt's grin faded. Dave did indeed put up with a hell of a lot. A year ago he'd been Dave Frost, a member of Kurt's Arcane Corps unit -- a tall, lanky blond with a wicked sense of humor. But that was before Dave had died, leaving his soul trapped in the body of Smilodon, his Familiar.

Another man might have surrendered to bitterness and grief for his lost humanity. Dave taught himself to talk by making the air vibrate with magic instead of human vocal cords. Now he was building a thriving career as a YouTube smartass.

"You got me all wet," a blonde volunteer complained, pretending to pout as she pulled at her soaked shirt.

The tiger gave her a toothy grin. "My pleasure."

"Ladies, quit flirting with the wildlife and finish cleaning the enclosures." Kurt put a little subsonic rumble in his voice. Dave wasn't the only one who could manipulate sound with his magic. "We don't want BFS to smell like the world's biggest litter box."

"Killjoy," Dave complained.

"You heard the man." Karla Morgen, the volunteer coordinator, made a shooing gesture at the women. "The poop won't scoop itself."

"You know," Kurt told Dave as the volunteers scattered, "you couldn't be any more a ham if you were Porky Pig."

"How else would I bring home the bacon?" Dave flicked a paw, and an invisible snare drum banged out a rimshot.

Kurt laughed. "You're getting scary with the magical sound effects."

"I live to terrify. Speaking of performances, how many tickets did we sell last night? Looked like every inch of the arena bleachers had somebody's butt on it."

"Pretty much." BFS's *Feral 101* show was designed to educate sanctuary visitors about big cats. They'd livened it up with a demonstration of Feral abilities, but the material had still been as dry as sawdust -- until Dave had taken the emcee job in his capable paws. "We brought in five thousand in ticket sales and donations, plus another thousand for selfies and souvenirs."

And they needed every dime. Keeping fifty-nine exotic cats fed and healthy wasn't something you did on a shoestring.

Dave gave him a smug smile. "I has skillz. I also has half a million followers."

"You're just lucky they don't know what an asshole you are."

"I'm a tiger. We're supposed to be assholes."

Movement across the lake drew Kurt's attention. In the next enclosure, a lion came to the water's edge, accompanied by his two lionesses. Staring at the tigers, the Familiar roared.

"What are you bitching about, Clarence?"

"He's probably missing Jake." Jake Nolan, like Dave, had served on Kurt's Arcane Corps team before becoming a Laurel County deputy sheriff. Kurt cupped his hands around his mouth and called, "He's at work, Clarence." Familiars had a grasp of English roughly equivalent to a four-year-old's.

The lion roared again, the low, moaning rumble rolling across the water.

"I don't want to hear it from you," Dave yelled back. "You've got a fucking harem to keep you company, you bastard." He eyed Kurt. "When are you going to find *me* a girl?"

"You'd eat her."

"Every single chance I got."

"I think that's illegal in this state."

"*Everything's* illegal in this state. Especially shit that's no business of the Bible-thumping populace. Why in the hell did you have to drag me to South Carolina? It's ninety degrees here in June. I have a fucking fur coat."

"You also weigh six hundred pounds. There aren't that many places that would take your fuzzy ass." There were other sanctuaries for exotic cats around the country, but BFS was the only one owned and operated by Ferals, for Ferals. Besides, Kurt owed Dave.

"I don't know why the hell I'm asking you," Dave grumbled. "You can't even find a woman for yourself."

Kurt flipped him off. "You really need to mind your own business."

"But minding yours is so much more fun." Dave grinned, all teeth. There'd been a reason they'd called Dave's tiger "Smilodon."

"Speaking of females, what's going on with Parvati?" Dave asked.

"Nothing good." When he'd gone to work for his father, Kurt had taken over supervising the cats' medical care. Sometimes it was a depressing job. "The vet says the cancer has spread to her bones. Add that to the fact she's fifteen…"

"Hey, watch it with the ageist shit," objected Dave, who was ten. Thirty, if he'd still been human. More seriously he asked, "Can the vet do surgery?"

"Not given the way it's spread. We may have to put Parvati down if this healer Dad found can't help."

"Let's hear it for Glenda the Good Witch." Dave emerged from the lake and shook himself, sending a thunderstorm's worth of water flying from his fur.

Kurt jumped back, but got sprayed with cold droplets anyway. "Damn it, Dave!"

"You looked so hot, I thought I'd help you cool off." The tiger smirked. "You're welcome."

"Bite me."

"You'd better hope not."

Before Kurt could retort, his father called, "Play nice, boys. We've got company."

Fred Briggs stood on the path just beyond Dave's enclosure. At his side a tall, pretty redhead gazed through the galvanized wire panels at them.

The newcomer's face had a fine angularity, with high cheekbones, a slim nose and a round, determined chin. In contrast to the elegant strength of her bone structure, her mouth looked lush and kissable. Her hair fell around her shoulders in auburn curls that gleamed in the afternoon sunlight, vivid against her Celtic pale skin. But it was her eyes that really captured Kurt's attention, a cool and watchful blue under straight auburn brows. She wore khaki shorts that displayed long, long legs, and her turquoise cotton top stretched across sweetly shaped breasts.

Intrigued, Kurt headed over to the fence for a closer look, both tigers padding at his heels. Fred turned to the woman with one of those old-fashioned Southern flourishes he did so well. "Genevieve, this is my son, Kurt, his friend Dave Frost, and Kurt's Familiar, Stoli." He looked at them. "Boys, this is Genevieve Reyes. She's the Arcanist healer who's volunteered to help Parvati."

"Or at least I'm going to try." A dimple flashed beside her smile. "Hi."

"Nice to meet you, Ms. Reyes."

"Call me Gen."

Kurt smiled back, more than a little dazzled. *Damn, she's gorgeous.*

Unfortunately, she was also a witch. In the Arcane Corps, he'd worked with a lot of magic users who'd been good people. *But then there's Mom.*

* * *

Though two tigers and a couple of humans stared at Genevieve, it was the younger man whose intense gaze made her feel shy. Kurt Briggs topped six feet by at least three inches, with a broad-shouldered, powerful build that reminded her of classical sculpture. Maybe a Roman centurion. His thick hair was the shade of a rich, dark espresso, cut short, as if he'd gotten used to wearing it that way in the military and had never gotten out of the habit.

His father's, on the other hand, fell to his shoulders in a gray-streaked mane. Otherwise the resemblance between the two was striking. Both had the same regal bone structure and wide mouth, the same deep-set eyes. It was the eyes that got to her. She itched to capture the shades of gold, umber and sunlit yellow that made Kurt's gaze so hypnotic.

Actually, all four of them -- Kurt, Fred and the two tigers -- shared that eye color. She knew it was a genetic marker of the ability to form spirit links between Feral-Talented humans and the animals bred to be their Familiars.

Annnnd the silence just got uncomfortable. Probably because I'm staring. And everyone else was staring right back. Purely to fill the silence, Gen blurted out the first thing that came to mind. "I'd love to paint you," she said to the nearest tiger. "You're beautiful."

"Why, thank you." The huge cat grinned, flashing more teeth than a Great White. "I'd be happy to sit for you." His voice crooned, so velvety and deep, he should be doing car commercials.

Dave. She felt her cheeks heat and knew her blush probably clashed with her hair. "I saw your video about Parvati on Facebook," she all but babbled. "That's why I decided to volunteer. Not sure I'll be able to cure her, but it's worth a try."

Several bars of "Eye of the Tiger" began to play. Fred Briggs pulled his phone out of his pocket, looked down at it, and cursed. "Excuse me, I have to take this." He walked off, his thumb swiping over his phone. "Fred Briggs, Briggs Feral Sanctuary... Hello, Senator. Thanks for returning my call..."

Kurt stared after his father, frowning, before turning back to Genevieve. Making a visible effort to change mental gears, he gestured along the enclosure fence that separated them. "The gate's this way. We really appreciate your taking time to help Parvati. Dad said you usually do portrait work."

She followed him and the tigers, moving parallel to the fence. "Magical face lifts for the rich and famous. Less dangerous than surgery or Botox, and the results look better."

"Sounds lucrative."

"Enough to let me do volunteer work healing sick kids."

"Why'd you move to Laurelton?" Kurt asked. "I'd think Hollywood would be a more logical choice."

She shrugged. "But Laurelton has the Faraday Children's Hospital. And a lot less access to Arcane healers."

Dave considered her, his tail tip flicking. "How many *have* you healed?"

"Not enough. I can do a lot, but only if my patient's magic is compatible with mine."

"It doesn't work with Normals?" Kurt lifted a thick, dark brow.

She waved a hand. "I'm talking about the aura everybody produces, Talent or not."

"'It surrounds us and penetrates us. It binds the galaxy together,'" Obi-wan Kenobi said.

Gen started, looking around for the source of the voice. "What the heck?"

Dave grinned. "I always thought George Lucas owed all us Talents royalties."

"That was dead on," Gen said, impressed. "How did you do that?"

"PFM."

"Is that some kind of weird military acronym?" She'd thought she knew them all.

"Yep. Stands for Pure Fucking Magic." He grinned at her, displaying a truly appalling number of teeth.

"Dave's an artist of geekery," Kurt told her. "He thinks he's funny."

"I *am* funny."

"What you are is a pain in the ass."

Dave lifted his head with a regal sniff and turned to Gen. "You were saying?"

She shrugged. "Not everyone's field is so compatible with mine that I can use it to induce healing. Hopefully I can work with your tiger's."

Fred rejoined them, tension visible in the set of his still-broad shoulders. "That was Senator Rich," he told his son. "He wants me to make calls to a list of his fellow senators. Evidently they've forgotten a lot of us 'sinister magic users' are military veterans."

Dave curled a lip to reveal one fang. "And NTRA is a giant 'Fuck-you-very-much-for-your-service.'"

"Jerks," Gen muttered. Unfortunately, the proposed National Talent Registration Act was a major plank in the Humanist Party platform. "I hate opportunistic bigots."

"You and me both." Fred grimaced, looking like a man who'd rather be doing anything but the job he faced. "I don't think listening to me argue with those guys would help your concentration. Kurt, would you mind escorting Genevieve to the Cat Clinic and staying with her until I can finish these calls?"

"Be glad to." His son hesitated, rubbing his thumb over that square jaw of his. He had big, calloused hands striped with intriguing scars. "I was supposed to go out for a beer with Jake tonight. You want me to call and cancel?"

"I don't think that's necessary. I should be done by then, assuming the healing even takes that long…" Fred lifted a graying brow at Genevieve.

"I've never done a healing on a tiger. But from what you've said about her condition, it'll probably take several hours to lay down all the layers of the spell. Unless you'd rather I came back tomorrow?"

"God, no. There's no reason whatsoever for that cat to be in pain any longer than necessary. We'll be happy to stay with you as long as necessary."

"That goes without saying." Kurt reached into his pocket and pulled out his cell phone.

His father growled, the sound a warning subsonic rumble no ordinary human could have produced. "Do not call Jake, at least not yet. I owe you a night off, damn it. I can knock this out in a couple of hours, tops."

"Do what you need to do, Dad. I'll take care of our guest."

"Okay, fine." Fred nodded at Genevieve. "Thank you. I know how much effort it's going to take. Means a lot."

"It's my pleasure. Good luck with the senators." She watched him hurry off, thumbing his phone as he went.

Kurt unlocked the padlock and stepped into the gap between the enclosure and the gravel path.

"What's with the two fences?"

"The inner fence is to keep the cats in," he explained, re-locking the gate. "The outer fence is to keep the humans out. Otherwise some dumbass would stick a hand into the enclosure and get it bitten off."

"Dave would bite somebody's hand off?"

"No, but Stoli might. When I'm around, I can keep him in line, but he's still a tiger. If some idiot antagonized him when our spirit link wasn't active, I might not realize what was happening in time."

"Okay, but Dave's human."

Dave spoke up, tail flipping back and forth. "Norms tend to freak when they see a tiger wandering around loose -- not that you can blame 'em. Besides, I could open that gate in less time than you could." A glowing human arm thrust out of the cat's shoulder and waved. The tip of one finger extruded, shaping itself into a key. "For one thing, I wouldn't have to look for my keys."

"I know, but it's the principle of the thing."

"What, no applause?" Dave gazed at her mournfully. "The least you could do is give me a hand." A snare drum clashed.

Gen groaned. "You ought to be ashamed of yourself."

"Dave is a man of many talents. Shame is not one of them."

"Nice rimshot, though. My Dad's in the Arcane Corps, so I grew up around Ferals, but I never saw any of them do sound effects." Though she supposed that trick was less impressive than creating animal manifestations from solidified magic.

"You're an Arcane Corps kid?" Kurt eyed her with interest. "Is your dad a Feral or an Arcanist?"

"Both my parents are Arcanists. Dad's Colonel Martin Reyes. He commands a Corps base in Germany. Mom's Major Diane Reyes, a magical demolitions expert." She frowned at a painful childhood memory. "When I was a kid, Dad's Feral teammates were like family. One of them was killed and trapped in his Familiar, and it really bugged the hell out of me. Especially after he was sent to the Corps retirement sanctuary. Didn't seem fair."

"Yeah, that place is a disgrace. BFS is a hell of a lot nicer." Dave waved his hand manifestation at the towering oak that dominated his enclosure. A ramp led up to a tree house constructed around the massive trunk, its log walls inset with long, low windows. "Hell, I've got a house and everything."

Gen studied it. "Must have a great view."

"Yep. Fred and Kurt built it for me, complete with electricity, plumbing, and an HVAC system." He bared his teeth in a wicked tiger smile. "And best of all, WiFi. Not being a biped anymore sucks, but considering my human body's six feet under, I consider it a win."

Kurt gave him a wry smile. "Nice speech. Wish I'd thought to record it so I could play it back to you when you whine."

The glowing hand shot him the finger.

"Sorry, Dave, I just don't like you like that." They could have been any pair of good friends giving each other hell.

"*Nobody* likes *you* like that, asshole." The hand disappeared as Dave turned back toward Gen. "Take care of Parvati, Ms. Reyes. She's suffered enough."

"I'll do my best."

Dave gave her a long, thoughtful look. "Yeah, I believe you will."

Kurt gestured for her to precede him, adding over his shoulder, "I'll let you know how it goes."

"Going to Potions?"

He shrugged. "Depends on how long it takes Dad to talk sense into those senate weasels."

"Well, if you drop by, bring me back a couple of bottles of Mellow Micro."

"You got it."

Gen fell silent as they walked through the sanctuary. Long, narrow enclosures snaked along on either side of the gravel path, big cats sprawled asleep under the trees or wending their way through the thick brush. "Are all these cats Familiars?"

Kurt shook his head. "No. BFS started as a Feral retirement home, but now all but five of our animals are rescues from backyard breeders and roadside zoos. We've even got one who used to belong to a drug dealer."

"Why would a drug dealer want a tiger?"

"Jaguar. And he figured it would keep the cops away."

"I gather it didn't work."

"Nope. The cops called us to come get the cat. One of the bennies of being a Feral. We're better than a tranq gun when it comes to calming down pissed-off animals."

"Handy talent." Genevieve hesitated a moment, then decided to just ask. "Playing devil's advocate here... why don't you just ship 'em back to Africa or India or wherever? Set them free?"

"Would if we could. They were raised in captivity. In the wild, they'd either starve to death or poachers would shoot them. They don't fear humans." He shrugged impressive shoulders. "It's a question we get a lot. All we can do is make sure we provide our cats with as rich an environment as possible." He paused to watch a jaguar rub her big spotted head against her enclosure fence. "But you're right, they're still locked up. It bothers the hell out of me, but we do the best we can."

"At least you're doing something about the problem."

He looked up at her and smiled. "So are you."

Genevieve found herself returning his warm smile -- and feeling a delicious little tingle when his eyes took on a sensual heat. *God, I really want to paint his eyes...*

Among other things.

Chapter Two

The one-story cinderblock building was covered with an elaborate mural of the BFS logo -- a lion's head, its eyes glowing Feral gold, mane flowing across the building in shades of sable, ocher and umber. A sign out front read BFS Cat Clinic.

"Here we are." Pulling out a ring of keys, Kurt unlocked the door. "This place is my dad's pride and joy. Before we built it, we had to transport the sickest cats to a facility in Charlotte, which was the closest clinic that could treat animals the size of ours. It's a two-hour trip, so we'd have to sedate the cat. That's stressful even for healthy animals."

Genevieve followed him into a short hallway with doors marked "OR," "Lab," "Treatment 1," "Treatment 2," and "Equipment." Huge color photos of exotic cats hung on the walls, obviously taken on the BFS grounds. "Nice place."

"Thanks. There's an operating room with a table that can support up to a thousand pound cat, portable x-ray and sonogram equipment -- pretty much anything we need this side of a CT scanner."

"Who does the actual treatment?"

"Vet from the North Carolina animal hospital drives down and donates his services. If not for him and the other volunteers, God knows how we'd keep this place afloat. Dad and I are salaried, but neither of us is going to get rich. We plow every dime we get back into BFS."

Genevieve smiled at him. "I'd be willing to pitch in too."

His handsome face lit. "Really? That'd be great. Most of the animals we get here have suffered some kind of abuse or neglect, so we need all the help we can get."

"My priority's always going to be the kids, but I'll do what I can for your cats. Healing tends to take a lot out of me, so it all depends on how much magic I've been doing."

"Anything you can do would be welcome." He unlocked the door at the end of the hall and opened it for her.

The smell of sick tiger was pungent in the enclosed space. The animal didn't even stir as they entered. She lay curled in a wheeled cage big enough to accommodate an even larger animal.

Genevieve knelt on the floor as close to the cage as she dared.

Dull yellow eyes opened and met hers. Parvati's hipbones jutted under thinning fur. But though her coat lacked the healthy, glorious sheen the other tigers had, at least she was clean.

"Do you think you're going to be able to help her?" There was a note of worry in Kurt's voice. He cared about this animal. Cared a great deal.

"Not sure yet. Let me take a look." She reached out, but a big male hand closed around her wrist.

"That isn't a good idea."

She slanted him a look, all too aware of the heat of his skin, the long fingers encircling her arm. "I wasn't going to stick my hand in the cage. I'm just trying to sense her magic."

"Sorry." Looking chagrined, Kurt released her. "It's just that sick animals can be more dangerous than healthy ones. And Parvati tends toward grumpy at the best of times."

"No, if you think I'm about to do something stupid, please let me know. Right now, I need to find out if her magic's compatible with mine." Keeping her hand where it was, Genevieve spread her fingers and closed her eyes, the better to see the cat.

A faintly glowing tiger lay in the darkness behind her lids in the same position as the physical animal. Her aura was so dim, it was barely visible. *If I'd waited even one more day, she'd have been too far gone to save.* Genevieve could do a lot, but her patient had to have enough strength to work with.

As she examined the tiger's aura, she realized something blazed at her elbow. Eyes still closed, Gen pivoted -- and froze, staring through her closed lids. Where Kurt should be, a tiger sat on his haunches.

Her eyes flew open to see the man watching at her, his expression puzzled. "What?"

She shook her head and closed her eyes again to study him. "Nothing."

Kurt's got a lot of power. And God, he's beautiful. Genevieve could have happily spent the next hour with her eyes closed, just watching the leap and play of his magic.

Which is not why you're here. Get your mind on the job and quit ogling the man.

Turning back to Parvati, she extended her hand again, and *reached*. A glowing tendril of magic extruded from her palm and slipped through the cage's thick steel mesh to touch the tiger's nose

The great head lifted, dim eyes widening. The animal growled feebly, but Gen stroked it with the tendril of magic, exploring. A large bright knot of painful red lay over the tiger's emaciated belly, which she recognized as the mammary tumor. More sparks of scarlet burned throughout Parvati's aura.

The vet was right. The cancer had spread. Gen thrust her magic into it and concentrated. The crimson obediently paled into orange as the pain dulled, responding to her magic.

The tiger made a soft, huffing sound, almost a sigh.

Gen opened her eyes and sat back on her heels in relief. If she could affect the pain, she could also do something about the cancer. "It's going to work. I can do this."

Kurt smiled brilliantly, his teeth a flash of white. "Good. That's really good."

She withdrew the tendril and the tiger moaned. "Shhhh. I'll make the pain go away again in just a minute."

Shrugging the messenger bag off her shoulder, she pulled out a pad of thick textured pastel paper, along with a pouch of pencils and her wooden box of pastels.

Kurt stood. "Let me get you a chair. If you sit on this floor for long, you're not going to be able to walk tomorrow."

"Hey, thank you. That'd be a big help." Focusing her attention on the cat again, she started roughing in the contours of Parvati's head and chest.

It was crucial to make the animal's likeness as accurate as possible. Every stripe and whisker had to be correct. Stylized or abstract work wasn't good enough when it came to healing magic.

Besides, the concentration of trying to capture the likeness as exactly as possible would help Gen focus her magic more effectively.

Wheels rattled over tile as Kurt pushed an office chair into the room. "Here you go."

"Thanks," Gen told him absently, sinking into it.

A moment later he wheeled a small table in front of her. "Figured this way you wouldn't have to hunch over that pad. Would you like something to drink? The vending machine's got Coke products."

"Water would be great." While he ducked out again, she put the pad on the table and started working in quick, sweeping strokes.

The trick was to capture the likeness while making the animal look as healthy as Dave or Stoli. She had to imagine Parvati healed, concentrate on that mental image, believe in it utterly as she laid down the layers of her magic.

Time seemed to fall away, until at last she sat back, eyes flicking from the sketch to the cat. *Yeah, that's pretty good. Now it's time for the magic.*

Gen reached for her box of pastels. Even before she flipped up the lid, she could feel their power as little electric tingles dancing over her skin. The colored sticks smelled of chalk and ozone, and ever so slightly of her own blood.

It had taken Genevieve the better part of a week to make the pastels in a ritual that stored her magic in each piece. She'd slept for a full day afterward, a heavy slumber born of pure exhaustion.

Taking a deep, slow breath, Gen gathered her magic, chose a white stick and began to lay down the highlights on the cat's fur.

Drawing deep from her well of magic, she sent power down her arm and through the pastel stick, magic building on magic with every stroke. She focused on the reality she wanted, believed in it with all her soul and power: cancer cells withering away, Parvati growing stronger. Becoming healthy and well until the tigress moved with the same fluid ease as Dave and Stoli.

Next came strokes of gold, ocher, and bronze to capture the contours of the animal's regal head. Between strokes, she used her pinkie to blend the color.

Slowly, layer by layer, she built up the image, fingers working power-infused chalk, each touch a part of the spell. That was the reason she worked in pastels rather than oils or watercolor -- paint would require the use of a brush. Greater physical contact strengthened the magic.

And with every stroke, she built a connection with Parvati's aura. Until she knew she could reinforce the animal's life force and eliminate each knot of lethal red energy.

Parvati became the axis of her world, the pivot point, the single focus.

Nothing else mattered.

* * *

Kurt watched Genevieve in fascination. Magic rolled off her in waves that swirled across his skin and filled the air with the clean ozone scent of magic. He'd worked with a lot of Arcanists in the Corps, but none of them had possessed so much raw power.

Gen rocked back to look down at her work, then back at the cat before bending over the drawing again.

Parvati had drifted into a deep sleep shortly after Genevieve began casting. The cat might not be Kurt's Familiar, but if he concentrated... He reached out with his Feral senses.

And smiled.

Genevieve's magic had indeed relieved the grinding pain of the cancer. Better yet, it was a natural sleep, not the sedation that could be dangerous for an animal already so weak.

He turned his attention to the Arcanist. Her blue eyes were narrow with concentration, but even as she worked, her lips curled in a smile. Curious, he brushed her aura with his.

Kurt couldn't always read human emotions as

easily as those of animals -- he couldn't read human thoughts at all -- but Gen's came through loud and clear. She was lost in the joy of her magic, in the pleasure of touching Parvati's aura and relieving her suffering. Her pleasure was intense, almost sensual. *God, she's sexy…*

And you're being borderline creepy. Besides, she's a witch. More Glenda the Good than Maleficent Mom, but still. With a sigh, he pulled out his phone and started checking email. Unfortunately, the effort at distracting himself didn't work. His gaze insisted on drifting her direction every time her magic flared and the hair on his arms rose.

And the hair wasn't the only thing, either. He could feel heat gathering in his groin, and his eyes flicked to the lush curve of her breasts. Realizing he was ogling her again, he forced his gaze away.

When was the last time he'd found a woman so intriguing? Even given the magic that would normally make him feel more wary than anything else? Except Gen had volunteered her normally expensive services to help one of their cats. A sacrifice she'd probably pay for tomorrow with exhaustion and an ugly headache. Even if Mom hadn't hated the cats, nobody would ever accuse her of random acts of self-sacrifice.

I could ask her out…

Except she's a witch.

Who heals cats. Besides, I want to get to know her better.

His mouth opened, but before he could get the words out of his mouth, a deep voice interrupted. "Kurt."

His father was standing in the doorway, powerful arms crossed, an expression of disapproval on his face. Fred tilted his head toward the hallway.

Kurt winced, but there was no getting around it, so he followed his father up the hall, and out of human earshot. "How'd the calls go?"

Fred shrugged. "Hell, who knows? They seemed receptive, but politicians lie." He studied Kurt, his Feral gaze luminous. "I'm more interested in the fact that I stood there for five minutes and you never even noticed. I don't think I've ever seen you react this way to a woman you've only known a couple of hours." He paused and lifted a brow. "Though considering she's a witch…"

"So she volunteered to heal Parvati so she could cast a spell on me? Been drinking the Humanist Kool-Aid?"

"Don't be insulting."

"Okay, cheap shot. Sorry."

Fred considered him a long moment before sighing. "I know you're lonely, Kurt…"

"Not with Stoli in my head."

"Stoli's not a woman. My point is that with the war ending, female Ferals will need a home for their retiring Familiars. BFS is the logical place for them to come. If you're patient…"

"For God's sake, I'm not planning to propose. All I'm thinking of doing is asking her out for a cup of coffee."

"I asked a pretty Bard out for a beer, and look how that turned out."

Kurt spread his arms. "Taaa-daaah!"

"Fair point, but… well, you need to think about the cats."

"What about the cats?"

"If you start something that ends badly, you could cost us a healer."

"And if we have this argument out in the

hallway, we won't have to worry about any theoretical bad romance, because she's going to hear us and never come back. Are you done with your calls?"

Fred, who looked on the verge of trying a new argument, nodded reluctantly. "Yeah."

"Then I'm going out for that beer." He gave his father a wave and headed off down the hall. "Night, Dad."

His father sighed. "Night, Kurt."

* * *

Faraday Square was Laurelton's funky heart, complete with a ten-foot bronze statue of Colton Faraday. The Arcanist millionaire stood hipshot and dapper on his granite pedestal, bronze eyes gazing up the brick walkway to a fountain spraying dancing water at the park's other end. Antique streetlights lined the sidewalks on either side, hung with huge baskets filled with rainbow cascades of wisteria, geraniums and begonias.

Shops and restaurants surrounded the park. A sign over one of them displayed a beer mug spilling sparkling neon foam that spelled the word Potions. Kurt parked and headed inside.

Huge steel brewing kettles lined half the room, pouring the scent of yeast and magic into the air. Booths and tables filled the rest, while a gleaming bar and shelves of bottles occupied the pub's rear. The usual crowd had gathered to enjoy the magical microbrews, just as they packed the place for the Saturday performances by local Bards.

Kurt never went to Potions on Saturdays.

He wound his way across the room to order an Arcane Ale at the bar. Accepting the icy bottle the bartender handed over, Kurt turned to find Jake Nolan watching him from one of the booths. When the other man tilted his own bottle in salute, he headed over.

The Feral cop wasn't a tall man, but he was built like a bull, with broad shoulders and powerful biceps. Jake wore his hair in a blond brush cut that made his broad features look even tougher and more uncompromising. His eyes glowed in the bar's dim lighting, shining with his link to his lion Familiar, Clarence.

"Yo." Jake's Mellow Microbrew was evidently doing its job -- he looked relaxed. Being off-duty, he'd changed out of his black uniform in favor of his usual geek gear: worn black jeans and a Deadpool T-shirt. It wasn't at all surprising that Jake's favorite superhero was basically a cross between Rambo and Bugs Bunny.

So was Jake.

Kurt slid into the booth. "So how was today's fight for truth, justice and chimichangas?"

"The usual. Encounters with assholes and idiots and idiotic assholes, and one or two hapless innocent bystanders." Jake studied him shrewdly. "You ain't happy."

"I did notice that."

"You want to tell me about it, or just glower?"

Kurt shrugged, only to discover that he did indeed want to vent. "Oh, you know, the usual. I showed an interest in a woman who wasn't a Feral..."

"And your Dad lost his shit."

"Nah, just booked me a flight on Guilt Air."

"Travelocity's got nothing on Fred. Who inspired this particular round trip?"

"You know that Arc who volunteered to help Parvati?"

At that, Jake straightened. "Wait, you're interested in a witch? Shit, I'll bet Fred did yark up a hairball."

"Actually, it was only about the size of a ping pong ball."

"As opposed to the Great Watermelon of 2015."

"He just warned me about ruining a good thing with somebody who could heal our cats."

Jake considered that, sipping his beer. "You do have a lot of old, sick kitties at BFS. What you don't have is a great track record when it comes to women."

Kurt eyed his very single friend. "So why aren't you home with *your* wife and kids?"

Jake flipped him off. "About this witch Juliet of yours…"

"Genevieve."

"Whatever. What's she like?"

"Well, she heals sick children and dying cats pro bono…"

"Which is cool and all, but is she hot?"

"She's…" Kurt broke off, struggling to put his reaction into words.

Jake sat back, impressed. "Sizzling, huh?"

"Yeah, and I'm not even sure why."

"Nice rack maybe?"

"Even you're not that shallow."

"I certainly am -- I have a dick. And since you do too, you ain't exactly a deep-sea diver yourself."

"You have a point."

"So? Give."

"Hell, I don't know. Big blue eyes and an incredible amount of red hair all…" He made a gesture around his shoulders. "Curly."

"You've got my attention."

"And yeah, nice rack. But what got me…" He fell silent for a moment, trying to puzzle it out. "While she was drawing Parvati, her magic… I never felt anything like it. It was intense."

Jake studied him. "We've worked with a lot of Arcs, but I don't remember you reacting like this to any of them."

Kurt turned his beer bottle between his fingers, listening to it scrape over the tabletop. "The Arcs in the service -- their magic was about death, about booby traps and demolition spells. Her magic feels like life. Something about it just made the hair stand up on the back of my neck. Even Stoli felt it. He was almost purring."

"Tigers don't purr."

"Neither do people, but I was doing it too." He paused, considering. "I'm going to ask her out."

"I see a watermelon in your future."

"Dad needs to remember he's not me. And every woman I meet is definitely not Mom."

"Big talk, but I haven't noticed you rushing to the altar."

Kurt shrugged. "None of them have been right."

"That why you haven't even tried in the last six months?"

"And when did you last get laid?"

"Wednesday. Brunette. Great tits. Likes to be tied up and spanked. I'm planning to introduce her to nipple clamps next."

"Pervert."

"You're one to talk." Jake grinned, slow and nasty, a sure indicator he was about to give Kurt hell. "If you decide not to grow a pair, I think I'll go make introductions with Witchy Woman myself. I don't have anything against Arcs. Maybe I'll even give her a spanking."

A surge of possessive anger took Kurt by surprise. As he wrestled it, a distinct scritch sounded over the laughter and chatter of the clientele. His fingertips vibrated. He looked down and saw glowing claws tipping his fingers, digging into the table. Startled, Kurt jerked his hand back and willed the claws away.

When he looked up, Jake was sitting back in the booth, giving him a long, considering look. "She did get under your skin didn't she? No wonder your dad freaked. How'd she get Stoli going so fast? It's not as if she's his type."

"That wasn't him, Jake. That was me." He tapped his now clawless fingertips on his beer bottle, frowning. "Maybe I should keep my distance. If she's already making me pop claws when I haven't even asked her out yet…"

"Jesus, don't give up before you even try."

"It can get ugly when Ferals lose control."

"Yeah." Jake's mouth took on a bitter twist. "Just look what happened to my brother."

"I wasn't talking about that."

"It's what you were thinking."

"You read minds now?"

"No, but I do know there's a difference between being careful and being in suspended animation. Risk the watermelon and ask the girl out." Jake gave him a long, serious stare. "Otherwise, the only pussy you're ever going to get is Stoli."

* * *

Genevieve sat back, studying the portrait. She could feel the magic radiating from the spell she'd built from layers of pastel, imagination, magic and will.

Fred Briggs moved to look over her shoulder. "Damn, that's good. You even got the stripe pattern right. Think it's going to work?"

"Depends on how she does over the next couple of days."

Parvati was awake now, her yellow eyes alert and interested, where before she'd shown only apathy and suffering. She extended her big, regal head toward Gen and chuffed.

"She looks the best I've seen her in weeks." Fred stepped up to the cage and dropped easily down on his haunches. "She's definitely not in any pain now -- I can feel that much." He grimaced. "The last time I touched her aura, I seriously considered having her put down right then. This is a real improvement."

Gen smiled in weary pleasure, enjoying the floating sense of accomplishment she always got after a successful healing. "Let's step out into the hall." She reached into her bag to pull out a can of fixative and picked up the drawing. "I need to spray this, and I don't want to do it around Parvati. She doesn't need to breathe this stuff."

But when she started to rise, her knees gave out halfway up and she sagged back down. Fred caught her forearm, his expression alarmed. "Are you okay?"

"I'm fine. Healing just takes a lot out of me." She rubbed the back of her hand across her aching forehead. *Probably just smudged pastel all over my face.* Every time she did a piece, she ended up leaving chalk fingerprints on everything she touched. "I'll be all right after a night's sleep."

This time when she tried to rise, Fred half-lifted her to her feet.

Damn, he's strong.

"Can I get you anything? Some more water, a candy bar?"

"Thanks, but I've got granola bars in my bag. My blood sugar gets a little low."

"I'm not surprised. You worked a hell of a lot of magic. Still feel it coming from that." He nodded down at the drawing.

Gen caught her balance and hobbled stiffly for the door, sketch and the spray can in either hand. "I'm used to it. I've been working spells like this for years."

He followed, obviously ready to catch her if she needed it. "So I gather. I checked you out -- I don't let just anybody around my cats. You've got a damned good reputation. But even so, I didn't expect you to pour this much power into Parvati. A child with cancer, yes, but most people wouldn't have gone that far for an animal."

She smiled up at him tiredly. "Why not? You do."

Fred smiled back, and she saw where his son got all the charm. "That's different. I'm a melded Feral -- I basically *am* a cat, biped or not." Power blazed up in his eyes, and in that instant, she saw something in their glowing depths that wasn't human. "I know what it's like to be an animal at the mercy of humans. You don't."

"No, but I am female. Us girls have to stick together." Gen handed the sketch to Fred while she pulled the top off the can and shook it hard enough to make the metal bead inside rattle vigorously.

Fred handed back the sketch, and she turned away from him. Holding her breath, Gen started coating the drawing with the plastic spray to prevent smudges that would destroy the spell. "We need to find a way to put this up. She has to stay close to it for at least a week while the cancer dies."

"I think I have something that will work." Fred disappeared into an office up the hall, coming back with a plastic sleeve used for medical records. He slid the sketch inside, then taped it to the wall beside the cage. By then, Parvati was asleep, her breathing deep and even. "Will that work?"

"Perfect." Gen started gathering up her pastels and putting them away in their case.

The big man watched her for a few minutes. "I can't tell you how much we…"

A roar rolled over the building, so loud Gen jumped. It wasn't the first time one of the cats had roared while she'd been in the clinic, but this one sounded as if the animal was right outside the door. "One of your fuzzy friends is not happy."

He stiffened, his expression hardening. "That wasn't a cat. That sounded more like a bear."

"I didn't know you had any bears here."

"We don't." He started toward the door. "Stay here. I'm going to see what's going on in my park."

Alarmed, she took a step after him. "You want me to call 911?"

Fred looked back at her. Magic blazed out of his body, surrounding him with the glowing form of a lion. Its massive head was even with his chest, its mane streamers of gold energy that bled sparks into the air. It was so bright she could see it even with her eyes open in the well-lit corridor.

"This is my park." His voice emerged in a rumbling growl. "Nobody comes in my park and roars at me." Whirling, Fred slammed out the door, adding over his shoulder, "Stay here. Do not set foot out of this building. I don't know who that bastard is, but I don't like the way he feels."

The door banged closed behind him.

Crap. Genevieve opened her consciousness. Dark magic hit her senses, and every hair on her body stood up. She must have been concentrating so hard on her own spell that she hadn't sensed it building.

Something dark and evil hung over the sanctuary

like a boiling funnel cloud. She knew the feel of Feral magic, and it didn't feel like this.

Arcanist magic. Incredibly strong, incredibly *evil* Arcanist magic.

What the hell's going on?

Chapter Three

Dave focused his magic to manifest a human hand. He used the power construct to pick up the remote control and point it at the flat screen television attached to the tree house wall.

Fred and Kurt had gone out of their way to make sure his quarters were as comfortable as possible for someone who wasn't physically human. As he'd told Gen, the house had air conditioning and central heat, not to mention electricity, a computer with voice recognition capability, an X-box, and a cable modem.

Then of course, there was Stoli, his combination pet and roommate.

The Briggs had offered to let Dave move in with them, but he'd drawn the line. He wanted a place of his own, somewhere he could kick back and be a tiger or a human, depending on his mood.

Turning the set on, Dave started flipping channels. Spotting a narrow, self-righteous face he knew a little too well, he stopped channel surfing to sneer.

"… We must be realists when it comes to these so-called Talents," the senator proclaimed in ringing tones. "Too many use their unnatural abilities to victimize law abiding, normal Americans. We need to know who these crooks are, what they can do, and where to find them when they commit crimes. Otherwise we're putting our children at…"

Dave stabbed the channel button with a mystical finger. "Fuck off, you bigoted bastard." He looked at Stoli, half-dozing in a huge padded cat bed that was the twin to his own. "We're loyal Americans when they need us to fight their fucking wars, and criminals when they need a convenient scapegoat. Pisses me…"

Something roared.

Dave's head jerked up as his ears flattened and his ruff rose. He knew the roar of every cat at BFS, and that hadn't been any of them.

Another deep, vibrating challenge rolled over the park.

"Fuck, that sounded like a bear." He padded over to the tiger-sized cat door and stuck his head out. He had to be mistaken…

But when Dave reached out with his magical senses, he found a sense of evil hanging over the sanctuary like a malevolent stench. He recoiled. "What the fuck?"

Another roar. That one was all too familiar. "Shit, that's Fred!"

If some Feral had slipped into the park who didn't belong there, Kurt's dad wouldn't take it well. He was too much a lion to tolerate invasions of his territory.

The two voices roared again, vicious with aggression and fury.

"Yeah, that's a fight." Dave turned toward Stoli, who'd followed him to the door. The Familiar's gold eyes blazed, tail lashing with agitation. "Fred needs backup before the situation goes south." He lifted a big paw, though he kept his claws sheathed. "Sorry, Stoli, but we've got to have Kurt for this one. And there's only one way to get his attention."

* * *

The psychic cuff caught Kurt across the head so hard he nearly fell out of the booth. *Get here, Kurt!* The spirit link carried an image of Dave snarling in Stoli's face. *I think your dad's in trouble.*

"What the hell?" Kurt reached into his link with Stoli until he could see through his Familiar's eyes.

Kurt, get over here! Dave hit him again in another lightning swipe. His claws were retracted, thank God, or he'd have laid Stoli's nose open.

The tiger backed away and roared at Dave, confused, not sure whether he was trying to fight or play.

Kurt, however, wasn't confused in the least. Dave wouldn't have jumped Stoli unless the situation was seriously fucked. He flung himself through the link, sending his spirit rushing into Stoli's body just as the cat had entered his own moments before. His consciousness merged with the tiger's, man and cat becoming one creature, twice as strong and fast as either alone. "Don't hit me again," Kurt growled, retreating out of range of another swipe. "What the hell's happening?"

"Finally! I was about to go without you. Come on." Dave leaped through the tiger door and bounded down the ramp to the ground.

Kurt/Stoli raced after his friend. Before he could again demand what was going on, Fred roared. Not a human shout, but a rolling, ear-shattering leonine roar felt in the bones as much as the ears.

A chill ran down Kurt's back, raising Stoli's hackles. He'd heard his father roar frequently over the years, but never with the fury and desperation of a lion fighting for his life.

Kurt leaped past Dave, paws thudding as he flung himself toward the locked door of the enclosure.

* * *

Fuck. Now what? Jake stared at Kurt, who'd slumped sideways in the booth mid-word. His friend's golden eyes stared at the wall, his face twisted in an involuntary grimace of fear and fury. "What the hell?" He surged out of the booth and moved around the table to check Kurt's pulse. It was fast, but steady.

Usually you pulled your cat into your body to draw on its power. It was rare to enter the cat's. Not unless, like Dave, you'd died and had nowhere else to go. Yet Kurt obviously *had* entered Stoli. One minute he'd been giving Jake hell, the next his head thumped against the wall as if something had knocked him cold.

It had to have something to do with BFS. Something bad.

Jake let his eyes slide out of focus as he reached for Clarence along their spirit link. He slid into the cat's head -- and heard Fred roar, Stoli and Dave echoing him in a deep, vibrating chorus of fury.

Oh, fuck. He jerked out of the link, snatched his phone off his belt clip, and called the Sheriff Department sergeant for Baker shift.

In a few crisp sentences, Jake told Sergeant Roger Johnson about what he'd heard, keeping one worried eye on Kurt. His friend's body twitched, eyes scanning back and forth, lips moving soundlessly. "Something ugly's going on, Sarge. Somebody needs to check it out. Now."

Johnson cursed. "I'll send Green to take a look."

Green? Jake had to bite back an insubordinate curse. Jake got along with most of his fellow deputies, but Green was a Humanist. Just what they didn't need if things were going south. Unfortunately, he couldn't afford to accuse his fellow deputy of being a bigot. "We may need more manpower than that, sir. It sounds like the situation is serious."

"Shit, Nolan, Briggs's a Feral. His daddy's a Feral. I think they can handle anybody dumb enough to try to give them a hard time."

Jake gritted his teeth. Johnson hadn't heard his friend's roar. "I'm going to back the deputy up just in case. I'm only five minutes away." *Maybe I can keep the asshole from doing anything stupid.*

"Probably overkill, but fine. I'll let him know." He could practically hear the sergeant's shrug. Johnson hung up.

"Idiot," Jake growled. He dropped a twenty on the table and hooked an arm around Kurt's shoulders. Manifesting Clarence's strength, he hoisted his friend into a fireman's carry and headed for the door.

The Briggs might be tigers, but sometimes even big cats needed backup with opposable thumbs. He just hoped Green wouldn't shoot the cats instead of the bad guys. *If there are bad guys.* Too late to second-guess myself now.

* * *

Kurt and Dave sprinted to the enclosure's gate. The guillotine-style door was secured with a padlock. The fifteen-foot high fence itself had a five-foot overhang that was angled inward 45-degrees, designed to stymie even a tiger's efforts to escape. There'd be no climbing it.

And they had to get the hell out. Now.

Dad's roars filled the compound, echoed by Jake's lion, Clarence. A savage alien bellow cut across theirs, deep and growling like a chainsaw.

Dave's ears flattened against his round feline skull. "How the hell did a bear get into the sanctuary?"

"It's got to be a Feral." Fear clawed at Kurt. "Can you get the door? I don't think I can concentrate."

"Yeah." Dave sat back on his haunches. Glowing, ghostly, a human arm extended from his shoulder and passed through the metal grate to thrust a thin tendril of magic into the padlock that mimicked the key. He inserted it, and the lock popped open a heartbeat later. He pushed the gate open just as Fred roared again, the sound edging a human cry of pain.

"Shit!" Kurt surged through the door and leaped into a run, Dave so close behind him, his tail brushed his friend's muzzle. They raced up the path that wound between the enclosures, following the sounds of battle.

Reaching the intersection between the enclosures, they paused, trying to work out which direction the sounds were coming from. It wasn't easy: the sanctuary's cats were in a frenzy, the bigger cats roaring, the smaller ones screaming and hissing. Kurt reached out with his psychic senses, trying to narrow it down.

And gasped.

Magic. Waves of it, a sudden throbbing pressure in his head.

"What the fuck?" Dave's striped tail whipped back and forth.

Kurt knew what he meant. It wasn't just the expected Feral magic, with its familiar psychic sense of fur and forest. That was present, but there was also something heavier. Darker.

Arcanist magic.

"It's coming from the arena." Kurt bounded off again, Dave right behind him. Fear raked him as they ran toward the stands.

The park's arena was used to educate BFS visitors on big cat conservation and abuse issues. An octagonal wire enclosure topped with a metal grate, it was surrounded by bleachers on seven sides. A gate took up the eighth.

Rounding the bleachers, Kurt skidded to a halt. "What the hell?"

"Oh, fuck me," Dave whispered.

Fred Briggs was in full combat manifestation,

surrounded by a glowing cocoon of magic in the shape of his spirit lion, Lahr. The great beast reared on its hind legs, striking out with claws of solidified magical force. Kurt had seen his father rip gouges in solid steel, something no purely physical cat could do. Enclosed in a magical lion two feet taller than his human body, Fred was a terrifying sight -- and a deadly warrior.

The creature he faced now was even bigger, a towering muscled monster almost twelve feet tall.

"Jesus H. Christ!" Dave gasped. "That's a fucking polar bear!"

"It'll kill him!" Kurt ran toward the open gate, knowing Fred was a dead man if they didn't help him.

"Wait!" Dave snapped. "It could be an ambush."

Too late. Magic flared directly in front of Kurt's eyes as something rebounded in his face. It picked up all six hundred pounds of him and flung him backward to hit the ground in a rolling tumble. He skidded to a halt, tasting copper from a bitten tongue.

Dave cursed. "Damn it, Kurt, I told you to wait!"

Fred bellowed in pain. The sound sent Kurt clawing to his feet, Stoli's fury and fear adding to his own. *I'm not going to let that bastard hurt Dad.*

There was no sign of whatever he'd hit, but he could sense power roiling the air. "It's got to be some kind of Arcanist barrier."

"Frosty's got a partner." Ferals couldn't cast that kind of magic.

Kurt swore. During the war, their Arcane Forces team had encountered some seriously nasty barriers, traps, and lethal magic mines created by Arc terrorists. Nobody but an idiot charged an Arcanist working. That was a good way to get your head blown off.

"So where the fuck is the Arc?" They needed to take the bastard out before…

Something flickered up at the top of the bleachers, but when Kurt looked straight toward it, he saw nothing.

Closing his eyes, he searched with his magical senses. A dimly glowing shape draped over one of the seats. He caught a whiff of Arcanist ozone. And over it all, the stench of magical rot. His tiger hackles rose.

He focused on the glow. Definitely an Arc, probably wearing a Spook Suit that bent light around him, making him effectively invisible.

Kurt's lips peeled off his fangs. *You're dead, asshole.*

Fred and the bear rammed together, tearing into each other's glowing shells with magical claws and teeth. The sound of the battle was deafening -- roars, snarls, energy crackling and snapping around them whenever one landed a strike.

We've got to get in there and help him -- which means we've got to take out that fucking Arc. Kurt shot Dave a look, catching his eye, then nodded toward the top of the bleachers.

Dave bared his teeth in something that definitely wasn't a grin.

Together they moved back from the gate and around behind the bleachers, moving in a low slink. Closing his eyes again, Kurt looked upward until he spotted that dim glow again. Focusing his gaze there, he opened his lids. *Looks like the top row, not far from the gate.* Gathering himself, he sprang six feet straight up.

Kurt landed as lightly as he could, but the bleachers still shook under the impact of his tiger's body. He charged toward the spot he'd pinpointed as the Arc's location in a clattering rush. Threw himself into a leap…

He was in mid-air when the muzzle flash went

off with a *BOOM* right in his face.

It was like being hit with a baseball bat. Kurt flew backward, slamming into a bleacher seat in an explosion of pain and stars. He tumbled down several seats to come to a stop draped across two of them on his back, dazed, panting in pain.

Dave roared. The bleachers shook furiously under Kurt as his friend went after the shooter.

"Kurt!" His father, voice echoing with the power of his cat.

The bear roared.

Fred screamed in agony.

Kurt jerked his head around, though pain radiated through his chest in frozen, agonizing waves. "Dad, no…"

The bear had his father down on the ground, muzzle buried in the lion's belly, ripping at the man inside the manifestation. Fred screamed again, the sound raw, all too human.

His voice choked off.

"Dad…" Kurt tried to flip over and roll to his feet, but he could barely lift his head.

Cold. He felt so fucking cold…

When he looked down the length of his body, he saw his white-furred chest was black with blood in the moonlight. The icy pain intensified, so searing he couldn't even breathe.

I've been shot. Sparks of darkness spangled his vision, and he knew his blood pressure was dropping. *I've been shot… and the bear got Dad…*

Stoli moaned, the sound rough with fear and pain.

We're dying. And they'll kill Dave and Dad. I can't let them… Won't.

But if he and Stoli didn't leave the cat's body

before it died, they'd both be lost. His human heart would go into cardiac arrest -- and they were finished. *If we die, we can't help Dad. Stoli, we have to go.* He sank his mystical fingers into his Familiar and threw himself into the Between, following the spirit link back to his own body.

With a psychic yowl, Stoli followed.

* * *

If I get my hands on that asshole, I'm going to eat him like a rib-eye! Dave bounded over the bleachers, headed for the spot he'd seen the Arc when he'd closed his eyes. A muzzle flash and flat crack announced the bastard was firing at him again, but he dodged right and the shot missed. The bleachers shook with the scrape and rattle of a body rolling across an aluminum bench.

Dave landed on the top seat plank, ducking barely in time to avoid a wild shot that whined past his head. He struck out, raking the air with lightning swipes of his claws.

Something thumped, and gravel rattled on the ground below the bleachers. The bastard must have leaped clear.

BOOM!

He ducked, taking cover as best a six-hundred-pound cat could, then threw a glance over the edge. Closed his eyes.

No glow. Dave scanned the blackness with his magical senses, but saw nothing whatsoever. *Where did the son of a bitch go*?

"Goddamnit! Kurt, the Arc's gone…" He turned, looking back down the bleachers. And froze. "Oh, fuck!"

A furry shape draped across one of the bleacher seat planks on its back, surrounded by a spray of something that gleamed like ink in the moonlight.

Blood.

"Kurt!" The shot he thought had missed hadn't been aimed at him. *Kurt's been hit*!

Down in the arena sand, another figure lay sprawled, surrounded by a spreading shadow, dark against the sand.

"Fred..." Dave moaned. "Shit, oh, shit!"

There was no sign of the bear. He'd fled while Dave had been busy with the sniper.

Dave bounded down the bleachers to Kurt/Stoli. His brother tiger lay far too still, the fur of his chest so wet with blood, the bullet wound wasn't even visible. The Arc must've shot him in mid-leap. Dave closed his eyes and looked for his friend's aura. He saw nothing but darkness. No magic, no flicker of life force.

"Fuck me." He wanted to throw up. *Kurt's not dead. He and Stoli fled to his human body. He's not dead. He can't be dead.*

But Fred had no other body to go to; his Familiar, Lahr, had died decades ago. The lion's spirit had shared his body ever since, just as Dave's spirit now inhabited his tiger.

If his human body died, Fred and his lion were lost.

Dave turned and ran to the end of the bleachers in a series of bounds that made the stands shake. Leaping down, he raced around the arena enclosure's fence. Just before he bulled through the arena gate, he remembered the booby trap that had knocked Kurt flying when they'd first arrived.

Closing his eyes, he scanned the darkness, but the spell across the gate was gone. Evidently the bastards were in the wind, having accomplished whatever they'd intended.

Dave slunk inside, fast and low. Closed his eyes. *Fuck.* Sigils floated in the air of the arena in a slow rotation, glowing bright red and stinking of dark magic.

Opening his eyes again, he hurried over to the Feral's side. "Fred!"

The big man moaned, the sound rough with pain. Relief rose, until Dave saw Fred's belly was as black as Stoli's. The sand around him reeked with blood. *Bear bit into him like a baby seal.*

Dave crouched over Kurt's father, manifesting a human form so he could sink an insubstantial hand into the wound. Curling his fingers into a fist, he formed a magical barrier to the bleeding, a first aid technique he'd learned in the Arcane Corps.

Golden Feral eyes opened. "Dave…" Fred gasped. "Kurt… is Kurt… Okay?"

"He was shot. Stoli's dead." Hastily, Dave added, "But I'm sure Kurt's gone back to his body." If he could just keep Fred talking, maybe the man could hang on until an ambulance arrived. "Do you have your cell? Can you call 911?" No way in hell could Dave dial the phone with his manifestation's fingers. Physical buttons, yes. A touch screen, no.

"I… think so." His voice sounded faint, breathy. Fred fumbled in a pocket, but the phone fell from his hand.

* * *

With a sense of relief, Jake spotted the BFS sign with its carved lion head logo. The tires of his battered Ford 150 pickup truck slung gravel as he took the turn a little too fast. He floored it down the tree-lined drive deeper into the property.

Kurt leaned against the passenger door, still out cold, only the seat belt holding him upright.

Distant roars sounded. When Jake reached out, he could feel his Familiar's agitation. Unfortunately, Clarence couldn't see what was going on, though Arc magic hung in the air like smoke. Jake could feel it all the way out in the sanctuary's drive.

Somebody had just worked one hell of a spell.

The first thing he saw when he pulled into the parking lot was a police car, its driver's door open, blue lights casting revolving beams. Shit, he'd hoped to beat the deputy there. If the poor bastard ran into an Arc booby trap...

But no sooner had he skidded the truck to a stop than Kurt began to convulse, his body arching, legs and arms thumping randomly against the car interior. His fist hit Jake's shoulder so hard it stung.

"Fuck!" Jake slapped the Ford into park and grabbed for his friend's wrist to keep him from hurting himself. Kurt wrenched free with a strangled scream and strength far greater than human.

Power filled the truck cab, and every hair on Jake's body bristled with the electric tingle. The psychic scent of tiger and ozone flooded the cab, much stronger than the Feral magic Kurt normally radiated. It felt more like Fred or Dave, people who'd completely melded with their Familiars. Jake's heart sank, knowing what that must mean.

If Kurt and his tiger had melded, Stoli was dead. Now his friend was going to have to deal with sharing his human body with his cat's spirit. Having witnessed Dave's struggles -- not to mention what had happened to Bobby -- Jake knew it would be a painful transition. And it could be downright lethal for innocent bystanders.

He caught his friend's shoulder. "Kurt? What's going on? What happened?"

Kurt straightened and looked at him, his eyes dazed, his expression devastated and grieving. "Sniper. There was a sniper. He shot me! Stoli's dead."

"Shit!"

"A bear Feral attacked Dad. He's been hurt. Hurt bad." He grabbed the door handle, scrabbled as if he couldn't quite make his fingers work. "We've got to get in there. They need us!"

He wrenched the door open and bolted out of the cab.

"Damn it, Kurt, wait!" Jake paused just long enough to grab his M&P SHIELD pistol from the glove compartment, then jumped out after him.

A bear Feral? Jesus, he wished the little nine-millimeter semi-auto was something with a lot more punch. Like maybe a surface to air missile.

As he raced after his friend, Jake shot a worried glance at the empty patrol car. In the distance, sirens wailed closer. Apparently the Sarge had decided they needed more backup after all.

Jake was no longer sure that was a good thing.

Bad as this situation was, it could get worse. When a cat spirit first entered a human host, the man had to deal with all the animal's power and instincts intensifying his own. And that could be incredibly fucking dangerous.

Just look at Bobby and Dave.

Given time, Ferals usually adjusted, but in a situation like this, all bets were off. And the cops knew it, which could make the situation even more dangerous. It was going to take all Jake's leadership skills and talent for bullshit to keep this mess from detonating. *I shouldn't have called it in.*

Too late now.

Jake poured on the speed, fighting to catch up to

his best friend. Who, God help him, seemed to be running faster than an Olympic sprinter. "Damn it, Kurt, slow down! You're going to get shot -- again!" For someone who'd just had a grand mal, the bastard could move. *Has to be manifesting his cat's magic.*

This is going to suck.

* * *

Genevieve paced the length of the clinic hallway in worry as the sense of dark magic grew denser. Outside, a chorus of feline anger and fear rolled over the park: everything from the thunderous roars of lions, tigers and jaguars to the screams of pumas and the smaller cats. They all knew something horrible had happened.

Goddamnit, I have to do something. There's an Arcanist out there working a really nasty spell.

And she'd just heard Fred scream in agony.

For God's sake, they're tigers, her common sense argued. *They can take care of themselves. You, on the other hand, could get yourself killed -- by a bear!*

She was also her parents' daughter. No kid of Martin and Diane Reyes was going to sit on her ass while people got hurt. But what could she do? The kind of healing magic she performed was no good for major trauma; it took too long.

An electric tingle built in the back of her brain. She'd thought the healing had drained her, but at the thought of Fred in danger, facing God knew what... Sheer adrenaline brought her power blazing to life.

Fuck it, I've got to try. She slammed through the door and stopped, listening. Her thoughts raced. Could some Caliphate terrorist have tracked Kurt back to the sanctuary looking for a little payback?

But that was crazy. The Caliphate's Ferals had access to lion and tiger Familiars, but the Arcane

Corps, the Chinese and the Russians were the only ones who bred Feral polar bears. This guy couldn't be a Caliphate sorcerer.

Still, someone had cast a major spell at the sanctuary. And like it or not, Genevieve was the most powerful Arc in town. She might be the only one who could deactivate whatever the hell it was.

Reaching out with her magic, she got a fix on the malicious working and started toward it.

* * *

Kurt skidded to a halt. *Fuck. Oh, fuck.*

A Sheriff's deputy faced off with Dave over his father's body. The tiger lay on his belly several feet away from Fred, but the officer still looked thoroughly freaked.

"I didn't attack Fred." Dave sounded utterly calm, despite the shaking gun trained on his head. "He's my friend."

"Then what are you doing out of your cage?"

"I came to investigate when I heard the fight."

"Bullshit. You're probably the one who took the bite out of him!"

Fred's head lifted weakly, yet his voice thundered, augmented by his magic. "Idiot, it was a Feral bear!" The amplified roar silenced absolutely everyone, even the sanctuary's agitated animals. His head dropped back to the sand, and he panted from the titanic effort.

"Dad!" Joy surged through Kurt. Forgetting the cop, he started for the gate.

The deputy snapped around, and Kurt broke step as the man aimed his gun at him. "Back *off*!"

Jake grabbed Kurt by the forearm and hauled him back. "Do you want to get shot?" he hissed before snapping at his fellow cop, "Holster your weapon and let this man talk to his father."

"This is a crime scene, Nolan. For all we know, he was involved."

"No, he wasn't, because I was with him at Potions when his father was attacked," Jake snarled. "Call dispatch and have them send an ambulance."

A hot flush colored the man's face, and he sneered. "You're not my sergeant, Feral. Hell, you're barely out of the Academy."

"Yeah, I *am* a Feral, which makes me better equipped to deal with Ferals than you. Go outside, wait for our backup to arrive, and then look for the damned killers," Jake said, enunciating every word. "We need to clear the park and make sure those bastards aren't still here."

They glared at each other savagely a long moment before the deputy's nerve broke. "You'd better be right, Nolan." Growling a curse, he turned and strode from the arena.

"Kurt?" Now Fred's voice sounded faint, broken and raspy. He'd evidently used the last of his strength to defend Dave. "Son?"

Kurt bolted into the arena and fell to his knees beside Fred. The smell of blood was choking this close. No surprise; his father's gore-soaked shirt lay in shreds, and there was a horrific wound over his belly. He must be in agony.

"Dad! Jesus!" He jerked his knit shirt off and pressed it to the deepest of the wounds, still sluggishly seeping blood.

Kurt was dimly conscious of Jake calling dispatch for that ambulance.

"Let me do that." Dave shouldered him aside. Generating a manifestation to block the blood, the tiger told Fred, "You shouldn't have used all that magic talking to him."

"Couldn't let him shoot... you," Fred gasped, somehow managing a strained smile.

"Don't talk. Save your strength." With an effort, Kurt managed to keep his voice level. Judging by his father's pale, sweating face, Fred had to be in shock. Especially given all the blood soaking into the arena sand. "The ambulance is on the way. Just..."

"Listen... Listen to me. Fuckers trapped me... Heard a bear... roar..." Fred wheezed. His eyes rolled as if he were looking at something that wasn't there. "Found him... in the arena. Polar bear. Arc trap..." He fell silent, panting with effort.

Kurt stroked his father's bloody forehead, his heart squeezing in his chest. "I'll make the bastards pay. They won't get away with this."

Fred didn't seem to hear. "Some kind of spell. Couldn't get out of the arena. Fought... I saw the Arc shoot... you... Bear ripped me up... Vanished... Spooks... Fucking spooks..."

"Dad, save your strength. Stay with us."

Fred's eyes rolled as he tried to cling to consciousness. "Sorry... Sorry about what I said... about girl..."

"What girl?"

"Gen... vieve..." His voice dropped to a cracked whisper. "Want you... be... happy... Love... you..." Fred sighed, a long exhalation. His eyes slid out of focus, going fixed.

Panic stabbed Kurt, Stoli's fear adding to his own. They'd both loved Fred. "Dad!" Closing his eyes, he stared hard with his magical senses just as his father's spirit -- that familiar Feral meld of lion and man -- whirled away into the night like sparks from a campfire.

"Dad!"

But it was too late. Fred was gone.

Kurt sat staring blindly after him. Dad couldn't be dead. Not like this. Not murdered. Trapped by a witch, batted around by a damned bear, ripped open when the Arc shot Kurt.

Those fuckers had come into Kurt's territory and killed his father.

Grief and rage tore through him, with Stoli echoing it until fury built fury like a stream of gasoline spraying across a forest fire. Opening his eyes, he grappled for discipline, sweat streaming down his face.

Dad's gone. They murdered him! Emotion thundered against his fraying self-control like a sandblaster. Kurt threw back his head and roared.

Chapter Four

"Look, I'm an Arcanist! Somebody cast a spell in there," Genevieve snapped. "I need to break it. Let me by!"

The beefy young cop glared down at her, one hand resting on his belt, not quite on his gun. "And how do I know you didn't cast the spell? Maybe you set that guy up to get ripped apart by that bear…"

"Fred? Fred's hurt? I can help!"

"Or you could make it worse." The deputy's eyes narrowed with frustrated anger under cropped, prematurely thinning hair. He curled his lip in a sneer. "Witch."

Oh, great, a Humanist. "I'm a healer," she gritted. "Maybe I can help him, if you'd just let me. Or we could just stand here while he dies."

The cop glared at her for a long minute. She glared back -- until, to her surprise, he started looking unnerved. "Fine! Go! Hell, he's just a fuckin' Feral. No skin off my nose if you kill him."

Outrage tightening her mouth, Genevieve hurried past him before he could change his mind. *He thought I was going to hex him.* But as she walked, a growing sense of evil rolled over her consciousness, and the hair on the back of her neck began to rise. No wonder the Humanist was so damned paranoid.

When she'd first arrived, entering BFS had felt like plunging into a river of magic from all the Ferals, human and otherwise, not to mention the purely animal cats. But now the energy had a leaden quality to it, a sense of seething darkness she knew indicated a very sinister spell.

Genevieve followed the psychic stench along the gravel path as fast as she dared. Fortunately, the walkway was brightly lit; she didn't have to worry about crashing headfirst into a tree. As she trotted along, she was conscious of glowing eyes watching her from the surrounding enclosures.

Fred's cats.

The roar rolled out over the park, a shattered cry of fury and grief. It seemed to stab right past Genevieve's twenty-first century intelligence to her inner small mammal. She jolted to a stop -- and found herself staring at a sign reading "BFS Educational Arena."

Spotting an open gate through the octagonal fence, Gen ran through it. And stopped dead, staring in sick horror.

Kurt knelt beside a body lying crumpled in a pool of blood. Dave stood beside him, his ears flat, his golden eyes too wide.

Oh, crap.

"You bastards!" Kurt leaped to his feet, magic snapping sparks around him. "I'm going to fuckin' kill you!" His tiger manifested in a golden explosion, forming a glowing shell of magic.

Ice slid through Genevieve's blood. *Oh, God, he's going to kill somebody.*

Gen wasn't the only one who was freaked out. Dave tensed, though whether he was going to run or do something to stop his friend, she had no idea. A blond man in a Deadpool t-shirt stood on the other side of the cat, watching Kurt as though he expected to be attacked.

There was a gun in his hand.

Kurt roared again, his tiger's rearing shell surrounding him, balanced weightlessly on its hind legs in a way that would have been impossible for a flesh and blood animal.

She had to do something or that blond guy was going to have to kill him.

"Kurt!" Even as she started toward him, Gen realized what a monumentally bad idea this was. She kept going anyway. It was too easy to imagine how she'd feel if Dad had been sacrificed in an Arcanist spell. "Kurt, I'm so sorry…"

"Lady, what are you doing? Get back." The blond man's gaze flicked to her, and he brought the gun up, aiming it at Kurt. He spoke in the dead flat tone of a man whose world had exploded as he desperately tried to contain the fallout. "Get out of here."

Dave slunk toward her, his gaze on Kurt's. "Go. He's out of control. He could hurt you."

"No, he won't." Her gaze locked on Kurt, silhouetted against the blaze of his manifestation. She reached out to him, using her own power to brush his aura. His grief slammed into her consciousness in a battering wave. The impact of it rocked her back on her heels. *He's in so much pain…*

"Kurt's tiger is dead," the blond man said in a carefully controlled voice. "I think he's trapped in a feedback loop."

Soldiers caught in feedback loops had been known to kill their teammates. *Oh, hell. We're screwed.*

And yet… Sometimes she could touch another's aura, reduce the pain, as she'd done for Parvati. She might be able to help Kurt, too. There wasn't time to draw the kind of intricate spell that would force him to calm down, but if she could reduce his pain enough, he could regain control.

Of course, if it doesn't work, he may kill me.

Licking dry lips, Genevieve moved slowly forward, sketching sigils in the air to focus her magic.

Extending her hands, she sent her aura sliding over his in a gentle brush. "Kurt? I can help you if you'll let me. I can help you control it."

The big man's eyes glowed from the burning mask of his tiger. The manifestation's mouth opened, displaying mystical teeth that could rip into her skin every bit as efficiently as the physical version. "Genevieve?" The voice sounded inhuman, reverberating as it did with his power. "He's dead, Genevieve. Dad's dead."

"I know, Kurt."

"Lady, back off!" Deadpool Shirt started toward her. Judging from the glow of his eyes, he was a Feral too.

Kurt's gaze whipped to him, hot and direct with aggression. He growled, the sound so deep it was almost subsonic.

The man swallowed, but kept coming, broad shoulders tensed to fight. "This is that girl, Genevieve? The witch you like, right?"

"Mine!" Kurt sprang, covering ten feet in an impossible leap as his magic drove his human body forward. Genevieve yelped, startled. His arms snapped around her like a trap clamping shut, and he jerked her against his side.

Gen found herself looking out at the world through the glowing tiger mask. *Crap!*

In a blur, Deadpool Shirt shifted his aim to follow his friend. "Kurt, stop. Don't hurt her. Don't make me shoot you."

"No!" Dave snapped, a rumbling growl rolling beneath the words. "Holster that weapon before you set him off."

"I'm not... going... to hurt... her..." Kurt growled.

"Step away!"

"No." He bared his teeth, and the huge fangs of his manifestation echoed the expression. "She's *mine*, Jake!"

"Kurt, you don't even know her! That's your cat talking. Let her go!"

"It's all right," Genevieve said, touching the powerful arm around her waist to draw his attention. He felt like Michelangelo's David cast in heated steel.

"No, it's not." Kurt met her gaze, his face limned in the glow of his manifestation. The mouth that should have looked sensual twisted in pain until her heart ached for him. "It can't get any *less* all right."

"It can if you hurt her." The muzzle of Jake's pistol tracked him steadily, but there was anguish in the Feral's eyes.

"Don't threaten me. This is my place. She's mine." Kurt tensed, focusing on his friend with the alien gaze of a cat on the edge of exploding into violence.

I've got to talk him down, or we're all screwed. "Look at me, Kurt." She poured her aura over his, using it to slow the furious churn of his power. "They're not going to hurt me, and neither are you."

He stared at her, nothing at all human in those golden Feral eyes.

* * *

Rage clawed for control, and Kurt grappled with it, trying to fight his way out the feedback loop. *I don't have the luxury of losing my shit. I'll hurt Genevieve.* He could feel her magic coiling around his, cooling, soothing. Slowing the feedback of his grief and rage. Reducing it just enough to let him fight it.

He had to fight it.

An image flashed through his mind: *Bobby*

Angela Knight   Arcane Kiss (Arcane Talents)

Nolan's Feral eyes, wide and insane, framed by the blaze of his lion manifestation as he reared over Dave Frost. Dave had still been human then. Still been alive.

Kurt brought his rifle up... And hesitated, unable to shoot his best friend's kid brother.

Bobby lunged for Dave's throat. Kurt fired. *A heartbeat too late.*

He fought the chaos ripping at his consciousness, staring down at Gen's lovely features, trying to concentrate on her, on the stakes of losing control. Reflected light from his manifestation painted the pretty contours of her face in gold, kissed the curve of her lips.

"You've got to be the master of your body, boy," his father told him, a stopwatch in his hand, timing him with dispassionate eyes. Kurt's hand burned, buried deep in a bucket of ice. He'd clenched his teeth, fighting the impulse to jerk it out. *"People die when a Feral loses control."*

He'd been eight years old. Some of the later lessons had been even worse.

Closing his eyes, Kurt drew in a deep breath, and held it for a count of three, then blew it out. Focusing all his attention on his breathing, he worked to slow his heartbeat.

Yet still rage swirled through him, feeding on Stoli's anger as well as his. Fighting his desperate attempts to rein himself in.

Then he felt it. *Magic.* Brushing his consciousness like a feather floating over his skin. *Genevieve.* Trying to work her magic on him, influence him, control him... *Like Mom.* Something hot and ugly detonated in the depths of his brain.

Before he could explode, her hand touched the side of his face, her skin cool and soft on his cheek. Her

- 58 -

blue eyes met his. "Shhhhh," she said softly.

Her magic stroked his. Not to force emotion on him, not to manipulate him with a Bard's magical song, but to soothe. To help. He remembered the way she'd reduced Parvati's physical pain, and knew she was doing the same for him.

Giving him space. Giving him the clarity he needed to exert control over himself. Closing his eyes, he drew in another deep breath. Held it. Blew it out. *In. Out. In. Out.* Combat breathing until the fury drained into the preternatural calm he'd come to know so well during the Caliphate War.

"There." Something brushed his lips, tender as a butterfly's wing. His eyes snapped open. Genevieve stood on her toes, her lips touching his in a chaste, almost sisterly kiss. Her blue eyes stared into his as she murmured against his lips, "I knew you could pull out of it."

And her aura brushed his again, making it thrum a deep, delicious note. She'd probably intended the kiss as a gesture of comfort, but despite his tearing pain, it somehow felt almost sensual.

In an instant, the pain twisted under the touch of her aura, transforming into something equally intimate. In the depths of his mind, heat leaped. Instinctively, he wrapped his arms around her narrow waist. His lips opened against hers, starved for the comfort she offered. Drinking in the taste of her, feeling the soft contours of her body.

That sweetness in the midst of this agony was as desperately welcome as an ice chip to a man burning in hell. Kurt focused on her, grateful for the distraction. But even more than that, there was the taste of her Arcanist magic, swirling all around them, making his skin tingle.

God, Kurt wanted her. Wanted to lose himself in her, to take shelter from the bitter agony of his father's death, if only for a moment. So he kissed Genevieve with all his desperate hunger to forget it all: his sins, his father's death. If only for this one moment. He kissed her, suckling the soft, damp velvet of her mouth, the taste of woman and magic.

By the time he lifted his head, both of them had begun to shake.

When Kurt glanced around, he saw they were standing in the simple illumination of the arena security lights. His tiger manifestation had vanished.

He was in control again.

Genevieve smiled up at him, though her face was wet with tears and her mouth trembled. "There. I knew you could do it."

Before Kurt could reply, a new voice spoke up, sounding dry. "Anybody want to tell me what's going on?"

Tensing, he instinctively drew her close as he looked toward the source of the voice. A dozen cops stood in the entrance of the arena enclosure. Every one of them had his gun drawn and pointed at them.

Oh, shit.

* * *

Genevieve's slowing heartbeat began to pound again as she stared in dismay at the cops. She was acutely aware of just how close Kurt was to the edge. If any of these men did anything aggressive, they could undo all her desperate work.

"Gen, what are you doing in the middle of this?" A man shouldered out from among the deputies. Unlike the uniformed officers, he wore khakis and a tan knit shirt with a Sheriff's Department logo. He was a little less than average height, with an athlete's powerful build and curly brown hair that made his handsome face look almost boyish. His calm, slow speech tended to defuse tense situations even as it made people underestimate his considerable intelligence.

"Grant!" She blew out a breath in relief at the sight of her friend. "Damn, I'm glad to see you."

"Wish it was under better circumstances." He turned and began to give a series of crisp orders to the men around him. He gestured at Jake and a tall, dark-skinned deputy. "Nolan and Williams, you're with me. The rest of you, spread out and search the park. Flag anything that doesn't belong, especially blood trails and weapons. Bad guys or witnesses would be even better."

"Grant?" Kurt murmured, gold eyes narrowing and taking on a dangerous glint. His magic boiled around them, and Genevieve realized he was about to manifest his tiger again.

Damn it, I just got him calmed down! Gen wrapped her fingers around his wrist, trying to reestablish their magical connection. His skin felt too warm, feverish with the magic he was using.

Fur seemed to brush across her mind -- Stoli, his spirit tiger, reaching out to her. There was something possessive about that elemental contact, as if the cat thought she somehow belonged to them.

Which probably explained the growl making Kurt's chest vibrate against hers. *Crap*. She started talking. Fast. "Grant Sawyer's a violent crimes detective with the Laurelton Sheriff's Office. I do forensic sketches and magical consulting for him. Nice guy."

As the other cops scattered, Sawyer walked past them to Fred's body. Careful not to step in the blood, he bent to search for a pulse, as calm as a man who wasn't being glared at by agitated Ferals.

When he straightened, his broad shoulders slumped. "He's gone." He looked down at the big sprawled body before turning to study them, his dark gaze cool. "This is Fred Briggs, isn't it? I've seen him on the news." He looked at Kurt, and his voice gentled. "I'm sorry for your loss."

To her relief, Genevieve felt the aggression bleed out of Kurt. "So am I." He closed his glowing eyes and swallowed, making an obvious effort to control the animal instincts that had driven him to assert a claim over Gen.

Sawyer turned to Jake. "Green said you called this in. What can you tell me?"

Jake didn't quite come to attention, but it was close. Evidently he respected the detective as much as Genevieve did. "A Feral and an Arcanist entered BFS tonight and trapped Mr. Briggs in the arena with some kind of spell. Fred manifested his lion and fought the Feral."

"Looked like a polar bear, based on the size," Kurt added in the clipped tone of a military briefing. "I'd estimate it was about twelve feet tall, based on the comparison to Dad's lion, which is... was... about eight feet standing reared."

Sawyer's brows lifted. "Damn. Big animal."

Jake nodded and continued, "Fred was badly wounded during the fight and died about ten minutes ago. Bled out."

"How much of that did you witness?"

"Not much. Fred managed to tell us what happened before he passed. Deputy Green was there." He grimaced. "Pointing a gun at Dave, who was trying to render first aid."

Sawyer glanced at the tiger, who'd moved over beside Kurt and Genevieve and lay down on his belly in an unsuccessful attempt to look harmless. "I can see why he might have been intimidated. Did Briggs have any idea who his attackers were?"

Jake shrugged. "He didn't give a description, just said it was an Arcanist and a bear Feral."

"They were wearing magical camo," Dave put in. When Sawyer looked at him, the tip of his striped tail twitched in irritation. "I was Arcane Corps before I went furry. I know a Spook Suit when somebody in one shoots at me. Couldn't see the Arc at all unless you looked for the magic."

"Did he have any idea why they attacked him?" The detective crouched to study Fred's body. He reached into a pocket, pulled out his cell phone, and started snapping photos. "Had he argued with anybody? There had to be some reason these guys killed a man everybody in town considers a saint."

"It definitely had something to do with magic," Genevieve said. "Really dark magic. I sensed it all the way out in the sanctuary." Glancing around the bloody arena, she again felt the swirl of alien power. Kurt's crisis had distracted her from it, but now she closed her eyes and *looked*.

Sigils appeared behind her lids, spinning in lazy malevolence. "Yeah, Arcanist magic. And the spell is still active."

Sawyer stiffened. "What? Now? There are a hell of a lot of Ferals here. You sure that's not what you're sensing?"

"No, she's right," Kurt said. "Dave and I ran right into a working at the entry to the arena -- must have been the same one that trapped Dad in with the bear. The Arc was up on the bleachers with a weapon.

Probably a sniper rifle. That's who shot my cat." He pointed up toward the bleachers where a furry still shape lay draped over a seat plank. A spasm of grief flashed over his face before he banished it. "I've got to get him down from there."

Sawyer followed his gaze and frowned. "We have to get a necropsy on that cat. I'll need the bullet for ballistics."

"I'll call the vet."

While they were talking, Genevieve started walking around the arena, holding her hands out at waist height, feeling the currents of energy swirling around her. Kurt paced her, the set of his shoulders protective as he stared around as though on the lookout for another attack. "It's definitely a working, and it's powerful as hell. But I can't quite tell what it's supposed to *do*." She looked up at him. "You said there was a barrier at the arena entrance?"

"I ran head-first into it. Felt like a brick wall." He strode across the bloody sand, head down, and gestured at a spot just before the gate. "Right about here. You can see my -- Stoli's -- paw prints."

Genevieve extended a palm over the churned sand. Someone with a lot of power had indeed cast a spell circle there. "We've got at least two different workings. This one is designed to block the gate entrance like a cork in a bottle. It's not active now or I doubt we could've gotten in. The killers must have deactivated it when they ran."

"And the second spell?" Sawyer asked. He'd followed them and stood taking notes in one of the narrow spiral notebooks he used at crime scenes.

"Let me take a look." Gen moved away from Kurt and started pacing along the inner perimeter of the fence. Energy roiled the air so violently she could almost see it with her eyes open. She hissed at the stinging electric tingle. "Damn, it's powerful! Strongest working I've ever encountered. And it's definitely death magic. I think they killed Fred to power the spell."

"So he was a human sacrifice?" Sawyer cursed viciously. "What kind of spell is it?"

"Booby-trap?" Dave trailed them, his tail whipping back and forth. "Do we need to get the fuck out before it blows?"

Genevieve shook her head; her mother had taught her how to spot mystical antipersonnel mines when she was a kid. "It's not a bomb… exactly. It does something nasty, but I can't tell what." She closed her eyes and turned her head, scanning the arena.

Glowing shapes seemed to hover in the darkness around her. Eyes still closed, she began working her way around the arena. Her shoulder raked across wire as she collided with the arena fence.

A firm male hand took her by the arm -- Sawyer, guiding her as he often did whenever she tried something like this. "Thanks…"

A menacing growl sounded in the air. Through her closed lids, Gen saw a tiger slinking toward her, head down, lips peeled off scimitar fangs.

Behind the manifestation, a glowing man snapped in Dave's voice, "Get it under control, Kurt!" He was tall, with the wiry build of a marathon runner. Big, bony hands, close-cropped hair, and rawboned features made him look as if he should be riding the range somewhere. He was dressed like a soldier in a tank shirt, camo pants and combat boots. Glowing dog tags hung around his neck.

Startled, Gen opened her eyes.

Kurt stood where she'd seen the tiger, while

Dave watched his friend warily from the location of the glowing soldier.

"Detective, get away from her," the tiger said in a very even, calm voice. "His control sucks just now."

"She has to keep her eyes closed to see the magic, so somebody's got to guide her," Sawyer objected.

"Then I'll do it." Kurt's growl was even lower than it had been before, naked menace in the sound.

The detective tensed, eying him. "I don't think that's a good idea." You couldn't be a cop and be a coward. "Are you sure you can be trusted with her? Because frankly it doesn't look that way to me."

Kurt growled louder, a savage light in his eyes.

Just what this situation doesn't need: a pissing contest. *Awesome*. "It's all right," Genevieve told Sawyer. "Kurt's not going to hurt me."

Reluctantly, the detective stepped back, though he didn't move far. Kurt glared at him, the air growling around him, reacting to his magic.

"Might want to give him some room," Jake suggested in a deeply careful voice. "He's going to be strung a little tight until he catches his balance. It's not a good idea to push him."

Sawyer studied Kurt coolly. "Did your dad push you too?"

"Frequently. But he wasn't the one who shot me, and I'm not the one who killed him."

The two men stared at each other, hostility sizzling between them like burning meat. At last, Sawyer stepped back even as Jake and Dave moved protectively closer. Gen couldn't tell who they were there to restrain, the cop or Kurt.

She gave them all the look they deserved. "Flex your testosterone later. I'm trying to work here. Kurt, are you going to help me or not?" Physical contact would make it easier to help him calm his roiling aura.

"I'll guide you." He took her arm.

She closed her eyes and went back to pacing along the perimeter of the enclosure, trying to ignore the glowing tiger that walked where Kurt should be. It was more than a little disconcerting, especially since she could feel Kurt's fingers cupping her elbow. It was as if he was both man and tiger.

Come to think of it, that was exactly what he was.

And I don't have time for this. Dragging her attention back to the matter at hand, Gen concentrated on the sigils burning like coals behind her closed lids. They floated in midair in three concentric rings, each a different shade of red, blazing almost as brightly as the Ferals. "I don't get this at all. I can't tell what the spell is supposed to do, other than something vicious."

"That's not exactly surprising, if they murdered my father to cast it."

She frowned, studying the sigils, which glowed in scarlet, ruby and crimson. Each shade of red probably formed a different layer of the spell, much as her own pastels did. Whatever it did, the working was complex as hell. "I've got to dispel this. I don't dare let it run, especially if we don't know what it's doing."

Opening her eyes, she turned to Sawyer, who was busily taking notes. "I'm going to have to look these sigils up. I need to go back to the cat clinic and get my sketchpad. I have to copy the sigils, and I need a big enough pad to do it."

"Where is it? I'll have one of the deputies get it."

"It's in my messenger bag. Just bring the whole bag. I left it in the Cat Clinic with the caged tiger."

"I'll get it," Jake said, starting for the gate. "I know the clinic better than your guys anyway."

"That'd be great."

He broke into a run, broad shoulders rolling, arms pumping.

Five minutes later he was back, the bag slung over one shoulder. He handed it over, not even breathing hard. The cop was in good shape -- but then, given that he was both a Feral and an Arcane Corps vet, that probably went without saying.

"Thanks." Gen pulled out the pad and three colored pencils of the same shades of red as the spell circles. Putting two of the pencils in her mouth, she used the third to sketch the first set of sigils, closing her eyes to study the shapes, then opening them to draw each as precisely as she could.

Each magical sigil represented an entire word or phrase, rather like ancient Egyptian hieroglyphics. The trouble was, most of the sigils that made up the working were so obscure, she had no idea what they meant.

Genevieve copied each set of sigils in their respective colors, then moved a little further and started drawing the next set. As she worked, she was careful not to infuse them with any of her own magic, since that would defeat the purpose of breaking the spell.

It was a slow process, but Genevieve didn't dare try to hurry. If she got one of the sigils wrong, it might be impossible to determine the working's purpose. Worse, she might think it did one thing when it did something entirely different.

"Once you figure out what it does, will you be able to tell who cast it?" Sawyer asked.

"Maybe." She paused to copy an elegant swirling pattern. "My mother specializes in magical theory. Chances are good she'll be able to decipher them. If that fails, I can always post this in an Arcane Internet forum, see if anybody sees something they recognize. Often there's a distinctive style to the way an Arc puts a spell together. Maybe someone will be able to ID the caster."

"Sounds like a long shot," Jake commented.

"Yeah, but it could also work. Gen's paid off for me before." Sawyer turned back to her. "Do you think you could sketch the attackers for me?" She'd done magical forensic sketches for him in the past that had helped him make arrests in major cases.

"Depends on how much breaking this spell takes out of me. I may not have enough left."

"May not work though," Dave pointed out. "Spook Suits are designed to block magic as well as visible light."

Sawyer shrugged. "Worth a try anyway."

By the time Gen finished walking the circle, her head was aching savagely from sheer effort. And she was nowhere near done. She only hoped she had the strength to break the working.

After checking to make sure her work was accurate, she tucked the pad and pencils back into her bag. Gen looped the strap over her shoulder and headed for the spell's dark heart.

Sullen arcane energy swirled above Fred Briggs' butchered body, making the hair on her arms stand up as she approached. When Genevieve closed her eyes, she could see glowing lines of force in scarlet, ruby, and crimson pouring down into the corpse and out again in great loops.

The magic felt greasy somehow, like rotting fish. Everything in her wanted to recoil.

Instead Gen reached out, found the point where the lines met over Fred's chest to shoot down into his heart. Sick pity blended with helpless anger at the thought of someone using the poor man's life force to power a spell this foul. Fred deserved better.

Damned if she'd let his killers get away with it.

In her mind, Gen visualized a glowing broadsword. She pictured taking it in both hands. Imagined the weapon's weight, its cool, steel purity, the feel of the leather wrapped around the hilt, until she could see the shining blade behind her closed lids, white against the sullen red glow of dark magic.

Gathering every bit of power that remained to her, she focused it and swung the mystical weapon with the full weight of her will behind the stroke.

BOOOOM!

The magical detonation hit her in the face like an enormous fist, knocking her backward. Kurt's strong, warm arms caught her before she could hit the ground.

"Take that, you son of a bitch," Gen gasped, and everything went dark.

Chapter Five

Indigo screamed.

Virgil Ford jumped in alarm and whirled in time to see his wife pitch forward. She hit the ground face-first and went into a grand mal seizure, back arching, limbs jerking. A high, wheezing cry tore from her contorted lips.

"Indigo!" He dove for her in a panic. He'd never seen her do that before.

Thank God for the spells on their Spook Suits, because they were barely out of the sanctuary. Without that magic, they would have been caught for sure. BFS was swarming with cops who would've heard her shrieks. As it was, the only reason Virgil could see or hear her was the exception built into the spell to let them perceive each other.

"Oh, Jesus!" He grabbed her wrists and held on as she bucked and heaved with that inhuman screech. Even as strong as he was, Virgil could barely control her. He ended up flinging a leg astride her hip and sitting on her to hold her down.

What the hell had gone wrong?

At last she collapsed, panting. Looking around to make sure nobody was close enough to see them, he grabbed the knit mask and dragged it off over her head. Which would probably make her look like a decapitated head, but it couldn't be helped.

Her face was agonized, her eyes staring blankly, wide with pain and shock. *Looks like some kind of spell backlash.*

He'd seen this once during the war, when someone had broken one of her spells. If so, she was in for one hell of a migraine, even apart from the aftereffects of the seizure.

She clamped her eyes shut, her teeth grinding together in an expression of agony.

"What happened?" He hoped it was only backlash. He didn't think the tiger had injured her, or she'd probably be dead already. "Talk to me, damn it!"

"Spell..." She gasped. "Somebody broke... the... fucking spell!"

"Which spell?" She had dozens of them running. He only hoped it wasn't connected with one of the sacrifices. He'd hate like hell for a sacrifice to have died for nothing.

She pried her lids open and glared at him. "What spell do you think? The one on Briggs." She reached out a shaking hand. "Give me that mask before they find us."

He slid it back on over her head himself, knowing her headache was probably too savage for her to manage it. "I thought you said the cops in this town didn't have an Arcanist."

"They don't. A department this size shouldn't be able to afford somebody with the kind of talent it would take to break one of my spells."

"He's that good?"

"Yes, he's that good. Get off me, we've got to get going."

Virgil rose and helped her to her feet. "What are we going to do?"

She swayed, then steadied herself and took a careful step in the direction of the BFS arena. "We've got to go back so I can kill that damned Arc. Then we'll have to lay low for a while until I can recast the spell."

He stared at her masked face. It glowed crimson with magic to his Feral senses. "Are you crazy? Every cop in the county has converged on this fucking place. There's no way in hell we're going to be able to..."

"We've got to," she snarled over her shoulder, still hobbling the way they came. "If we don't, it's all for nothing. The master spell won't work without this section. Everything we've done, everyone we've sacrificed will be for nothing."

He could tell by the tone of her voice that she was wearing that chilly fanatic gleam he hated. Virgil loved her, but sometimes he thought she really was crazy. God knew she had reason to be. "Maybe we should just forget this."

"That's not an option. Those Humanist bastards are about to ram through NTRA. This is the only way to stop them. Where's my fucking weapon?" She glanced around, spotted the rifle she'd evidently dropped, and pointed at it imperiously.

With a sigh, he picked it up and handed it to her. "I thought the idea was to keep down the collateral damage. Maybe we have to make another sacrifice, but that doesn't mean we've got to kill the Arc."

"If this guy is as good as I suspect, he'll realize the spell he broke is part of a larger working. If he hasn't, somebody will. They'll start looking for patterns, and once they do, they'll figure it all out. They'll track us down, Virgil. And some of those states have the death penalty."

"And we'd be separated." His gut twisted at the thought. He'd never see her again. Both of them would disappear into some Talent prison, never to see the light of day again, even if they weren't executed. "Christ, Indigo, let's just forget this."

He saw again the face of the man he'd just killed. The faces of all the Ferals he'd killed to make her vision reality. *I should never have let her talk me into this.*

She turned her head with an effort, as if fighting the aftereffects of the backlash. "I'm not giving up! I have *seen* this, Virgil. If they pass NTRA, internment camps are the next step. We have to stop them!"

"But what if what we're doing guarantees NTRA passes? I'm tired of killing, Indigo! Look, we can leave the country, go somewhere without an extradition treaty with the US. We can finally retire, sit in the sun and drink those froufrou drinks you like."

"And the people we killed will still be dead! For *nothing*. Or we can finish it and build a better world. Just one more and it will be done." Her gloved hand touched the side of his face. He felt it even through the mask he wore, the tingle of her power, stronger and more seductive than any he'd ever felt.

Virgil's entire body leaped in response. She'd always had that effect on him. But..."I'm tired, Indy. I'm afraid we're going to go down in history like that fuckin' Caliphate sorcerer bin Laden."

"Please." His heart wrenched at the pain and pleading in her voice. "Please help me. I can't do this without you. If we just have courage a little longer, it will all be worth it. I swear to you."

His shoulders slumped. "You can't just kill that Arc in front of a dozen cops. They'll bring in the Feds, and when they do..."

"None of the others brought in the Feds. My magic worked on them, and it'll work on this bunch once the Arc's out of the picture. I'll cast another spell, get them all under control. If we do it fast enough, they won't have time to call anybody. We'll be able to finish it."

How the hell did she talk him into this shit? "All right, damn it. Let's get it done."

* * *

Kurt put Genevieve down just as she started coming around. He pushed her hair back from her face and studied her in worry. She was paler than the sand she lay on, and her blue eyes looked dazed. He wasn't surprised. He could still feel his teeth vibrating from the shock of that spell snapping. "Genevieve?"

She moaned. "Not so loud. My head…"

"I'll get the paramedics," Sawyer said and turned to gesture to the ambulance team who'd arrived to transport Fred's body. The pair, a weedy Latino man and a plump blonde, grabbed their stretcher and started inside the enclosure with it.

"Wait…" Gen gasped. "Have your guys… Check the park again. Whoever cast that spell probably collapsed. If they're still here… you may be able to catch them."

Kurt frowned. "Given the Spook Suits, I doubt they'll be able to see the killer even if he is out cold. And given what kind of bastards we're dealing with, that may be a good thing. Not only do they have serious power, but if they're some kind of wetwork team…"

"Professional assassins?" Sawyer frowned uneasily. "You think that's likely?"

"That was a hell of a shot. Not many people could've stayed cool enough to make it with a tiger jumping them." Dave's tail flicked. "On the other hand, this is the South, and a lot of people are good shots with a long gun."

"Yeah, but Spook Suits are a lot harder to create," Kurt argued, stepping back to let the paramedics get to Genevieve. "They're not the kind of thing you just whip up on your mom's sewing machine."

"Neither was that spell." Genevieve flinched as one of the medics shone the light into her eyes while the other took her blood pressure. "Whoever cast it had to be a heavy hitter. It had multiple layers of complexity, and he laid it fast. Otherwise Fred would have caught him at it." She paused thoughtfully. "Or her. Could have been a female Arc, I suppose."

Kurt frowned at her, running a thumb over his lower lip. "But why? Why do this? Why fight my father and kill him? Or for that matter, why do it with a manifestation? Why not shoot him from a distance?"

"Hard to penetrate a manifestation with a bullet," Jake pointed out.

Dave sat back on his haunches and cocked his head. "Depends on how many times you shoot him. If you hang back and blast him long enough, you can punch through."

Kurt waved an impatient hand. "Point is, that bear Feral took a big chance. Dad could easily have killed the bastard -- he fought hard." His gaze flicked toward his father's body, then away again as pain shafted his heart. "If I hadn't distracted him by getting myself shot…"

"Oh, bullshit," Dave growled. "I'm so tired of watching you flog yourself. First about me and Bobby, now your dad. You're a Feral, not fucking Superman."

Jake folded his arms, frowning deeply. "No, but Kurt does have a point. Why *didn't* they shoot Fred?"

"They needed it for the magical charge," Genevieve told them, ignoring the paramedics, who murmured quietly to each other. "Different kinds of death provide varying magical charges. Killing somebody in combat while risking death yourself is about as big as it gets." She frowned. "I reiterate, what the heck did that spell do?"

"Ask your little witchy friends," Sawyer told her. "In the meantime, we need to get out of this arena and let my forensics team get to work before we destroy what little evidence survives."

Kurt rubbed a hand over his aching forehead. He knew the man was right, but the idea of leaving his father's body went against the grain. Although…"We can help with the search. Just tell your guys not to shoot us." A wave of blood lust rolled through him. Once he found the shooter and that murdering bear Feral, the police wouldn't have to worry about putting anybody on trial.

Jake, unsurprisingly, seemed to know exactly what he was thinking. "Why don't you let me take care of that? I can see magic too, and I'm a cop. You're not."

Kurt opened his mouth to snarl, but Dave interrupted. "Do we really want to leave Genevieve by herself? Considering that she just broke the spell they killed Fred to cast? What if they come back and try for *her* now?"

Shit. He stared at his friend, feeling sick. "I should've thought of that."

"You're not thinking straight." Dave flicked a fuzzy ear. "I sure as hell wasn't after I died, and nobody'd murdered my father right in front of me."

Before Kurt could reply, Sawyer pointed at the bulbous housing mounted on a nearby light pole. "Is that a camera? Do you have security video in this place?"

"Sure. Security cams, plus web cams carrying live feeds of the enclosures."

"People love to watch the kitties," Dave observed. "But I doubt any of them will show much. Spook suits are designed to bend most electromagnetic energy, so cams don't pick them up any better than eyes."

"Yeah, but suits can't hide manifestations, and I saw that bear," Kurt said. "The cameras'll pick up the fight."

"Could you burn a copy of the footage for me?" Sawyer looked down at Genevieve, his gaze searching and concerned. "Do you think you'd feel like reviewing the arena footage with me?"

Kurt stiffened. *And watch Dad die?*

"Of course." But there was something a little tight in her expression. She obviously liked the idea no better than he did.

Sawyer gave her a relieved smile. "Thanks. Maybe you can spot something that will help us catch these guys."

"I'll give it my best shot."

Which was a damned good point. If she could find anything at all to let them catch these bastards... *they need to die.*

Unfortunately, there was a hint of acridity to Genevieve's scent he knew meant pain. Kurt frowned at her and asked the paramedics, "Does she need to go to the hospital?"

The EMT shrugged. "Her pupils are equal. Blood pressure is a little elevated, but..." She looked at Genevieve. "How about it. You want to go to the hospital?"

"Heck, no, it's just a headache from breaking that spell." She grimaced. "It was one hell of a spell."

"Then let's get you inside." Dave's tail whipped once. "My shoulder blades are itching."

"Yeah, mine too." She started to sit up, grimacing.

Kurt rose, bent, and swept her into his arms. She felt almost weightless, probably a result of his new strength.

She glowered up at him with a mix of pain and offended pride. "I can walk."

"You can't even sit up." His arms tightened.

"Lighten… up a little, Kurt," she gasped. "You're hurting me."

He almost dropped her, then had to shift her weight in his arms, making her suck in a breath.

Jake looked up as he crouched near Fred's body, where he was attempting to get the killer's scent. "They talked about that in training, remember? It takes some time to get used to the increased strength your cat gives you."

Carefully, Kurt eased his grip and shifted her weight to avoid jolting her more than he had to. "Yeah. Yeah, all right. Is that better?"

"Look, just put me down. I can walk."

"I don't think so. Besides, in the shape you're in, you can't walk fast enough."

"And the longer we're out here, the more danger we're all in," Dave put in.

She sighed. "All right, damn it."

As they walked, Sawyer snapped orders into his radio. "We're looking for two subjects, probably dressed in magical camo designed to make them invisible. Keep an eye out for anything moving with no visible cause, because one of them may be moving it. One subject is a Feral bear, and the other is an Arc with a long gun. If you see a glowing lion, that's our Feral deputy…"

"And don't shoot the tiger either," Dave muttered. "Last time, I didn't like it at all."

Kurt snorted. "I didn't think much of it either."

* * *

"It's a woman." Simmering rage heated Indigo's voice as they crouched in the brush, watching Briggs' son walk past carrying a slender redhead in his arms. A tiger and someone who was probably a cop followed. "I think I recognize her. It's Genevieve

Reyes. She's an Arcanist painter -- I read an article about her in *The New York Times*. It didn't say anything about her working with the local cops." Her voice dropped into a snarl. "Traitorous bitch."

"If we try to take her out now, we're going to get caught," Virgil pointed out uneasily. "And then your spell will never be finished. If you know who she is, we can find out where she lives and pick her off later."

Indigo considered that a long nerve-racking moment. "All right." The words sounded as if she bit them off between her teeth. "We'll wait. It'll give me more time to think of a really good way to make her pay." She turned back toward the park exit, passing unseen between two cops. "Whoever we have to kill to make up for Briggs is going to be on her head."

* * *

Kurt crossed the central green with Genevieve in his arms, passing the Gift Shop and the Cat Clinic. Cops worked their way through the trees, radios crackling, flashlights throwing dancing beams of illumination as they searched for the killers.

He climbed the steps of a long, low building painted rustic brown with a wrap-around porch. A wooden sign with the lion logo stood out front with the words *BFS Offices* scrolled in gold.

Decades before, it had been a farmhouse belonging to one of Kurt's great uncles. Dad had renovated it for use as an office soon after he'd opened BFS.

Kurt had to put Genevieve down to unlock the door. She leaned against the wall, looking tired and a little pale, while he dug out his keys.

"You sensing anything?" he asked Dave as his friend peered out at the darkness around them. The tiger's night vision was better than his -- at least, without resorting to magic.

"I'm not sure," the tiger grumbled. "She may have broken that fuckin' spell, but the mojo lingers. I feel like somebody's drawing a bead on my furry ass."

"Me too." The door creaked as he swung it open, releasing a blessed wave of air conditioning.

He led the way down the narrow hallway into the video suite.

A cheap black semicircular desk presided over a bank of monitors that showed video from both security cameras and live Web Cams. A humming PC tower stood under the desk, while a mic, keyboard, mouse, and a pen tablet waited on top of it.

All the gear was used; Fred tended to go as cheap as possible when it came to anything not directly related to the cats. Yet video production was crucial to generating public interest and the donations that kept the sanctuary going.

Kurt logged in and pulled up the file of the arena camera footage as Sawyer and Genevieve settled into a couple of rolling office chairs. Dave settled onto his haunches at Kurt's elbow in a silent gesture of comfort.

"You don't have to sit here and watch this with us, Kurt," Sawyer told him softly.

Stoli growled in the depths of his mind, and he turned to snarl before he recognized the compassion in the detective's gaze. Kurt swallowed his anger. "You don't know the equipment."

"I can handle it," Dave said. "You're a little bit too raw to do this right now."

Kurt knew Dave was right, but leaving felt like cowardice. His father had been murdered. He should have the balls to try to help Sawyer catch the killers, especially since he had magical combat experience the cop didn't. "I can manage."

"Of course you can." Dave's tone was surprisingly gentle, given his usual sarcasm. "Nobody is more aware of what you can do -- what you're willing to do -- than I am. That isn't the point. Your control is justifiably shaky right now, and you don't need to push it."

It was true, and yet... One hand curled into a fist around the computer mouse. "If I leave this room, I'm going to drive myself crazy imagining what happened to him. I'd be better off staying put. If I have to, I'll look away."

Dave shook his great head in a very human gesture. "Do you really think you can *not* watch?"

"Besides, you're assuming I'm going to let you stay," Sawyer said coolly. "You do realize that under normal circumstances, you'd be a suspect?"

In the depths of Kurt's mind, Stoli snarled. He felt like snarling himself. *Shit, maybe Dave was right.* "I'm not a damn bear," he managed anyway. "And when my dad was attacked, I was at Potions -- with Jake."

Sawyer sighed. "I am aware of that. I don't really consider you a suspect. But I can guarantee you that if we catch this asshole, his lawyer is going to be looking for every possible excuse to throw doubt on our conclusions and our investigation. He'll suggest you hired a hit man to give yourself an alibi, then he'll use that doubt to try to get the real killer off. And since the first suspects in anybody's death are always the immediate family, you'd make the perfect distraction."

"So I shot my own Familiar, is that it?"

"Kurt." Dave's voice sounded very soft, very calm.

His legs stung as something sharp dug into his skin. Kurt looked down to see he was gripping both thighs with claws glowing on the tips of his fingers. He hadn't fully manifested his cat, but he was entirely too damned close to it.

He dropped his head, closed his eyes and began combat breathing. The slow, even rhythm would force his heartbeat to slow and control his terror and rage.

The detective started to say something, but Dave snapped, "Wait. Give him a minute." Manifesting an arm, Dave grabbed the mouse and started cueing up the arena camera footage.

To buy himself time to cool off, Kurt stood and stalked into the hall. "I'll get you an external drive to burn that video to."

He ducked into the supply room a couple of doors away. Metal shelving lined the walls, covered with everything from packs of paper, notebooks, and pens to assorted electronics. Kurt crouched to examine the section that held the external drives. It would take a lot of storage space to record the hours of video from all hundred-plus cameras.

"Are you going to be all right?" Genevieve asked from behind him.

Surprisingly, Stoli didn't want to snarl at her. "I'll be fine." Spotting a two terabyte drive, he picked it up and rose to his feet.

Gen folded her arms and considered him, her red hair shifting around her shoulders as her head tilted. "You really don't lie very well."

Kurt gave her a faint smile. "Dad never encouraged it."

"Yeah, I can see how intimidating it would be to lie to Fred Briggs."

A pang knifed through him. "He did set very high standards. And lived up to every last one of them."

Genevieve moved to join him, glistening eyes blinking rapidly. "I know how inadequate this is, but I am so sorry for what happened to him. If there's anything I can do…"

"You're doing it." Despite his own pain, he felt a twinge of worry. She looked far too pale. Probably still feeling the aftereffects of breaking that spell. "Would you like a soft drink? Maybe a candy bar or something?"

She flashed a weary smile. "That'd help. And if you happen to have a couple of Excedrin lying around…"

"I'm sure I can find something." Carrying the drive, he led the way back down the hall.

Genevieve followed him into the kitchen, where he got soft drinks out of the refrigerator and grabbed a couple of granola bars before filling a bowl with ice water. She carried the bowl while he juggled the rest.

The first thing they heard when they stepped back inside the suite was a shattering roar. The arena cameras had audio, as did the web cams, though some of the security cameras didn't.

"I was right," Dave told him grimly. "The Spook Suit hid the fucker, at least until he triggered his polar bear manifestation. No sign of the Arc so far."

The creature glowed, an enormous, muscular shape with a relatively small, bullet-like head and enormous paws. It stood on its massive hind legs, roaring, the sound loud enough to make the security cameras vibrate.

Less than a minute later, Fred ran into the arena in full lion manifestation. He blazed so brightly it was impossible to see the man inside the magical shell, as if he was more Hollywood special effect than human.

The bear charged him with a deep-throated roar.

The two crashed together in an explosion of magical sparks and the grating boom of conflicting fields.

The Ferals ripped at one another with claws and fangs, sometimes on their hind legs, sometimes a snarling knot of rage, leaping apart only to ram each other again. The two slashed and roared, exchanging blows with vicious, blinding speed.

It was hard to see exactly what happened, because video cameras didn't perceive the frequencies of magic as well as the human eye and mind did.

Kurt dropped down into a chair in front of the screen, dumping his armload without another thought.

"We brought you some water," Genevieve told Dave.

"Thank you," the tiger said absently. "Put it down in the corner where it won't get knocked over. I'll get to it in a minute."

"Jesus Christ," Sawyer breathed. He shook his head, sounding dazed. "I've never seen Ferals go at each other full out. I had no idea it was anything like this..." He leaned closer to the screen, frowning in puzzlement as if trying to make out the details. "But the manifestations are magic, right? I mean, they're clawing at each other, but is that doing anything to the human bodies underneath the manifestations?"

"That's complicated," Dave told him. "Animal manifestations -- or for that matter, when I manifest a human body part -- create kinetic fields..."

"Kinetic fields." He frowned. "Like telekinesis?"

"Exactly. The manifestations shield the Feral's physical body from direct contact, but it takes an enormous amount of concentration and energy to create one."

"It's every bit as taxing as physical combat," Kurt put in. "You can exhaust yourself pretty quickly. The longer you fight, the thinner the shields get."

"I've never understood why you have to have a spirit link with an animal to do this to begin with. I mean, why can't Genevieve create manifestations? She's pretty damned powerful."

Gen looked up from the energy bar she was unwrapping. "Not by Feral standards. I don't have the kind of raw power these guys have, which is why I've got to layer my magic to achieve the effects I do. As it is, it takes both the Feral and his Familiar to create a manifestation."

Sawyer blinked. "Oh. Yeah, that makes sense."

Dave took up the explanation. "Familiars like Stoli have access to greater native magic than normal animals do, just as Feral humans have greater talent than Norms. When you spirit link with your Familiar, you blend that magic, more than doubling it. Otherwise, we'd never be able to do it."

"There's another thing I don't understand." Sawyer tilted his chin at the screen. "Fred created a lion manifestation, but you make human body parts. What's the difference?"

"When one member of a Feral bond dies, the spirit is drawn into the surviving body. My human body died, and my spirit was forced into my cat, Smilodon. Since I don't have hands, I have to create a human manifestation. When Fred's lion died, its spirit entered Fred. Fred drew on its energy to create lion manifestations that were considerably stronger than his human body."

"Could you create a tiger manifestation?"

He hesitated a long moment. "Some melds have done it, when they were really desperate. Doesn't last long, though. Running a human mind inside a tiger's brain uses so much magic, there's not much left for the shell. The most you can ordinarily manage is a human manifestation considerably smaller and weaker than your tiger."

"Huh. Well, I guess that does make sense."

Kurt jolted as his own recorded voice bellowed, "Dad!"

One of the cameras pointed at the arena stands picked up a rush of motion as Stoli leaped onto the bleachers and charged toward the invisible Arc. A shot rang out, sounding oddly flat. The tiger slammed into the bleachers and tumbled back down several benches, making the stands shake.

Fred's leonine head turned. "Kurt!"

In that moment of lethal distraction, the bear pounced, slamming Fred to the sand and ripping into his belly. He screamed as the manifestation winked out like a bulb going dark, leaving only a vulnerable human body behind.

The bear dived on him. Fred howled in agony.

Kurt stared at the screen in numb horror. He'd feared his fall had distracted his father at the wrong moment, but to know it without question…

Oh, God, Dad…

Chapter Six

Genevieve stared at the screen in sick horror as Fred went down in a spray of blood and the crackle of dying magic. She'd known the man had been murdered, but actually watching him die was so much worse than she'd imagined. And the fact that his son being shot was what had distracted him...

She'd barely known Fred, and she felt like throwing up. How much worse must it be for Kurt? Gen looked over at him to find his handsome face set like stone, even as sickened guilt filled his eyes.

"Fuck," Dave growled. "Goddamnit, Kurt, I told you..." He was on his feet, his tail lashing in agitation, his round ears pinned back. His golden eyes were wide and round as he stared at the other Feral, his ruff bristling.

Kurt's eyes began to blaze golden. His hands gripped his knees, knuckles going white. Glowing claws protruded from his fingertips, digging into his thighs so hard, blood spotted his jeans.

Her gaze flicked back up, colliding with Grant Sawyer's on the other side. The detective's hand rested on the butt of his gun, and a muscle in his jaw worked, eyes grim and narrow as he stared at the magical claws. He looked up into Kurt's face, tensing.

Ready to draw his weapon.

No. Oh, hell no.

She rolled out of the desk chair without even stopping to think about what she was doing and dropped into Kurt's lap, trapping those clawed hands under her ass. Sending her magic flooding across his aura, she swooped in for a desperate kiss. He stiffened against her in shock as she sent her magic flooding over his aura.

"Don't," she murmured against his mouth. "Hold it together." And deepened the kiss, powering it with her own grief and fear and sympathy.

If I've miscalculated, he's going to rip me apart. She kissed him anyway, counting on surprise and magic to knock him out of his feedback loop long enough for him to regain control. It had worked in the arena. It could work now. Would work now. Because if it didn't..."One good man died tonight. That's one too many," she whispered.

"What the fuck?" Sawyer sounded utterly confused. "This is a hell of a time to make out."

"Shut the hell up!" Dave growled. "She's trying to shock him out of it, and she's doing a good job. Don't distract them."

Though his hands were trapped, Kurt managed to lift her enough to cup her ass, the gesture part possession, part blind need, part pleading, like a drowning man grabbing for a lifeboat.

Gen tasted tears in her mouth and knew they were his.

At last Kurt drew in a ragged breath and sat back. "Thank you."

"Hell yeah, thank you. That wasn't a fucking fight I was going to win," Dave said.

Sawyer eyed him. "Dude, you're a tiger."

"Yeah, a flesh and blood tiger. I bleed if he rips into me. It'd take me a good five minutes to claw my way through his manifestation. He could easily kill me before I got to him."

Genevieve barely heard them, all her attention on Kurt, acutely aware of his body between her thighs, strong and hard and very male even in his pain. Grief vibrated through his magic, a deep and grinding ache.

Then he visibly shook off the emotion and

straightened his shoulders. "I've got to burn that video for Sawyer." He lifted her off his lap as if she was a toddler.

Picking up the external drive, he ripped into the theft-resistant plastic as if it were tissue paper. He plugged the drive into one of the tower's USB ports and started dragging the files over. Something wet gleamed on his cheek, and he wiped it away with an impatient grunt.

Genevieve sat there, staring blankly at the video screens that showed multiple views of the arena. She felt battered, and her eyes stung.

Fred charged into the arena in his doomed bid to drive the Feral bear out of BFS. In an empty section of the arena, sand flew up in a fine spray.

What the hell's that? Gen leaned forward and stared at the screen. It looked as if something was moving over the arena sand, though there didn't seem to be anything there. She hadn't noticed that the first time through because her attention had been locked on the fighting Ferals. "Kurt, rewind Arena 1, would you? It looks like something's…"

He shot her a glance and touched the video screen, rewinding the recording a few seconds.

And there it was again, a spray of sand flying up beside the fence as Fred entered. In the same area where she'd detected the death spell. "There he is," she told Sawyer. "That's got to be the Arc."

Without having to be told, Kurt backed it up even further. All four of them stared intently as Fred charged into the arena again. Sand flew.

"Dad must have startled the Arc. See how he kicked up the sand when he jumped?" Kurt rewound the video as Gen watched, keeping her eyes on the spot where the Arc must have stood.

"Are those footprints?" She pointed at a trail of disturbed sand just inside the arena fence.

"Maybe."

Sawyer swore. "Jesus, the resolution on that camera sucks."

"That's a security cam." Kurt slowed the video to half-speed and backed it up even more. "We don't use it for production purposes. Not like the main cam."

"Arena cameras need an upgrade," Dave said.

"Yeah."

It took them another twenty minutes of running the video back and forth to pinpoint the moment when the footprints first appeared.

"Two hours," Kurt growled. "It took the Arc two fucking hours to lay that spell before the bear lured Dad into the arena."

Genevieve sat back in her chair, frowning. "That's really not good."

"Why?" Sawyer asked.

"There were three layers to that spell. The Arc must have a lot of juice to work something that complex, that fast." Genevieve chewed on her upper lip. "I'm not sure I could have done it. He's got to be a hell of a lot more powerful than me."

"These guys are definitely professional hitters," Kurt growled. "Probably military."

Dave grunted in agreement. "Where else would he have gotten a polar bear Familiar?"

"But why the hell would the military want to kill your dad?" Sawyer demanded.

"Didn't say it was *our* military," Kurt said.

"Caliphate?" Dave suggested.

"Given the bear…"

"Somebody could have sold them a bear," Dave retorted.

"Or it could be the Russians or the Chinese."

"But why would any of those guys want to kill a man whose main reason for living is saving exotic cats?" Sawyer growled in frustration.

"The key is that spell." Genevieve leaned back in her chair to stretch out her legs and cross her ankles. "Once we know what it was supposed to do, we'll know why they sacrificed him."

"And that will give us a better chance of figuring out who did it." Sawyer frowned in thought.

"Are you sure you want to get involved in this?" Kurt studied her. "If these assholes realize you're the key to solving this thing, they're going to kill you."

Gen sat forward and rubbed her hands over her face. "That ship has sailed. The minute I broke the spell, they were going to come gunning for me. Especially if they'd done this before anywhere else."

"I don't buy that. If somebody had been committing magical murders, we'd know about it," Sawyer argued. "It'd be all over the news. Hell, it'd be all over Facebook."

Dave chuffed. "And *then* it'd be all over the news."

Kurt reached out and covered Gen's hand with his. It felt warm, strong. "I think you'd better stay here tonight. If you go home and they track you there, you're not going to be able to fight off that bear by yourself."

She swallowed sickly, remembering blood flying from Fred's ripped belly. "I can probably create wards around my house to keep them out."

"Tonight? After everything else you did today?"

He had a point. Gen rubbed her aching forehead. Her temples banged and she felt the last dregs of energy from her adrenaline jag vanishing like water down a drain. "Maybe once I get some sleep."

"I can make up the guest room for you."

Sawyer gave Kurt a flat look. "Under the circumstances, I don't think that's a good idea. The department can…"

Kurt glowered right back. "Fight off a polar bear -- while investigating Dad's murder?"

"Because you guys did such a good job of spotting the killers before they left the park," Dave said sweetly. "Assuming they have."

"Well, there's always Nolan."

"Working as a team, Dave, Jake and I might be able to take the bear down. Him alone, not so much." Kurt shook his head. "The sheer power the killer had… Yeah, polar bears are the world's biggest land predator, but he seemed to have even more juice than that."

Genevieve stared at the glowing bear on the nearest screen. "There were three levels to that spell. Maybe one of them amplified his magic."

"Then you definitely need Feral backup," Dave told her.

She sighed and yielded to the inevitable. "Sounds like it. I'd appreciate the help."

Kurt smiled. Just for a moment, his gold eyes glowed so brightly, she wasn't quite sure his intentions were as innocent as all that.

And why the hell do I find that idea so intriguing?

Chapter Seven

Kurt's home sat on the back of the BFS property, a sprawling Victorian farmhouse that looked like something out of an old Western. The porch lights were on, revealing a wide wrap-around porch. The house's wooden siding was a soft gray with a hint of green, a shade that would match the bark of the surrounding pines in daylight, while the shutters and trim were slate gray. A sense of weathered peace surrounded the place, as if it were part of nature rather than a man-made construction.

"What a gorgeous house," Genevieve told Kurt as they walked up the short paved drive, Dave pacing beside them.

"Thanks. My great-great grandfather built the house at the turn of the twentieth century after Colton Faraday gave him the surrounding hundred acres of farmland for moving to Laurelton." Kurt moved to unlock the door.

"Faraday? The Arcanist railroad guy?"

"Right. He dreamed of turning Laurelton into a haven for Southern Talents, so he bought up a bunch of farmland and went recruiting. The town was just a wide space in the road then, so it wasn't hard. We've still got more Talents per capita than any other city in South Carolina." Pushing the door open, Kurt started inside, only to stop in mid-step. "You know, I think I'd better check the house. Hang on a minute."

"Make it fast," Dave told him. "I feel this burning sensation on the back of my head. Kinda like a laser sight."

Kurt snorted and vanished. Five minutes later he was back to open the door again. "Nothing," he said, as he stepped back to let them enter.

Gen entered to find herself in a short narrow hall that led to a flight of stairs. Faded rugs covered the dark wooden floor, and a big framed photograph of a lion hung on one wall. The air smelled faintly musty in a way she associated with old houses.

Kurt flipped the deadbolt and hung his keys on a pegboard by the door. "You want anything? Soft drink or whatever?"

"The only thing I need is a horizontal surface."

"I'll make up the guest room." He turned to the tiger. "Dave, mind playing bodyguard for an hour or so? I've got to take care of Stoli. I can't just leave him draped over the bleachers."

"How the hell are you going to get him down? He outweighs me."

"I'll text Jake, see if we can get some of the cops to help. We need to get Stoli into the refrigeration unit until the vet can get that bullet for Sawyer."

"Okay. Sure." Dave's whiskers drooped. "Yeah, I'll be glad to hang out with Gen."

"Thanks. Give me a minute to take care of the bedroom." He pulled out his phone and started texting as he took the stairs at the end of the hall.

Gen watched him go, blinking eyes that stung as she imagined the job that faced him in the arena. "Think they'll have moved Fred yet?"

"I have no idea. I do know it feels really weird handling your Familiar's body when he's now in yours instead. It's kind of like a sneak preview of being dead."

Gen winced.

Shortly Kurt descended the stairs again, headed for the door with the grim air of a man headed to an ugly job. "Good night, Gen."

"Is Jake going to be able to help?"

"Yeah. I'll be back as soon as I can."

When he was gone, Dave shook his great head and padded off down the narrow hall, the wooden floor creaking under his weight. "I need some water. Sure you don't want anything?"

"I'm good." She followed him.

The tiger walked into the darkened kitchen. An arm thrust out of his striped back, reached up, flicked on the lights, and disappeared again.

Genevieve looked around at the kitchen. A double oven, a massive refrigerator, and a dishwasher, all stainless steel, stood between white cupboards with gleaming black counter tops. Copper-bottomed pots hung from a ceiling rack over an island bar that served as a breakfast table. "This looks a lot newer than I expected."

"Fred renovated it for Kurt's mom." He grimaced. "Trying to make up for the fact that she did not get along with Lahr, his lion. She'd threatened to walk." His eyes narrowed. "Some singing was probably involved."

"Fred could sing?"

"No, but Kurt's mom did."

Normally Gen would have asked what he meant by that, but just now she didn't much care. "I can't believe this." She climbed up on one of the black leather bar stools around the central island. "One minute I was talking to Fred about Parvati. Next thing I know, he's dead." She sighed. "And I liked him, damn it."

"Fred was a hell of a man. I'm going to miss him." Dave headed for the kitchen sink. "Though I have to admit he could be a son of a bitch at times. God knows he complicated the shit out of Kurt's love life."

"How so?"

"By trying to keep his son from making the same mistakes he did."

"Are you being intentionally mysterious?"

"Nah, just an intentional pain in the ass." All the teeth in that grin were downright terrifying. "It's my superpower." Rising onto his hind legs, he braced his forepaws on the sink. Again, the glowing hand emerged, opened a cupboard and pulled out a bowl, put it in the stainless-steel sink and turned on the tap. "Mind setting the bowl down for me so it won't splash everywhere?" His voice dropped to a grumble. "Being a quadruped is a pain in my striped ass."

"Oh. Of course." She hopped down to reach past him and pick it up. But when she started to carry it back to the bar, Dave laid a big paw on her wrist.

"I need it on the floor. I'm not exactly built for stools -- and the stools are sure as hell not built for six hundred pounds of me."

Gen put the bowl where he indicated and took her seat again, watching as he settled onto his belly and started lapping. "How long have you known Kurt?"

"Ten years now. Met him in Arcane Corps basic training. Our tigers -- Stoli and Smilodon -- were brothers," Dave said as he lapped. Since he produced his voice magically, he could drink and talk at the same time. "I don't mind telling you, at first I hated his guts."

"Why?"

"He was my competition. The Arcane Corps only takes the most physically fit, mentally qualified, and magically talented Ferals. Particularly when it comes to getting one of the really big predators like a lion, a tiger or a bear."

And it was always predators, she knew. "When I

was a kid, I always fantasized about being a Feral with a horse Familiar."

Dave looked up, gold eyes round and appalled. "Oh, God, no."

"Hey, people rode horses into combat for thousands of years."

"You grew up reading *Black Beauty*, didn't you?"

"It shows?"

"You do know the whole point of spirit linking a human to an animal is to gain abilities humans don't have?"

"Like claws, fangs and several hundred pounds of muscle."

"Plus the psychological qualities of their Familiars. If the animal's instinctive response to threats is to run away -- which is precisely what horses have evolved to do -- you can actually end up making a soldier less effective than he would have been alone. Which is the exact opposite of what the Arcane Corps is going for."

"I know -- Dad explained it. But at twelve, I didn't give a damn. I wanted a horse Familiar. Much cooler magic than spending hours with a sketch pad."

"Well, spirit linking is pretty amazing." Dave flopped down on his belly, then stretched out his forelegs, looking like the world's biggest house cat. "The Corps put us through hell trying to find out which of us was the most deserving of the best Familiars. Out of the two hundred Ferals in our class that year, only eight of us got a big predator, though another fifty got wolves and smaller cats like pumas and jaguars. Kurt and I ended up magically bonded to littermates, so the Corps assigned us to the same Feral team. Along with Jake Nolan and his brother, Bobby, who got a pair of lions."

"That brings up a point that has always bugged me," Genevieve said, propping a foot on the stool so she could drape an arm across her knee. "Fred spent a lot of time cussing Parvati's original owner for breeding cubs to use as props. But how is that different from breeding them to use as weapons? I mean, you're risking the cats' lives, right? Even if Familiars don't go into combat, their Feral partners do."

That was actually more for the safety of the soldiers than the Familiars, because if the human partner died, the Familiar might turn on his teammates. Familiars did need to be kept fairly close, of course -- within a few miles -- in order for the spirit link to operate. That usually meant being transported in an aircraft just within range. Which meant that though they technically weren't in combat, they couldn't be said to be safe either.

Dave paused so long, Gen started wondering if she'd offended him. Finally he said, "Yeeeah... but Feral animals aren't just animals. They're the product of rituals and selective breeding that make them the most intelligent creatures on the planet this side of humans. They crave spirit links as much as we do. Another thing: the life expectancy of a tiger is only about twenty years. Familiars get to live three times longer than they otherwise would by sharing their human's body after theirs die."

Gen stared at him. "But... does that mean you..."

"Only have about ten more years?" He shrugged. "Still ten more years than I would have had."

"Yeah, but..."

"Which doesn't mean I'm happy about it," Dave said. "In fact, I'm pretty much the poster child when it comes to the dangers of dealing with a newly melded tiger Feral. That's how I died."

A chill rolled over her. "What?"

"Bobby's cat was killed when his plane was shot down during a mission. He melded with Selena's spirit as she died, so she wasn't lost. Unfortunately, then he had to deal with the same psychological adjustment Kurt faces now. It's not easy to deal with having somebody else in your head 24/7."

"But I thought that's what a spirit link is."

"Not entirely. When you and your Familiar are two separate physical beings, there's still some distance. You link only when one of you reaches out. Once you've melded, he's there all the time."

"Yeah, I can see how that would be an adjustment."

"At first, it went pretty well. Bobby seemed to be handling the transition, and a couple of months later, the shrinks cleared him to go out on a mission."

He rested his big head on his forepaws. "HQ sent us into these caves on the borders between Afghanistan and Pakistan…"

"Where they thought Osama bin Laden was hiding?"

He tilted his head. "Different network of caves, but basically, yeah. Our target was an Arc terrorist. The bastard created some of the most vicious magical traps I've ever seen." He stared into the distance, his golden eyes very wide with remembered pain. "Bobby managed to walk right into one of them. This trap was designed to flood him with murderous rage. Which it did, just as I bumped into him."

"Oh," Genevieve winced. "Oh, crap."

"Yeah. Bobby manifested his cat, whirled on me, and went for my throat in a magic-induced rage. Snapped my neck like a twig before I could even think about manifesting Smilodon. It was all I could do to meld with my cat in time, or I'd be gone."

She stared at him, not sure what to say. "I'm so sorry."

"It gets worse. The minute I was down, Bobby went after Jake and Kurt. Jake was so shocked at what his brother had done, he was late getting up his manifestation. He'd have died too, but Kurt shot Bobby about half a heartbeat before he could rip out his brother's throat. And none of us have ever gotten over it. Kurt still feels guilty."

"But why? It sounds as if Bobby would have killed Jake."

"Kurt grew up with them. They were his best friends. He did what he had to do, but he keeps thinking he should have manifested, fought Bobby off, maybe bought him time to regain control. And he blames himself for not being fast enough to keep Bobby from killing me."

"Somebody needs to buy that man a red cape with a big S."

"Yup. That's the problem with being raised by a saint. Especially one that could be a little bit of a son of a bitch."

Genevieve shook her head. "All these tragedies in his life, brought about by Arcs. I'm surprised he kissed me."

Dave snorted. "Even Fred knew you're nothing like those bastards. For one thing, you volunteered your very valuable skills to heal Parvati. That gets you automatic good people points."

God, I hope so. Then she frowned, wondering why she wanted Kurt to see her as different from the Arcanists who'd inflicted so much pain in his life. What difference did it make? It wasn't as if he was a friend…

But I'd like him to be.

* * *

Kurt stroked a hand over Stoli's big head. The cat's eyes were fixed, glassy, and his tongue protruded from his mouth. His fur felt thick and coarse under his hand, without the vital warmth Kurt associated with the tiger since the first time he'd touched him ten years ago.

He sat in the magic circle, the two-month-old cub a warm, furry weight in his arms. Glowing arcane sigils rotated through the air around them as amber eyes met his. Eager. Longing.

The cub's magic swirled against his, tender as a breath. Awe rose in Kurt as he touched Stoli's almost human intelligence. They flowed together, life force twining with life force, forming a mystic braid not even death could break.

Suddenly Kurt was looking up at himself, and he and the cub were one.

And now that part of Stoli was gone.

Kurt set his teeth and turned toward Jake and the four cops who'd volunteered to help. The two Ferals could have managed the weight, but the tiger's long body would be almost impossible to maneuver without help. "Let's get this done."

Kurt took his Familiar's head while Jake lifted his hindquarters and the cops helped steady him. Together, they made their way carefully down over the bleachers toward Jake's pickup for the trip to the Cat Clinic.

In the depths of his mind, Stoli moaned.

* * *

The guest bedroom was located at the top of the stairs, up the hall from Kurt's and the master that had been his father's. It was almost painfully neat, though sparsely furnished, with a double bed, a chest of drawers, and a mirrored bureau, all of sturdy pine. The bed was so tightly made, it looked as if you could bounce a quarter off the spread. Apparently Kurt had never gotten out of the habit of making a bed the way he'd been taught in the Corps.

"Want a shower?" Dave asked. "I'll wash your back."

"I have a rule," Gen told him, "I only have sex with people who have the same number of legs."

"You're no fun. Seriously, bathroom's the next door on the right."

"I doubt I could stay awake through it. I'd probably end up water-boarding myself." More softly she added, "Thank you for helping me with... everything."

"We're the ones who owe you. Especially if you can help us catch these bastards." Then he padded out. "Good night, Genevieve."

"Good night." Throat tight, she closed the door behind him. And thought of Kurt and Fred and Stoli, of Bobby Nolan and Dave.

God, what a mess.

* * *

Kurt came to her in the darkness, his mouth finding hers in a rush of masculine heat and animal passion. Need exploded in her in a conflagration that sent her awareness ablaze.

Her arms snapped up, wrapping around his shoulders, feeling the warm roll of muscle under his skin. The springy hair on his chest teased her nipples, and she gasped as his mouth moved on hers, his tongue thrusting deep in slow, luscious strokes, suggestive and primal.

"God, Kurt..." It had been so long, so very long since she'd had a lover. Loneliness had made her nights as hollow as bells, nothing inside but ringing emptiness.

But Kurt filled her senses now, and her body cried out for his in desperate craving.

His hands cupped her face, the skin on them rough with calluses, as he cradled her jaw.

The length and weight of him pressed against her, so much bigger than she was. "Help me forget," he breathed against her mouth. "I need you. I need you…"

"Yeah, me too. I've been so lonely…" She surged upward, pressing up into his kiss as her hips pumped against his erection, silently begging. "So very lonely."

And he rolled right back at her, letting her feel the thick, engorged width of him pressing against her bare belly.

Panting, he pulled out of the kiss, staring down at her. Those Feral gold eyes glowed in the room's velvet dark, bright. Brighter.

Until the gold seemed to explode in a blinding flash. The great glowing muzzle of a tiger reared over her, fanged jaws opening to reveal three-inch daggers of light.

She screamed.

* * *

Genevieve jerked awake with the sound of her own scream ringing in her ears, disoriented, terrified, her heart pounding in thick lunges. It was pitch black, but somehow she knew it wasn't her bedroom. She didn't recognize the smells, couldn't make out anything in the darkness.

Flinging out a hand, she groped for the lamp, terrified Kurt was still in the room with her, playing with her like a cat in the dark. Her fingertips hit something hard -- the lamp base -- and she grabbed it, lifting it like a weapon even as she used her left hand to search for its switch.

Light burst into the room. She was alone in the Briggs' guest bedroom. Blowing out a breath in relief, Gen rolled to her feet, still holding the lamp as she peered around warily.

Alone. I'm alone, I'm safe. She lowered the lamp to the nightstand and sank down on the mattress again to rake trembling hands over her clammy face. Her heart thundered in her chest. *Jesus Christ, that was a bad one.*

The flip side of artistic creativity was horrific nightmares. She'd learned to accept them as the price of being what she was. As Dad had always told her, there was no such thing as a free lunch. Even Normals with purely non-magical talents paid for them with nightmares worse than those endured by the less talented. In Gen's waking hours, she believed the gifts her talents gave her made up for the price they exacted. But on nights like tonight, it didn't feel that way.

Then again, anybody would have had nightmares after what had happened to Fred. *Especially after that nasty little bedtime story of Dave's.* Still, she supposed she should be grateful for the warning. Of course, she'd known battles between Ferals could get ugly -- she'd been listening to her parents' war stories for years.

But to actually watch Fred get torn apart on that recording… she shuddered.

What the hell am I going to do?

A calm, cold voice in the back of her mind told her it had been stupid to involve herself in this ugly mess. If she had any sense, she'd get her ass back home and avoid Kurt and his furry friends like the plague from here on out.

She'd find out what the spell did and give the

information to Sawyer. Then she'd head to New York, visit the gallery that carried her work. Maybe do some sightseeing and get her head back on straight.

What if those assholes track me down? If Fred and his lion couldn't fight that bear off, I'd have no chance whatsoever.

And then there was the Arcanist. Spell-casters might not have as much raw magical power, but Ferals had no defense against Arc booby traps.

If she cut and run, and something happened to Kurt or Dave -- or hell, anybody else -- because she wasn't here to help, she wouldn't be able to live with herself.

So no, she wasn't going to run. She was going to stay in Laurelton and do what she could to keep the Arcanist from killing anybody else. *And I may get myself killed doing it.*

Yeah, well, everybody dies. The trick was to make sure you didn't spend the rest of your life regretting your actions because the result was somebody else's death.

The nightmares from that would make tonight's look like an episode of *Sesame Street*.

On the other hand, that didn't mean she had to be stupid about it. Trouble was, she could control her actions, but her emotions were the real problem. Kurt had already touched her with his pain and heroism. If she wasn't damned careful, she'd fall in love with him.

Especially since he was exactly the kind of man she'd always looked for. Kurt was far too much like her father -- a hero with a strong sense of responsibility and honor.

Plus he's gorgeous. Too bad she'd met him at the worst possible time.

Becoming   one   with   a   big   cat   did   not

automatically make you crazy. After all, Fred had been melded with his lion for twenty years since the animal's death, but there was no indication he'd had any problems with self-control. Given what an extremely public person he'd been, there would have been rumors if he'd ever lost it.

But Kurt's meld was too fresh, leaving him vulnerable to his tiger's instincts. If she followed up on this attraction, he could easily become even more dangerously possessive -- as male cats tended to be. Considering he'd already come close to attacking both Sawyer and Jake…

"No! Goddamn you, you bastard!" Feet thudded to the floor, accompanied by a snarl that had not come from a human throat.

Genevieve froze, staring at the wall opposite the bed, her heart thundering.

The bear. Had the bear assassin broken in and attacked Kurt? For a long moment, she heard nothing more than her own ragged panting.

"You fucking idiot," Kurt's voice growled.

She strained her ears, but seconds ticked by in ringing silence.

Her shoulders slumped in relief and she settled back against the headboard, swinging her legs up. Apparently she wasn't the only one who'd had bad dreams. Though his would probably have been even worse. At least hers hadn't featured her father's murder.

A door opened and closed in the hallway, and the floor creaked as he walked past her door and started down the stairs.

I need to go back to bed.

But what she really wanted was to follow him down the stairs. *Dumbass. Didn't we just go through that?*

Getting involved with the magical were-tiger is not a good idea.

But there'd been such defeated pain in that "You fucking idiot."

"He's not the only one," she growled, and rolled out of bed. She'd worn her turquoise top to bed, so she put on her shorts and padded barefoot out into the hall.

Gen was midway down the stairs when Kurt looked out at her from one of the downstairs rooms. "Sorry I woke you. Everything's fine. You can go back to bed."

But everything wasn't fine. He looked haggard, his handsome face drawn under disheveled dark hair that looked as if he'd been raking his fingers through it. He was shirtless, his glorious chest bare.

She tried to ignore the view. "Actually, I was already awake. Had a nightmare."

"Yeah, there's a lot of that going around. You want something to drink? Dad's bourbon is really…" He broke off. His expression twisted before going controlled again. "… good."

"Sure." As she followed him into the parlor, she thought, *I am such a moron.*

If the house was Victorian, its decor was not. An oxblood leather sectional couch faced a flat screen television on an entertainment center. On shelves beneath that sat a satellite box and a video game console with a pair of controllers. At the opposite end of the room, a gas fireplace had replaced one that had obviously once burned wood.

But it was the walls that caught her attention. They were covered in photos of lions, tigers, jaguars, pumas, leopards, lynxes -- all kinds of cats, including species she didn't even know the names for.

Compelled, Genevieve walked over to the nearest of them, a lion with bright Feral gold eyes. Judging by the skillful composition and quality of the print, it was obviously professional work. "These must have set Fred back some serious cash."

"Actually, no. Dad was an amateur photographer. Did photos of every cat BFS ever housed. There've been a lot of them over the past twenty years." He moved closer. "That's Lahr, Dad's lion. He's the one you see in the BFS logo."

She looked around at him. "Lahr?"

"As in Bert Lahr, the actor that played the Cowardly Lion in the *Wizard of Oz*." He grinned. "Which was something of a joke. Lahr loved a good fight. He had a roar that could vibrate the paint off a wall."

"Sounds intimidating."

"Yeah, but deep down, he was a softy. Especially with me. He's the reason I was so determined to join the Corps and get my own cat. I loved him." His smile faded. "Mom, not so much."

"Your mom didn't like him?"

"Mom hated him. I think she was actually glad when he died -- testicular cancer. It wrecked Dad and me. I was ten."

"I'm so sorry." Her gaze drifted back to the lion's hypnotic gaze. There was more than an animal's intelligence in that intense stare. "Your father had real talent."

"He loved his subjects. That always helps." Kurt moved over to a walnut bar that ran beside the television and poured himself a glass of something amber from a cut-glass decanter. "Want any? Aged Kentucky bourbon. Dad loves… loved the stuff."

"Sure." Maybe it would help her get back to

sleep.

As he filled a second glass, she asked, "Where's Dave?"

"Took the first watch. He's probably skulking in the bushes outside the house."

"Is that safe? I mean, between witches and polar bears…"

His mouth pulled into a flat line as he handed her the glass. "We fought a war, Gen. We know how not to be seen." He nodded toward the sectional, and she followed him over to it to sit down. "What did you dream about?"

Genevieve froze. And knew by the heat in her cheeks that she was blushing.

Kurt blinked and looked startled. His nostrils flared. Almost like an animal scenting…

He looked quickly away, downing a deep swallow of his bourbon.

I need to get my ass back to bed. Instead she took a sip of the bourbon. Liquid fire detonated in her mouth, smoky and dark. It burned all the way down. She coughed, acutely aware of him, sitting bare-chested and handsome in the light of the single lamp he'd turned on.

God, that chest. *I'd love to paint him.* It wasn't the first time tonight she'd had that thought. But then she hadn't known what a bad idea it was.

He almost lost it twice tonight. Only an idiot would go for three. She forced herself to look away. But a moment later her gaze drifted back to dwell on the ridged muscle of Kurt's flat abdomen and broad chest. His biceps flexed as he lifted his glass for another sip. Heat rolled through her, and she swallowed. *Bad idea.*

Really, really bad.

Really.

Chapter Eight

The smell of her arousal seemed to sink right into Kurt's brain. In the depths of his mind, Stoli rumbled in hunger. His eyes swept the length of her body in the dim light, taking in the soft curve of her cheek, her plump lower lip, her straight, slim nose.

Her hair was sleep-tousled, as if she'd just rolled out of bed -- which she had. The rich auburn shone, a dozen shades of copper, bronze and red burnished by the glow of the single lamp he'd turned on. Curls foamed around her slim, pale throat, leading his gaze down to the cotton turquoise top she wore. The fabric bore fingerprint smudges of pastel dust from drawing Parvati.

She'd taken her bra off to go to bed. He could see the small points of her nipples pressing against the fabric like little bullets.

Her nipples are hard. His imagination instantly began spinning erotic speculation about the way they'd look without that top. What color were the tips -- rose, candy-pink, soft brown? *How would she taste?*

Stoli chuffed in his head, reacting to the burst of hunger with a blaze of pure need. The tiger's arousal built his own, and Kurt barely bit back a groan. It seemed anger wasn't the only emotion that could set off a feedback loop. *I need to get the hell away from her.*

But before he could force his reluctant feet into motion, she lifted her glass for another sip of the bourbon, and those soft breasts swayed, looking full and touchable beneath the thin fabric.

The scent of her need intensified, a teasing bloom of female musk in the air as she grew more aroused. He caught a flash of blue as her gaze flicked toward him, then instantly away.

Kurt asked the question knowing perfectly well he shouldn't. "What did you dream about?" His voice sounded a trifle hoarse. "Was it me?"

Genevieve laughed, but it wasn't at all convincing. "Conceited much?"

"Was it?" Stoli sent him a vivid mental image of Gen on her hands and knees, her ass lifted in invitation.

Or maybe that was his own imagination.

"What were we doing?" He'd intended the question to sound teasing, but the words came out darkly suggestive.

The blush drained from her cheeks, leaving them too pale. Gen looked away, taking a deeper slug of the bourbon. She didn't even shudder this time. Unfortunately, the line of her lips looked tight rather than sensual.

Something clenched his belly in an icy fist. "Did I hurt you?"

Gen raised the glass and drained it. A tiger's nose wasn't as sensitive as a dog's, but he could still detect the faint acridity of her fear. She still didn't answer.

"I wouldn't hurt you." He felt sick. "I would never hurt you."

"Not intentionally." She turned back and met his gaze. Despite the fear, there was sympathy in those crystalline eyes. "Dave told me what happened to Bobby."

Goddamnit, Dave. "My dad trained me to be a lot more disciplined than Bobby. Nothing against Bobby's mom -- she was a single mother, and she didn't have a Familiar. I don't think she realized how important it was to be tough on a Feral kid."

She sighed. "It was just a nightmare, Kurt. It

didn't mean anything."

"There's fear in your scent."

"It was just a bad dream."

He sank back on the couch and rubbed his eyes with one hand. In his own dream, he'd been the one to trip the Arc's booby trap in that cave. He'd been the one to go mad when someone bumped him from behind, reacting in blind animal rage. Except it hadn't been Dave he'd killed.

It had been Genevieve.

I've got to get out of here before I do something really stupid. Like kiss her again. Kurt dropped his hand, shoulders slumping. "I don't blame you for being afraid, especially after the way I acted tonight. Look, I'm going back to…"

Gen touched him, shutting him up in mid-word. Her silken fingers curled along his cheek. "I'm not afraid." Her blue eyes gazed into his, vivid and steady. "You didn't lose control, Kurt. Your father was just murdered, but you still held on. You didn't hurt anybody. I'm not sure I could have said the same if somebody'd killed my dad."

He inhaled sharply. Her scent flooded his head, and he realized she meant it. The acridity was gone, leaving only her personal scent, all magical ozone and Genevieve.

But if the fear had faded, the need had not. It still rolled from her, smoky and tempting as incense. "I'm not afraid," she repeated softly.

"You were."

"I had a bad dream. It's been that kind of night. But if you were really going to lose control, you'd have done it in the arena when your dad died. If you didn't then, I don't think you're going to."

Kurt closed his eyes, fighting temptation, and

saw her magic glowing behind his lids. It wasn't just gold like his, but a hundred other shades, colors chasing each other across her aura like the aurora borealis.

The glowing woman leaned toward him. His eyes flew wide as Genevieve kissed him. It might have been their third kiss of the night, but it didn't feel like either of the others. Those had been kisses of desperation, of grief, of pain and sympathy. This was a gentle exploration of a kiss, slow and soft.

Her tongue slipped into his mouth in a teasing lick that burned smoky with bourbon. Kurt closed his lips and suckled her gently, tasting her with senses both feline and human. Her lips brushed back and forth across his in slow seduction. He returned the swirling stroke of her tongue, sliding his own into her mouth, tilting his head as he explored her.

At last she eased back from him. Kurt stared at her, fighting the need that burned hot in his groin, his and Stoli's desire flaring like gasoline teased with a torch.

Cool little fingers touched his hand and took the glass away. Leaning forward, she put both their empty glasses on the coffee table with a clink. His eyes caught on the sinuous curve of her back, leading down to the swell of her ass.

Genevieve turned back to him, and he took her in his arms. She felt perfect, skin soft and smooth and lush.

That image flashed through his mind: Gen on her hands and knees. Stoli wanted her to pull her under him, but he refused. *Not after the fear I saw in her eyes. I am not going to scare this woman again.* He was going to make love to her. Despite common sense, despite his better judgment, he wanted her. Needed her.

Craved her.

But he wasn't an animal. He eased back and looked deep in those cornflower eyes. "You trust me. But do you want me?"

She caught his shoulders in both hands and pushed him back against the couch, then slung a leg astride his lap. "Yes."

Kurt stiffened… in more than one sense of the word. His cock leaped as her soft weight came down on his thighs. She felt so delicious, he groaned. Gen covered his mouth with hers and drank the sound, kissing him harder this time, demanding, tongue swirling around his.

Closing his eyes, he watched her glow as the heat in his veins blazed.

She stroked him as she kissed him, tracing the cords of his throat, the thick muscle of biceps and shoulders.

He cupped the rise of her hips, slid one palm up to the dip of her narrow waist. Pushing up the hem of her shirt, he found bare skin, warm and smooth and soft under his fingertips.

Stoli rumbled, and Kurt had to suppress a magical echo. He had no intention of killing this mood with a growl, even a growl of hunger. *Especially a growl of hunger.* "Are you sure this is what you want? Because I'll go if you're not."

She pulled back just enough to glare. "Don't you dare." Sharp little nails dug into his chest.

"All right, all right!" Laughing, he reached up to cup her breast. *Soft.* God, she was so incredibly soft. The smooth, warm curve filled his hand with pure erotic delight. He groaned.

So did she.

He caressed her gently, squeezed, stroked.

Found the stiff little nipples that had been driving him crazy since she'd walked into the room. Made them even stiffer with gentle tugs between thumb and forefinger.

Genevieve pulled away from his mouth and let her head tilt back, eyes slipping closed. "I do love a man with talent."

"Thank you." He pulled the top up, revealing both lovely breasts. With pleasure, he saw her nipples were a luscious candy pink, furled tight in arousal. "See what you think of this…"

Leaning forward, he closed his mouth around one delightful bud. The taste of her was more intoxicating than the bourbon, sending fire roaring along his veins like a flame following a trail of gasoline.

A cool low voice that sounded like his father said, *This is a really bad idea.*

He ignored it.

* * *

Genevieve moaned as Kurt tongued one exquisitely sensitive nipple in erotic little swirls. Each wet stroke created sensations as fragile as soap bubbles, all weightless iridescence.

She cupped his head in both hands, dark hair curling cool against her fingers like rough silk as she pulled him closer. He nibbled gently, then drew back, raking the tip in delicious little bites.

Kurt took his time as he stroked the other breast, gentle fingers cupping, pressing.

Gen tried to remember the last time it had been this good. But it never had been.

Ever.

He released her breast, and switched his attention to the other nipple. "Don't want you to feel neglected," he told it, and closed his lips for a suckle and a slow swirling lick that sent another jolt of pure arousal rocketing through her.

She looked down at him, at the dark fan of his lashes as he closed his eyes in an expression of pure sensual bliss. Sweet, piercing tugs that sent sparks of pleasure zinging along her nervous system.

Genevieve stroked him right back, running her fingers down his body along the curve and dip of powerful muscle. "You've got to let me paint you."

Feral gold eyes flashed up at her. He gave her a wicked little smile. "I don't think so. I'm already under your spell as it is."

He tightened his arms around her, turned her on his lap and spilled her down on the sectional. Dropping to his knees on the floor, he pulled off her shorts.

Kurt drew back, his glowing eyes dwelling on her nude body, Feral gold and hot with male appreciation.

He positioned her diagonally so he could kneel between her spread thighs. Bending his handsome head to stare in absorbed interest, he cupped her between the legs, making her draw in a breath. "What a pretty pussy. Lovely red curls."

Kurt found the seam between her vaginal lips and slowly, slowly slid his finger inside in a lusciously arousing stroke. His thumb circled her clit, sending tightening coils of heat through her sex.

"God, that feels so goooooood," she breathed.

He pumped in and out a few times, then pulled his finger away and bent to cover her pussy with his mouth. Licking up and down her outer lips, he teased out incredible sensations with every flick of his tongue -- sensations so intense, her eyes fell closed in delight.

And started at what she saw with her magical senses. The tiger's great head glowed above Kurt's, watching her with wide golden eyes. There shouldn't have been room, but part of the insubstantial beast seemed to be inside her thighs.

She jerked, disconcerted, as Kurt went right on licking, apparently unaware his Familiar watched her.

His mouth drew hard on her clit, sending brilliant pulses of pleasure flashing up her body. But even as her body responded to his carnal ministrations, her heart leaped in fear at the memory of the dream.

Stoli made a soft sound. Not with Kurt's magic or vocal cords, but as if the tiger touched her aura, projecting a sense of approval and affection. The cat's wasn't a human mind, but it didn't feel as purely animal as Parvati's either.

As if to reinforce that encouragement, Kurt's big hands cradled her thighs, and she felt the warmth of his strong body between her legs... and a fierce male need -- Kurt's, as communicated by Stoli. In a rush of emotion and images, the tiger told her she was safe, let her feel Kurt's desire rising like a tide rolling up a summer beach.

They wanted her.

Gen found herself relaxing, surrendering to his mouth, his hands, the heat of him. His tongue swirled around her clit in teasing circles -- around and around, back and forth...

He closed his lips around the nubbin and sucked ruthlessly. The merciless pleasure hit her just as she relaxed from the anxiety of a moment before, and pushed her right over.

Pleasure roared up in a dancing conflagration that ripped a shout out of her. She came, stunningly quick and hard, her body arching up as she drowned in fire. Screaming.

As she came, her aura flared, and she felt both Stoli's wordless feline satisfaction, and the dark intensity of Kurt's hunger.

He growled in lust, the air reverberating around them. Yet this time she felt no fear.

Kurt released her and surged to his feet. Reaching for the zipper of his jeans, he tugged it down carefully to avoid snagging the thick cock jutting against the fabric. The shaft sprang free as he pushed his pants down brawny legs and kicked them impatiently aside. His golden eyes stared into hers, as wild as Lahr's had been in that photo.

Her heart leaped in anticipation, her eyes dropping to the long, curving shaft.

"Ooh," she breathed.

"God," he growled, his gaze savage. "I need you!"

He pounced, landing on hands and knees astride her on the sectional. Panting, still dazed with pleasure, she looked up at him, at the width of his shoulders, the shifting muscle in his strong arms. His eyes glowed through strands of dark hair shadowing his angular face.

Pressing against her full length, Kurt lowered his head and kissed her, his mouth open, hungry, searching.

Genevieve moaned into his mouth, coiling her arms around him. He felt so deliciously broad and hard, all thick brawn and smooth skin. She stroked her hands along his body, feeling the deep vibration in her aura interacting with his. She caught her breath in need.

She'd never made love to a Talent with the kind of power Kurt had, and she was startled at the way his magic intensified her own need. Though she'd just climaxed, her anticipation bloomed hot again.

By the time he pulled away from the kiss, they were both panting. He stared down into her face with those brilliant eyes. "You're so fucking beautiful."

"So're you. And…"

He wrapped a big hand around that gorgeous dick, pressed it to her opening, and entered in one powerful lunge. They groaned in unison.

"Oh, God!" She arched up with a gasp in reaction to their joined need. "You feel so thick!" He stretched her wide enough to sting, yet there was something incredibly satisfying about being filled by him.

He drew out slowly, a muscle flexing in his jaw as if he fought for control. Fought to take his time and make it good.

And it was. So, so good.

He began to ride her hard, lunging deep, dragging out, plunging again. And with every thrust, their auras sparked, energy leaping between them. Gen's skin tingled in waves with every stroke, echoing the pulse of her engorged clit.

She gasped with his merciless thrusts, the grind of his pelvis between her legs. A second orgasm coiled within her, tighter and tighter.

He threw back his head with a shout. His magic burst against hers, spurring it hard, his pleasure rocketing into her mind through the mystical conduit.

Genevieve came again, screaming, her voice spiraling so high it cracked.

In her mind -- in her aura -- she felt the vibration of Stoli's roar.

* * *

If a tiger could have purred, Stoli would've been doing it. So would Kurt.

The seat was too narrow for them to lay by side-by-side, so he picked Genevieve up, lay down, and draped her over him. She barely stirred, apparently concentrating too hard on breathing. So was he.

"You made me see stars." Genevieve's voice sounded throaty with a note of laughter.

Kurt stroked a hand through her glorious red mane, enjoying the tangled silk of it under his hands. He wanted to brush it out for her, if only for the pleasure of playing with it -- and knowing he'd been the one to tangle it. "I can truthfully say the same to you." *Of course Dad won't be pleased...*

An instant after the thought, grief hit like a blow to the head. No, his dad wouldn't be pleased. His dad would never be pleased again. What Kurt wouldn't give for another one of his father's *She's-not-a-Feral-girl lectures.* He let his head fall back, his eyes stinging.

He blinked the tears away. *I don't have time for this. I'm going to find those bastards, however many of them there are, and kill every last one of them.*

But first he had to make sure Genevieve was protected. Had to convince her to stay with him.

Though it might make his life easier -- and certainly simpler -- if she left. He wouldn't have to worry about keeping his distance or controlling Stoli's unpredictable emotions.

Not to mention yours, boy. The mental voice sounded like Fred.

But the point wasn't his comfort, it was Genevieve safety. "I'd like you to consider doing one of two things for me."

Genevieve turned her head on his chest and pulled her thick mane out of the way so she could look up at him. "Anything."

"Leave town."

"Except that." Giving him a narrow-eyed look, she sat up. "I'm not going anywhere until those two are caught."

"Genevieve…"

"If I'd gone with your father when he went to the arena, maybe I could have broken that spell when they trapped him." Her mouth tight, she looked around for her clothes. Spotting her shorts, she got up and put them on. "Instead I kept myself safe, and he was killed."

Kurt frowned and bent to pick up his own jeans. "More likely, he wouldn't be the only one in a body bag right now. That Arc had a high-powered rifle. If he'd seen you start to break that spell, he would've shot you."

Genevieve tugged the top over her head. "Or she. Could just as likely be a woman."

"Don't split hairs."

"Don't make assumptions."

"Okay, granted." He'd worked with plenty of women Arcanists. Come to think of it, he'd probably known more female Arcs than male. "But that still doesn't negate my original point, which is that he -- or she -- would've shot you."

"Maybe. And maybe your dad wouldn't be dead."

"I can tell you right now that you giving your life for his is not the way Fred Briggs would have wanted it. It's sure as hell not the way I'd want it. Besides, even assuming he could've killed that bear, the Arc would've shot him anyway. I think that's why he or she was set up on the bleachers, to take Dad out if he won."

She sighed. "Damn, I'd like to believe that."

"Believe it. Look, don't feel driven to get

involved in this mess out of guilt. I would not want that even if it means these two don't get caught at all."

"There's no way in hell I'm staying out of this. If I sat on my thumb and they killed somebody else, that death would be on my head as much as theirs. What if the spell they're trying to cast kills even more people? What if Fred wasn't their first sacrifice?"

"What are you getting at?"

"I have a feeling the arena working was part of an even larger spell. If so, they may have committed other sacrificial murders. Those victims deserve justice, and their killers deserve to pay."

"Of course they do, but that doesn't mean you have to put yourself in the cross hairs."

"I notice *you* didn't hesitate."

"Fred was my father, Gen. Of course I didn't hesitate. But I'm a soldier…"

"And I'm a woman." A dangerous glint lit her eyes. "Is that it?"

"Hey, I fought beside plenty of women in the Corps. But they were trained to fight, and you're not."

"If I was a male Arcanist, would you be worried about whether I'd had combat training?"

He winced before he could suppress it.

"Yeah, that's what I thought. My gender doesn't mean my sense of duty is less than yours."

Kurt stared at her in exasperation. "You do realize there's no way I can respond to that without sounding like a sexist asshole?"

"Maybe that should tell you something." She did him the favor of changing the subject. "You said there were two things you wanted to ask me to consider. What's the other one?"

He eyed her a moment, trying to decide if he was about to piss her off again. "If you won't leave, would you consider staying here at BFS? Just until we get these people stopped."

She hesitated, and a flicker of longing flashed over her face.

In the depths of his thoughts, Stoli chuffed in triumph. If Kurt were honest, so did he.

Then, damn it, she shook her head regretfully. "I'm not sure that's a good idea."

"I'm not going to push you into going to bed with me. If you want me to keep my distance, I will."

She snorted. "I touched your aura, Kurt. You're not the kind of guy who stoops to that sort of manipulation."

"So what's the objection?"

"It's just not necessary. I can create a warding spell around my house. They wouldn't be able to get in any more than Fred was able to get out of the arena."

"You don't have wards around your house now?"

"Nope. I'd have to burn magic to cast a spell like that, and I prefer to save my power for healing people and making money. Besides, I have good locks. And a security system. And a gun."

"You own a gun?"

"My folks are military. You bet your ass I have a gun. And Mom made sure I'm a crack shot."

"Remind me not to piss you off." More seriously he asked, "Could you ward this house like your own?"

She hesitated, looking thoughtful. "Easier. Your house's footprint isn't as large as mine. The bigger the circle, the harder the spell is to cast because it requires more magic. That's probably why the Arc laid the spell in the arena."

"That, and the bleachers hid what they were doing. Even if you went home, you'd have to leave your wards -- and then you'd be in danger."

"On the other hand, if I warded this place, you and Dave wouldn't have to spend all night standing watch. We'd be able to protect each other." She hesitated, considering. "Okay, you talked me into it. I appreciate the protection."

"I promise I'll keep my distance."

Gen flashed him a wicked little grin. "I wouldn't go that far. I..." Before she could finish, a huge yawn forced her to cover her mouth with her fist. She shook her head. "Wish I could lay those wards now, so we could all crash. Unfortunately, I doubt I have the juice."

"Why don't you go back to bed? It's time for my watch."

She frowned, hesitating. "I'd offer to take a turn, but if I do, I won't be able to light a candle, much less create those wards." Standing on tiptoe, Gen pressed a quick kiss to his lips and gave him a smile. "I'll see you in the morning. Good night."

He caught her chin and pulled her in for a deeper kiss, then released her and put an arm around her waist and walked her to the stairs. "Sleep well."

Kurt watched her climb the stairs, admiring the roll of her deliciously curvy ass. He'd love some sleep himself, but he knew even if he went to bed, he'd only have another nightmare.

Besides it was his turn to stand watch.

Chapter Nine

When he stepped outside, he found the porch lights were off.

"Sounds like you two had an interesting night, you lucky bastard," the tiger's deep voice said from the dark.

Kurt moved to the railing to find Dave among the bushes beside the porch steps. He wouldn't have seen the tiger at all if not for Stoli's magical night vision. "Lying in wait?"

"Ambush predator. And I can think of at least two fuckers I would love to ambush. Besides, I have no interest in freaking the po-po."

"Are they still searching the park?"

"I heard a bunch of units pull out an hour ago, but I'm sure they left a couple of guys to guard the scene."

The scene of Dad's murder.

Kurt wondered when the reality of his father's death would quit ambushing him. When would the pain begin to dull?

He'd lost friends in the service: Bobby, Dave's human form, other men he'd fought beside over the years. Their deaths still hurt, but were no longer so agonizing. He wasn't sure he'd ever get over this.

Kurt sank down in one of the porch rocking chairs, feeling weary to the bone. "You expect to lose your dad sooner or later. But not like this."

The bushes rustled as Dave emerged. He padded up the cement steps to flop down on the floor beside Kurt's rocker. The wooden boards groaned. "Fred was a good man. I can't tell you how grateful I am that he took me in after my medical discharge."

Kurt shrugged. "Vets like you are the whole

reason Dad opened BFS to begin with."

"I still owe him -- and you. Which is why I feel a duty to say this even though I know you don't want to hear it." Gold eyes narrowed. "What the fuck do you think you're doing with that girl?"

"Are you really about to give me Dad's 'She's not a Feral girl' speech?"

"No. I'm about to give you the 'You're spraying her with gasoline and about to light a match,' speech." His tail thumped once against the porch floorboards. "Remember what happened the last time somebody's cat was trapped in his body when he triggered an Arcanist trap? Now we've got an Arcanist building traps in the damned arena, you've just gone through a major emotional trauma, *and* you pick now to start having sex with Genevieve?"

His temper leaped. "Goddamnit, Dave, she's nothing like Mom!"

"Hell, I know that. If anybody could hack being in love with a Feral, it's Genevieve. She's got entirely too much guts for her own good. She sure as hell won't cut and run the way your mother did. Even Fred would have realized that, if he'd had enough time." He looked up at Kurt, gold eyes glowing. "The problem is not Genevieve."

"I don't fall in love with every girl I have sex with," Kurt told him impatiently. "And tigers do not mate for life. I am not going to lose my shit just because I slept with her." But even as he said the words, he was uncomfortably conscious of his own growing anger.

And in the depths of his mind, Stoli snarled with possessive rage in the depths of his mind.

Back off. He's our friend.

"You need to send her away," Dave insisted

stubbornly. "Get her the hell out of town."

"Damn it, I know that. I tried to talk her into it, but she won't go. What the fuck do you expect me to do, tie her up and throw her into the trunk of a car?"

"Reason with her. Or, hell, be a son of a bitch. Be the kind of sexist asshole women hate and she'll leave on her own."

Unable to sit still any longer, Kurt leaped to his feet and began to pace. "And what happens if the killers go after her? Do you have any idea how long she would last? I'm thinking about twenty, twenty-five seconds. Tops."

"They can't get to her if she wards her house. All they'd be able to do is pace around outside the way we did when they had Fred trapped in the arena."

"And what happens when she has to go out and get a gallon of milk? When they ambush her in a convenience store parking lot and rip her to pieces?"

"Tell her you'll buy the damned milk."

Turning, he leaned back against the porch rail and tipped his head back, staring at the ceiling. "Look, she can ward this house as easily as she can ward her own. And then she'd have us for bodyguards."

Dave rose to his feet and paced toward him, tail lashing. Stoli's snarl grew louder. "Oh, yeah, she'll be safe then," he said sarcastically. "From everybody but the people in the house with her."

He kept his voice low, steady. Resisted the urge to roar. "I am not going to hurt her."

"It's not just her I'm worried about, dumbass." He flattened his ears and glared up at Kurt. "Look, under normal circumstances, there is no Feral I know with more discipline. Your self-control was always better than mine. But these are not ordinary circumstances. Fred was murdered tonight, and you and Stoli were shot. As if that's not enough, we're pretty sure the bastards are going to be coming after us next."

Kurt stalked restlessly to the other side of the porch. "I can handle myself."

"Against any ordinary Feral -- even a bear Feral -- yes. But that was not an ordinary Feral we saw tonight. That son of a bitch has more power than I have ever seen. It was all Fred could do to stay alive as long as he did."

"Dad would have been fine if I hadn't distracted him by getting shot."

"Bullshit, Kurt. You could see the difference in their manifestations on the damned video. The bear was twice as bright. That fucker would have still had a full manifestation when Fred's lion collapsed. And your dad would still have died."

Kurt raked both hands through his hair in angry frustration, wishing like hell he could believe Dave was right. "You don't know that. And if I'd killed that bastard Arc, we could have gotten in to help him fight off the bear."

"Who died and made you Clark Kent?" Dave's tail whipped back and forth as his whiskers bristled in irritation. "It's Bobby and me all over again. I died because of *me*. I wasn't paying attention to where I was going and ran into Bobby. I didn't even see him touch that damn wall. And then I was too fuckin' slow to manifest and fight him off. Or even shoot him."

"For God's sake, it all happened in a fraction of a second! I was able to react in time solely because I was farther back and he was busy with you."

"And you're so damned fast. Which is why Jake Nolan ain't inhabiting Clarence right now. But you don't give yourself credit for that. You just play *coulda-*

woulda-shoulda until I want to bite you. Which is exactly why I don't want to see you kill that girl, either because you're unstable, or because you walk into the fucking Arc's booby-trap."

"I doubt these guys will do the same thing that Caliphate sorcerer did."

"Really? Because if I were that asshole and I wanted Genevieve dead, that's how I'd do it. Then you'd self-medicate with a nine-mil and he'd have both problems solved." Dave started pacing the porch as if trapped in a very small cage. "What happens to the rest of us then? Me, Clarence, Parvati, all the cats here?"

That silenced even Stoli. "I'll write a new will. I can leave BFS to Jake."

"Jake's a cop, Kurt. Yeah, he'd take over running the sanctuary, because that's what kind of guy he is. But he hasn't trained for it, and running BFS isn't his passion the way it is yours. He likes being a cop. His thing is saving people, not cats."

"Jake's a Feral, damn it. He *is* a cat."

Dave huffed, an impatient sound. "My point is that we need you. And that girl needs to avoid catching anybody's bullets -- or claws."

"And I'm telling you she won't leave. I tried desperately to convince her, but she feels guilty because she didn't go out to the arena with Fred."

"No wonder you like her. She's got just as big a Jesus complex as you do. The two of you should go waltz on the lake." He shook his head and began to pace again. "Damn it, I could've sworn I talked some sense into her when I told her about Bobby."

"So you did do that on purpose."

Dave didn't even have the grace to look ashamed. "Hell yeah. I don't want to see her get fed into the meat grinder with us. And if you were thinking straight, neither would you. You know damned well what Fred would say about this, even aside from her lack of Ferality. He wouldn't want her involved for the exact same reason I don't. It's a monumentally bad idea."

"Then you talk to her, since you're so determined to stick your oar in."

"I'm going to. But the job would've been a hell of a lot easier if you'd kept your dick zipped up."

"My dick is none of your business."

"No, evidently it's Stoli's, because he's leading you around by it."

"I have had enough!" Kurt's voice emerged in the deep growling rumble that was barely understandable for its subsonic vibrations. "*She is mine.*"

Dave turned and stalked right up to him. "Was that you talking, or Stoli? Because it sounded a fuck of a lot like Stoli. Maybe you'd better think about what it says when your cat starts controlling your body instead of the other way around."

He manifested before he even knew he was going to do it, magic bursting out of his body in a soundless explosion.

Dave bounded off the porch in a single long leap, whirling to crouch on the walk, gold eyes blazing with his magic. "Get a grip, Kurt, or I'm going to hurt you."

Snarling, Kurt vaulted over the porch, Stoli blazing out around him like a torch.

"What are you going to do, Kurt? Kill me? And what do you think you'd do to her?"

A roar building in his throat, Kurt crouched to spring.

Light bare feet thumped down the house's

interior stairs, headed for the door.

"Genevieve?" Dave's eyes rounded in horror. "Control that cat, Kurt!"

Stoli didn't give a shit. Hell, he wanted to kill Dave in front of his female. It was exactly the kind of thing male tigers did in the wild.

The sheer inhumanity of that thought shocked Kurt still. *Dave's my best friend!* He'd failed to save the man once; he wasn't going to fail him this time. Clenching his eyes shut, he grappled for control. The manifestation vanished just as he heard the door bang open.

"The hell?" Genevieve stared wildly at them, then around into the surrounding darkness. "I thought the damned bear was out here! Scared the crap out of me!"

Kurt concentrated on combat breathing until he could manage words. "I'm sorry we woke you."

"I was just trying to explain to Romeo here that you need to go home and ward your house." Dave manifested a human arm, and held its thumb and forefinger a fraction of an inch apart. "And he came about this far from tearing my head off. I am a hell of a lot better able to defend myself than you are. Go the hell home and ward your house..." His voice vibrated the air like a set of amps turned up to 11. "And stay there."

Genevieve straightened and gave Dave a cool look. "So that's what the Bobby story was about. You want me gone."

Dave rumbled in frustration. "I want you *safe.* What I don't want is my best friend eating a bullet because he lost his shit and killed you."

She folded her arms and glared down at them from the porch. "Kurt's not going to kill me. He could have, several times tonight. He didn't. In fact, I seem to do a better job of helping him retain control than you. You're the one out here trying to start a fight."

Stoli growled. Kurt concentrated on keeping his breathing slow and even. *Shut up, cat.*

"Tell me something, Genevieve," Dave said quietly. "How many fights with your boyfriends have you had? Did you ever say anything you regretted? Did one of them ever say anything he had to apologize for because he was pissed? How much worse would that have been if he'd weighed six hundred pounds and had three-inch claws?"

She made a point of studying Kurt. "I'd say it's closer to two hundred, actually."

"Not in terms of magical force. You keep treating us like humans with special effects, but we're not. Humans are social animals. Tigers are ambush predators, and we're solitary."

Genevieve snorted. "Yeah, you're real solitary. I can tell that by all the videos on YouTube. You wouldn't love giving everybody a good laugh if you were all that damned solitary."

"That's my human half, Gen. I've got a hell of a lot more experience in dealing with this than you do. When I tell you that you need to leave, you need to leave."

"I'm not going anywhere," she growled. "I'm going to ward this house and make sure that the next time the fucking Arc shows up, I break whatever spell he casts. And for the record, if you'd had an Arcanist on that mission, he'd have sensed the trap and disarmed it. All of you would still be human and Bobby would still be alive."

"Our team Arc was breaking a trap elsewhere in the cave, but even if she'd been there, it happened in seconds," Dave told her. "There wouldn't have been time."

"But it wouldn't have mattered, because she'd have seen the booby trap and kept you from tripping it in the first place. So I'm staying, and I'm going to help you avoid any more traps."

Dave rumbled in disgust. "Then I hope you like having a fuzzy striped shadow, because I'm going to keep you alive if you don't have the common sense to do it yourself."

"Keep up the condescension and you'll be the only bald tiger in North America." She turned on her heel, walked into the house and slammed the door behind her.

Kurt and Dave stood there in silence for a moment, listening to her stomp back up the stairs. Dave sighed. "I'm sorry about that, but I'm not going to let you destroy yourself."

"Thank you, Dave," Kurt said, shaken and meaning it. That had been entirely too damned close. "I'd appreciate all the help I can get. If you can convince her to leave, do it."

* * *

Genevieve woke the next morning to the sound of voices. A lot of voices. It sounded as if the house was full of people. "What the heck?" She rolled out of bed, pulled on her shorts again and headed for the bathroom at the end of the hall. They'd done renovations on the house at some point, installing indoor plumbing and adding a couple of bathrooms. The claw-footed tub was the oldest she'd seen outside of a television show, with cracked white enamel and an actual stopper you inserted in the drain.

She stood under the spray a long time, trying to come alive again. Which was probably a bad choice of words, given Fred.

Coffee, Genevieve thought, shampooing her hair. *I need coffee*. Which was only the first item on her to-do list. Next was heading back to her house to pack.

Along with making a few calls to do some rescheduling. Like that trip to Palm Springs next week to paint the A-list actress who'd hired her to perform a magical face lift. That one needed to be moved into next month.

Genevieve frowned as she soaped herself down. She'd heard the longer a crime went unsolved, the less likely cops were to solve it. And they *had* to solve this one before anyone else got killed. *Then I can go home and get the hell away from these people before I do anything I regret. Or at least, anything else I regret.*

Her hands slowed their sweep over her body, remembering Kurt's touch, Kurt's mouth. She supposed she couldn't really say she regretted making love to him; it had been too damn sweet.

And too damn dangerous to more than her heart. She was afraid the tiger was right about Kurt eating a bullet if he lost control and hurt her.

Kurt was not the sort of man to just shrug something like that off.

Gen shut off the tap with a vicious twist and got out to towel off her wet hair. She made use of a brush from her bag, then got dressed, grimacing as she pulled on the clothes she'd worn the day before.

Not only were the shorts and top wrinkled, they were covered in pastel dust. She always ended up looking like one big smudge after a working, since blending the drawing with her fingers was crucial to the magic.

"I'm going to make a great impression on those people downstairs." Spotting a bottle of mouthwash, she poured some into her palm and rinsed her mouth, wishing she'd thought to bring a toothbrush.

This, however, was about the best she could do to get some of the nasty out of her mouth and avoid revolting anyone who stood too close.

Downstairs, the house was indeed full of people, most of them women who looked like they'd been crying. So did the pair of elderly male retirees who seemed as shell shocked as everyone else. They all wore T-shirts in different colors with the BFS lion logo on one breast, with the word "Volunteer" across the back in white lettering.

Genevieve followed the sound of Kurt's voice to the den where they'd made love the night before. He stood with his back to the fireplace in a fresh BFS T-shirt and jeans, a pair of thick work boots on his big feet.

"I want to thank you all for coming in today," he told them, his voice clear, his expression carefully controlled. "No matter what's happened overnight, we have fifty-nine cats who still need to be fed. I'm obviously going to be pretty distracted for the next few days, so I'm going to have to count on y'all to take care of things for me."

There was a general murmur of assurances that they were all more than happy to help.

"Be aware, there are going to be a lot of cops on the premises. I want you to give them your full cooperation." Kurt grimaced as his voice dropped to a growl. "There are also reporters hanging around outside the gates. Please avoid them as much as possible." As if on cue, his cell phone rang. He plucked it out of his back pocket, eyed the screen, and put it back without answering. "Speak of the devil."

"Vultures," somebody muttered.

"Yeah, you can hear the flapping from here. Point is, you're going to be approached by people looking for quotes. I can't tell you what to say, and wouldn't even if I could. You're volunteers, and I'm grateful for all the help you have given us over the years."

"We're glad to do whatever we can," a graying woman murmured. Tears gleamed on her face. "Your father…" Her voice cracked. "was a remarkable man."

Kurt's gaze softened. "He thought a lot of you too, Karla. He often told me how much he appreciated all your hard work."

The woman's shoulders shook. Another volunteer wrapped an arm around her.

He looked around the room, meeting the tearing eyes of the crowd. "Remember anything we say is almost guaranteed to go viral. We don't want to make it harder for the cops to catch Dad's killers." A muscle ticked in his broad jaw. "And we don't want to damage BFS's reputation. We count on the thirty bucks a head we get from tours to keep our cats fed and healthy. If our income takes a big hit, I'll have to find other sanctuaries that will take them. Fifty-nine cats would be extremely difficult to find safe homes for."

"But wouldn't the Feds help?" asked one earnest young blonde. "I mean, we have a grant to take care of the Ferals, right?"

"Right, but most of our cats aren't Familiars. They're old and retired from circuses or roadside zoos, and they could wind up in places a hell of a lot worse than this one. I don't want to see that happen."

Karla wiped her eyes with a tissue. "I think I'm speaking for all of us when I say we'll all keep our mouths shut to the press." She turned to sweep a hard gaze over the volunteers. "Won't we?"

A ragged chorus assured her that they would.

"If somebody asks you for a quote, you send them to me," she said firmly. "And for God's sake, don't say anything inflammatory on Facebook or Twitter or whatever social media you belong to. That'd go viral quicker than a television interview."

She clapped her hands in a brisk gesture, looking for all the world like a football coach before the big game. "Let's go get those cats fed and their enclosures cleaned."

It wasn't quite that easy. People walked up to hug Kurt and talk to him a moment before heading out.

Heart aching, Genevieve made her way into the kitchen for the cup of coffee she'd been craving since she woke up.

Instead of the pot she was expecting, there was a huge stainless steel urn, and the kitchen table was covered in open boxes of donuts and plates of cookies, some of which smelled as if they'd been baked just that morning. This being the South the day after a death, she knew there would be a constant stream of visitors with food and condolences.

As she made for the coffee, Gen had to circle around Dave, who sprawled on the floor. He'd buried his muzzle in a huge bowl full of bacon, eggs, sausage patties, and a whole cooked chicken.

"Morning." He did not, of course, sound as if his mouth was full. "How'd you sleep?"

She sighed as she filled a Styrofoam cup and doctored it with Splenda and creamer. "Better than Kurt did."

"Yeah, that's a pretty safe bet. Sawyer came by this morning to tell him to keep his mouth shut about the investigation. Which is going to be damned uncomfortable, since he's got to talk to the press or people are going to think he was involved."

"But the cops'll speak up for him, right?"

"I hope so, but you never know. I think it would be a good idea if the two of us stood out there with him. The press is going to ask asshole questions in hopes of getting a rise out of him, and if he gives them one -- especially one with claws -- we're all fucked."

Genevieve frowned. "Why doesn't he just have one of the volunteers read a press release? Hell, I could write it. I'm used to dealing with media. Part of the job." She'd done a lot of interviews over the years, many with major media outlets. Her work had attracted a lot of attention, as much because of her client list as her talent.

"The press release is already up on the website. Kurt wrote it on his cell phone while he stood watch. It's a masterpiece of restraint. He didn't even announce he's gonna mount a magic polar bear head over the couch with its own glowing dick sticking out of its mouth."

"That was diplomatic of him."

"Nah, that's what we call plausible deniability. 'No, officer, I don't know who shoved that sniper rifle up the terrorist's ass and emptied the clip.'" He bared his teeth in a ferocious grin. "'Somebody call Sherlock Holmes.'"

Gen snickered, only to frown as her attention fell on her smudged shirt. "When's the press conference? I'd like to go home and change first. I'm covered in more chalk than a blackboard."

"Unfortunately, the press conference is in half an hour, so that probably won't work." Kurt walked in and handed her a bundle of emerald green cloth. "But you can see if this fits. I figured you'd like to change your shirt."

"Hey, thanks!" Genevieve put down her coffee cup and shook out the bundle. It turned out to be a BFS T-shirt with "volunteer" printed in white lettering across the back. She smiled up at him, touched by his thoughtfulness, and checked the collar tag. "Bless you! And it's the right size, too."

He poured himself a cup of coffee. "Been helping volunteers find the right shirt since I was ten."

"Man of many talents."

Dave looked up with a grin and contributed a rimshot.

"Actually, I didn't even intend that as a pun."

He looked horrified. "First rule of comedy, kid: it's always intentional, especially when it ain't."

Gen snorted and turned to Kurt. "You want my help with the press conference? I was telling Dave I'm used to dealing with the media."

"I'm afraid it's going to get pretty nasty. Plus, we don't want to make it any easier for the killers to track you down."

She considered the idea, then nodded reluctantly. "Okay, that's a good point."

"After we get done, I'll drive you back to your house to pack your things."

"We can take Fred's SUV," Dave suggested. "I'll go with you."

Gen wanted to object that that was overkill, but unfortunately it probably wasn't.

Another thought occurred to her. "I also need to check on Parvati at some point."

He brightened. "I've already been by the Cat Clinic -- I had to meet with the vet who's doing the necropsy on Stoli. Doc Bryson said Parvati's out of the woods. She even ate all her food for once."

"At least I accomplished one thing last night."

His smile warmed her. "Don't sell yourself short."

Chapter Ten

There were cops and reporters all over the sanctuary when the three of them started for the office.

Dave wore an orange safety vest that reminded Genevieve of the kind of thing you put on service dogs. It had his name across the sides in ten-inch white lettering; she'd seen him wear it in some of his YouTube videos.

"I don't want anybody to freak the fuck out," he'd explained, balancing on his haunches as he buckled it on with manifested hands. "I wish I'd thought to put it on last night."

Of course, the minute he appeared in it, reporters came running.

Dave gave his voice a rolling amplified rumble that sounded more than a little menacing. "No. Comment."

Every one of the reporters stopped dead and took a step back, though the cameras remained focused on the tiger as he stalked past in regal disdain.

"Maybe we should have him do the press conference," Genevieve murmured to Kurt.

"The idea is to kill any rumors I was involved in Dad's death. If I don't answer questions, that's exactly what they're going to think."

"I could always eat a reporter." Dave gave the nearest camera his best terrifying smile. "That'd get rid of the bastards. The cops won't care; they hate 'em worse than we do."

"Don't tempt me. They've been calling all morning. I'm not even sure how they got my personal cell."

They circled around to the office's back door and ducked inside. Sawyer waited for them at the end of the corridor in a dark blue suit, though judging by the shadows under his eyes, he hadn't gone to bed at all. He shook Kurt's hand with a searching look. "You sure you're ready for this?"

"No, but it doesn't particularly matter whether I am or not."

"I've already emailed your statement out to all the reporters. I'd suggest restricting your comments to describing the kind of man your dad was, why he did what he did, that kind of thing. If they ask you any questions about the crime itself, I'll handle it."

"Yeah. Let's get this over with. I've got a lot to do today."

"You and me both." The detective turned to Genevieve. "Are you participating in this thing?"

"Not this time. I'm going to hang back and wait." She gave Kurt a smile. "Moral support."

* * *

Kurt took a deep breath and opened the door, then stepped back to allow Sawyer and Dave to walk out onto the porch ahead of him.

A soft hand touched his forearm. "I'll be right here," Gen said softly, her blue eyes steady and level. "If you need me."

"Thanks." Damn, he wished he could afford her calming presence at his side, but she was in enough danger as it was. He was going to have to hold it together unassisted. And by God, he would. He'd handled a lot worse in combat under a lot more pressure. No matter how ugly their questions got, none of the reporters were literally trying to kill him. He could handle them.

To Stoli, he added, *And for God's sake, keep quiet. They want us to get mad, and if we do, we'll all pay, including the cats.*

Kurt visualized being forced to watch the animals packed up and trucked away, maybe even euthanized. Stoli's building rumble of anger cut off as if he'd shut it down with a switch. The knots between his shoulder blades loosened fractionally as he stepped out onto the porch.

If he could just keep the consequences in mind, he might be able to get through this. He followed Sawyer to the cluster of mics attached to a stand. Four separate television cameras pointed at them, manned by people in shirts with TV station logos. More formally dressed on-air reporters clustered among them, along with several local newspaper and radio reporters -- even a couple of bloggers he'd met before. Except for the cameramen, everybody had a cell aimed in his direction.

Sawyer swept his gaze over the crowd. "At 11 PM last night, the owner of Briggs Feral Sanctuary, Fred Briggs..." He stopped to spell the name, "was attacked in the BFS arena by another Feral, who assumed the manifestation of a polar bear..." He summarized the incident in as little detail as he could, including Kurt's becoming aware of the attack thanks to Dave and his bond with Stoli.

"Dave Frost and Kurt Briggs, in his Familiar's body, attempted to come to Fred Briggs' rescue. Kurt's Familiar was shot and killed by a gunman, and Fred Briggs suffered fatal injuries and died on the scene. Dave attempted to pursue the killers, but they escaped. My officers have spent all night searching the park. I'm requesting that anyone who knows anything about these murders, please contact the Laurel County Sheriff's Office..." He rattled off the department's phone numbers and email addresses.

Then the questions started, and Kurt tensed.

"We've heard reports that Briggs was a human sacrifice," one of the reporters yelled. "Were the killers Satanists?"

Sawyer didn't turn a hair. "I can confidently say there is no satanic involvement in this crime."

"There's a lot of security cameras around this place, not to mention a ton of web cams," another reporter called. "Is there surveillance video of the attack?"

Stoli snarled, and Kurt tensed at the thought of watching his father's murder over and over and over again on television. He drew in a deep breath and blew it out again, concentrating on combat breathing.

"We are not releasing the video at this time," Sawyer said.

"How was he killed?"

Questions flew hard and fast after that, many of them answered with "No comment." Kurt focused on breathing and imagined what would happen to his cats if he lost control.

Finally, Sawyer cut them off when they started repeating the same questions. "I'll be releasing more information when we have it." He turned to Kurt and gave him a slight nod.

Kurt stepped up to the microphones and began to read a statement. "I'm Kurt Briggs. My father, Fred Briggs, was a veteran of an elite Arcane Corps team in the 1990s. He and his lion, Lahr, participated in missions around the world, including Desert Storm, where he was awarded an Arcane Service Medal.

"When my father left the service, he learned that several of his fellow Ferals couldn't find homes for their Familiars." He grimaced. "Turns out people aren't crazy about big cats moving into the neighborhood, military veterans or not. So he converted the farm that had been in our family for a century into Briggs Feral Sanctuary, intending it as a home for retired Familiars like Lahr.

"Then when I was about ten years old, we went to the circus. It was the kind where the performing animals were kept in tiny cages. Dad was appalled anyone would keep cats that big in cages that small. He was even more appalled when he got a good look at one of the lions and realized the marks across its shoulders and flanks were whip scars. My father pulled out a camera and took pictures.

"We found out why the cat was scarred in the big top that night, when the lion tamer used a whip on his animals." Kurt remembered the rage on his father's face, and his own bewilderment.

He glanced around. The reporters were scribbling furiously. "Not all circuses beat their animals, but that one did. When we got home, my father reported what he'd seen to the US Department of Agriculture, photographs and all. The USDA went in and shut the circus down after discovering that many of the animals had suffered similar abuse. Dad offered to take the cats in, though BFS had never housed non-Familiars before. He had to take out a loan to do it, since our grant provided for Feral cats, not natural animals. That was why we had to start conducting tours of the sanctuary to raise money, because otherwise we wouldn't have been able to take care of them all."

Kurt's eyes had begun to sting. He blinked, impatient with himself. "Dad was an idealist, intelligent and passionate about ensuring that animals who'd been abused or neglected could live out the rest of their lives in safety. As he told me, he knew how it felt to be an animal.

"Now he's dead. Murdered. Gutted by…" He broke off. "My father deserved better. He was a hero who fought and bled for this country. We're devastated by his loss, but BFS will continue as a sanctuary for the cats Dad loved."

Pausing, he scanned the attentive faces ranged around the porch steps. "I ask that anyone who knows anything about this crime report it to the Sheriff's Office. But please be aware these are dangerous individuals, and do not underestimate them."

One of the reporters called, "So one of the attackers actually shot and killed you -- or rather, your Familiar?"

In a flash, Kurt remembered the slamming impact of the bullet, the blazing anguish of it. "Yes, that's correct."

"So you saw them? Could you describe them?"

"They were wearing magical camouflage. I never saw their faces."

"Did your father have any enemies?"

"Of course. There were a lot of people Fred worked to shut down. Abusers who breed tigers for sale to mall photographers for use as props, or owners of traveling circuses who mistreat their animals. There are also canned hunts where wealthy people pay a lot of money for the opportunity to hunt and kill captive tigers. Often these animals were raised by humans, and walk right up to the people who shoot them to mount their heads on the wall."

He shut his mouth, realizing his voice had taken on a deep thrumming growl.

Dave stepped to the edge of the stairs.

Instantly every one of the cameras swiveled to the tiger as he smoothly took up the story. "No matter how many enemies he had, Fred also had a lot of friends. I'm proud to be one of them. I owe him and his son more than I can ever repay. I was trapped in my cat when I was killed in action during a mission in Afghanistan. Kurt served with me on the same Feral team, and he asked his father to take me in. I am incredibly grateful to them both, because this place gave me a reason to live, a home where I'm accepted, and a place where I can help both Familiars and natural animals."

The tiger scanned the crowd, his tone for once lacking its usual note of cynical humor. "Fred was a decent man, like his son. I'm going to do everything I can to help the police catch his killers. And I ask you to do the same."

They pelted him with questions, which he answered with uncharacteristic patience.

"If Mr. Briggs was a human sacrifice, what was the spell supposed to do?"

"We're still investigating that," Sawyer said, stepping back to the mic. Dave melted back with obvious relief. "We'll keep you posted when we have more information."

"Have there been any other sacrifices?"

"Let's get the hell out of here," Dave muttered, "while the getting's good."

Kurt opened the office door, and the two of them escaped while the reporters tried to pry a few last bits of information out of the detective. Gen gave him a smile and whispered "You did good."

He dredged up a smile of his own, if with an effort. "At least I didn't eat anybody."

* * *

"You sense anything?" Kurt asked Gen as they pulled up in front of the house.

She frowned, studying it with narrowed eyes.

"Nothing."

"Nice place," Dave commented from where he lay, curled across the back seat.

And it was. Genevieve's house was a mix of traditional and contemporary styles, with clean lines that reminded Kurt of a Spanish mission -- not a common look for this part of South Carolina. White and gray stone covered the lower third of the façade, with white wooden siding above that. Stone fronted the arched porch, and the big windows were framed in steel. The black roof had just enough pitch to shed rain.

Huge azalea bushes flanked the porch and circled the massive trees of the front yard. During the spring, they'd be bright with pink and white blooms, but now their leaves were a deep, glossy green.

"Let's get it done. I need to get those wards up." She opened the SUV door and got out.

Kurt frowned and drew his weapon from the holster at his hip. "I'm going to need to clear the house first."

"I told you, I didn't sense anyone."

"I'd rather not find out you're wrong the hard way. Stay out on the porch with Dave."

"And if they planted booby-traps, all you'd be able to do is trip them."

Well, he couldn't argue with that.

Inside, the house fairly vibrated with magic in a constant tingling stroke across Kurt's skin he found almost arousing. He had to fight to ignore the sensation as he checked for unwelcome visitors, his magical senses extended. The only Feral he sensed was Dave, pacing around outside the building checking for scents or magic that didn't belong.

As he worked his way through the house with Gen right behind him, one part of him registered the decor. It was as deliberately simple as the exterior, with pale gray walls accented by white baseboard and trim. Pewter gray curtains hung at the windows, and the floors were a silvery wood. The furnishings had modern, geometric lines, thickly upholstered in white, black, or shades of silver.

But what grabbed his attention was the art that hung on every wall. Not just pastels, but oil paintings, watercolors, and pen and ink sketches. Looking around, he realized the house was designed to complement the art, not the other way around.

The colors were vivid -- deep greens, yellows, reds and blues in countless shades. The subjects were just as eclectic: portraits, nudes, and landscapes. He spotted several fantasy images featuring mermaids, dragons and knights, a little too wild and dark to be kitsch. Most of the work was Genevieve's, but there were other artists featured as well.

He cleared the house in the familiar routine he'd used to check for would-be ambushers during the battles with the Caliphate. Gun leading the way in a two-handed grip, he moved rapidly through every room, checking closets and under beds, magical senses alert for any whiff of energy that didn't belong. "There's no one here."

"I told you that before we walked in the door."

As he holstered his gun, Gen strode into the bedroom, where a king-sized bed with a cherry frame stood beneath a pile of pillows and a comforter in dove gray and metallic silver. The floor was a short-piled gray carpeting with a dark steel-gray pattern.

A huge painting of a forest scene sprawled across the wall over the bed, the emerald green of the leaves drawing his eyes. As he stared in fascination, he saw animals amid the trees: deer, squirrels, a raccoon, an owl. A big gray wolf stared out from a cluster of leaves, yellow eyes glowing like a Feral's.

As Kurt studied the painting in fascination -- what he'd first taken for a lightning bug turned out to be a fairy -- Gen started packing.

After tossing a medium-sized suitcase on the bed, she unzipped it, then started bustling around the room. Her movements economical, she collected jeans and tops in vivid blues, greens, and sunny yellows that complemented her dramatic redhead's coloring.

When she started picking out underwear, Kurt glanced away. It probably wasn't a good idea to watch, especially not with a bed so close.

Genevieve ducked into the bathroom and emerged five minutes later with toiletries, a tackle box, and a hairdryer.

"Planning to do much fishing?"

She gave him a dry look. "It's makeup."

He grinned back. "I thought it might be."

She started to pick up the suitcase, but he shot her a look and nudged her aside. "This all you're going to need?"

She shook her head. "I've got to pick up the supplies for casting the wards. Then I need to shoot a photo of the spell I sketched to send to my mom."

Oh, that's right, Genevieve's parents were Arcane Corps career military. They might even have encountered Fred when he was active duty; the Corps wasn't a particularly large branch of the military. "Wonder if they knew my dad?"

Gen shrugged. "It's entirely possible. They were in the field during the first Gulf War at about the same time."

As she headed to her studio to collect her spell supplies, Kurt claimed the suitcase and headed off to put it in the SUV.

"I gather by the lack of cursing there were no bears lying in ambush," Dave observed dryly, emerging from the bushes as he popped the trunk and stowed the suitcase away.

Kurt slammed the hatch. "Not so far. I'll let you know if that changes. You spotted anything?"

"Nada." Dave looked around at the surrounding homes, all of which looked fully as expensive as Gen's. "Nice neighborhood. Looks like our girl has money."

"Considering what Dad said she charges everybody but us, she ought to."

Dave snorted. "Lucky us. I think I'll go sniff around a little more. Make sure we don't get any murderous visitors." He padded off, big feet silent on the lush grass.

"Stay out of sight while you do it," Kurt called after him. "We don't want the neighbors to call 911."

Returning inside, he found Genevieve in a huge, high-ceilinged room that served as her studio. Skylights and an entire wall of windows poured natural light over an easel, a drafting table, and a computer station mounted with two huge flat screen monitors.

Genevieve stood working at a table with a pair of lights mounted over it at forty-five degree angles. The same metal frame held a camera pointed straight down at the table. She was shooting pictures of the sketch she'd done of the Arcanist spell.

As he watched, she turned to the computer and switched it on. While it booted, she went to the corner to a cylindrical tank with some kind of bulky gear attached.

"Let me get that." He walked over and lifted the tank's handle, tilting it onto its rear wheels. "What is this thing?"

"Air compressor. I need it to run my airbrush."

He gave her a teasing grin. "Planning to make T-shirts?"

"I can't exactly use pastels around your house. I've got to draw the wards with something."

"Most of the Arcs I worked with did that with a brush."

"Not for a ward that big."

He frowned. "So what did the assassins use? If they'd used an airbrush, we would've heard it."

Genevieve shrugged. "Maybe not. A regular air compressor makes a lot of noise, but this one isn't much louder than a refrigerator. Plus he probably used stencils to make the work faster." She pursed her lips. "Must have used ultraviolet paint, since I didn't see any visible marks on the sand."

He frowned as a new thought occurred to him. "Wouldn't he have had to use his blood? Because if he did, once the cops catch him, they'll have all the DNA they need to convict his ass."

"You don't have to use your own blood to cast magic. You can use a sacrifice's. Probably an animal's to set the trap spell in the arena gate, then your father's blood to activate the main casting."

"I'm going to kill that fucker when I catch him."

"Might not want to joke about that."

"Who's joking?" Pushing the compressor, he headed outside to the SUV as Genevieve picked up her cell phone and started dialing.

When he came back, the call wasn't going well.

"Dad, I'm not trying to play hero here." Her voice was raised, her tone hot and frustrated.

Kurt's tiger hearing easily picked up the male baritone on the other end of the call. "We saw the press conference on CNN, but I didn't realize you were there. What the hell are you doing getting involved in something like this?"

"Look, they had a sick cat, a tiger. I was at BFS trying to heal the animal when that bear Feral showed up and started roaring. Fred Briggs went out to investigate..."

"And you just went out there with him? Are you out of your mind? You know what that thing could have done to you?"

"Give me credit for a little sense, Dad. I stayed in the clinic." Her voice took on that note of anguished guilt he'd heard before. "But if I'd gone with him, maybe he wouldn't have died. Maybe I could have broken that spell and helped him escape. Instead he got trapped, his son got shot, and he ended up a human sacrifice."

"Which wasn't your fault, honey," a woman said, in the strained tone of someone trying to be the voice of reason. "The killers are the ones who are at fault here."

"And if they could kill a Feral lion and a tiger Familiar, what chance do you think you'd have?" the colonel demanded.

"He has a point, dear. This isn't a good situation."

"And that's aside from this Briggs character. You don't even know the man."

"Dad..."

He ignored her attempt to cut him off. "Your mother and I have served in the Corps for thirty years, and we've worked with a lot of Ferals. Briggs could be every bit as big a danger to you as that bear."

"Oh, come on! The man is a decorated war hero..."

"Which means absolutely nothing! If his tiger just died, at this point they're barely melded. He's got zero self-control right now, even without his father having just been murdered. If he loses it, you'll be screwed."

Kurt froze, staring at her. Everything her father was saying was the absolute truth; he should be rooting for Colonel Reyes to talk her into leaving.

But he didn't want her to go.

Stoli's anxiety echoed his, exacerbating his frustration and anger. He drew in a deep breath and blew it out slowly.

"It's too late for me to cut and run, Dad. I broke the spell. They're going to be targeting me now."

"You don't know that. But if you stay there and keep involving yourself, they will target you. You're going to end up getting yourself killed."

"And what if I leave and they come after me anyway? Dave and Kurt can do a hell of a lot more to defend me against that freaking bear than I can. Kurt asked me to stay at his house and I'm going to do it."

"Oh, I'm sure he has."

Kurt felt his face go hot at the insinuation in the colonel's tone. Never mind that the man was right. Or at least not completely wrong. He did want Genevieve, more than he should. *Enough to put her at risk?*

"If you need a bodyguard, we can hire one for you. We've got connections."

"And just stand back and let the assassins cast whatever spell they're trying to cast -- kill whoever they want to kill? If Kurt trips some kind of spell and gets killed the way his father did when I could have prevented it, it'll be my fault."

"No, it'll be the fucking Arc's fault," her father snarled.

"If it was you, what would you do? And don't tell me that you'd put your tail between your legs and run, because I know better. If you'd been that kind of man, you wouldn't still be in the Corps."

"I'm a man. You're not."

"Sexist much?"

"I've served with plenty of women, including your mother. You don't have the temperament for combat, Genevieve. You're not good with confrontation. That's why you let those assholes in high school give you such a hard time."

"So now I'm not just female, I'm cowardly."

"Of course not. You always put the worst possible interpretation on everything I say."

"Oh, for God's sakes, Martin," her mother snapped. "You're not helping. Genevieve, I need to take a closer look at the spell. I'll call you back as soon as I get something figured out."

"I'd appreciate it."

"We can still hire a bodyguard."

"I don't need a bodyguard. Look, Dad, I'm a grown woman. You're the one who's always told me to stand on my own two feet."

"Not against a polar bear! And not by staying with that damned Feral! Those men are dangerous, Genevieve. The military spends a lot of time and money making sure they are just as deadly as possible."

"Exactly. So I've got more than enough bodyguards. Mom, give me a call when you get something figured out. I appreciate all the help I can get." Her tone softened. "I love you guys. 'Bye."

Her father began another hot interruption, but she hit the END button and sank down in her chair, rubbing her forehead as she muttered, "Well, that could have gone better."

Kurt stepped around the corner, and she looked up as he said, "He's worried about you."

"I know that, but sometimes they still make me crazy. My dad's first reaction to any conflict is to take over."

"Believe me, I feel your pain." His voice dropped to a muttered, "And I'd give anything to still have that problem."

Chapter Eleven

Genevieve sat cross-legged in a circle she had drawn in chalk on the cement of Kurt's drive. The afternoon sunlight turned her long hair into a cloak of copper fire as she sat there, eyes closed, slim and straight in cream shorts and a T-shirt. Her long, long legs looked tan and lovely, with the kind of elegant muscle that suggested she ran or lifted weights. Maybe both, given her military family. Her full lips moved as she chanted something in Latin. For once, he couldn't feel the spell she was casting. The magic was contained by the circle.

Three containers of paint sat in front of Gen's knees, and she held a glass vial full of dark brown powder -- her own dried blood.

Still chanting, Genevieve tipped the vial over each of the paint containers and tapped out a careful quantity of the powder. Her gestures smooth, she picked up a glass rod engraved with intricate magical sigils and stirred the mixture with precise circles of her wrist.

When she was finished, she picked up one of the containers, rose to her feet and stepped out of the circle, leaving the other two inside. The circle would maintain the power of the spelled paint while she worked.

Kurt handed over the airbrush gun -- a wand-shaped device attached to the coil of tubing. She screwed the container onto the brush, and turned on the air compressor. It started with a soft sigh as she walked to the circle she'd sprayed on the ground with non-magical paint. The design was nothing more than a guide to the placement of the actual spell. It needed to be as close to round as possible to avoid irregularities that would create weaknesses the Arc could exploit.

Kurt followed her, playing out the tubing as she started painting symbols along the circumference of the circle in sweeping strokes, creating the intricate sigils that comprised the language of magic. She chanted as she worked, her voice rising pure and clear over the hiss of the compressor. Each step and sweep of her hand seemed more dance than anything else, and her eyes stared into the distance, as if she gazed at something only she could see.

It took more than two hours to lay the spell -- three complete circuits of the house, one for each of the three colors.

It was a hot afternoon, and the sun beat down on their shoulders. It wasn't long before sweat streamed down Kurt's spine and dewed Gen's skin as if she'd been oiled. Yet she didn't pause, never seemed to let her concentration flag.

With every sigil, the strength of the spell grew, until it felt like a second sun beating on his face. Genevieve had given him a charm designed to fool the spell into thinking he was a part of her, or the spell would have shoved him right out of the circle.

God she really is powerful, he thought. Something about the feel of her magic lapping against his skin felt intensely erotic. His cock throbbed, thick and heavy behind his zipper, and his balls ached.

Kurt tried to remember the last time he'd felt so aroused for so long. Memories kept flashing through his mind of Genevieve sitting slim and naked astride his lap, her blue eyes shining like gemstones with power, a wicked little smile on her lips.

Stoli wanted to jump her. Just pounce on her, taste her pink nipples and sweet mouth. He had to keep reminding himself if he interrupted her, he'd disrupt the spell. They'd have to start all over again. *And she'd kill me.*

Kurt dragged his gaze away from her lushly tempting ass and tried to think of something else.

He needed to make a call to the American Association for Feral Rights. If anyone knew whether there had been similar crimes, it would be someone at AAFR, which collected statistics on crimes committed by and against Ferals. Then he'd need to start making funeral arrangements for his father. That thought sent a wave of such grieving pain through him, his lingering arousal instantly vanished. *I think I prefer blue balls.*

Genevieve bent to paint another sigil. He let his eyes drift back to her sweetly curving ass. The need was maddening, but it was better than the pain.

* * *

Gen had to use her left hand to steady her right as she painted the last sigil.

With a mental pop that felt like the sensation her ears produced inside a climbing plane, the spell activated. Magic swirled around her, and she closed her eyes to watch the sigils revolve, intricate symbols of blue, red and green swimming through the air.

Her sense of the magic radiating from the surrounding life of BFS -- the cats, the Ferals, even the plants -- muted as if someone had turned the volume down on the world.

Gen took a staggering step to one side, abruptly exhausted. Her legs gave out and she went down. Before she even hit the ground, muscled arms closed around her for the second time in two days. Or was it the third? She couldn't remember.

"You can't keep making a habit out of this,

Kurt," Genevieve muttered into his warm, sweating neck.

"I can if you keep falling on your ass," he told her tartly, striding toward the front door.

Dave emerged from the bushes to join them. "You do know how to sweep a girl off her feet, Rhett," he said in a dead-on Vivian-Leigh-as-Scarlet drawl.

Genevieve chuckled and closed her eyes. Her head ached with a kettledrum throb.

Kurt lengthened his stride, forcing even Dave to break into a trot. "I don't think I like your coloring," he told her grimly.

The world made a slow, sickening revolution around her, forcing her to close her eyes and admit, "I'm not feeling great."

The air-conditioned house felt like a freezer after so long in the hot sun. She started to shiver as he deposited her on a chair in the kitchen. Leaning her elbows on the kitchen table, Genevieve rested her aching head on her hands and let herself savor the numb relief of doing nothing whatsoever.

Kurt's hand appeared in front of her face holding a bottle of water. "Drain that."

"Thanks." She took it gratefully and drank it down.

Dave studied her. "Think she's got heat exhaustion?"

"Nah." She pressed the cool bottle against her face. "I'm a little hot, but most of it is magic drain."

Kurt got her a bottle of Gatorade, then filled a bowl for Dave before dropping into a chair with his own drink. For the next ten minutes, they all concentrated on hydrating.

"I can't remember the last time I felt this whipped," Gen admitted. "Too many major spells too close together. I seriously need to recharge my psychic batteries."

Kurt flashed her a wicked smile. "Need some help with that?"

"Uh..." Genevieve felt her cheeks heat. Usually you recovered from a big magical effort the way you would any other kind of exertion -- rest and sleep. But there was another way. Sex with another Talent could be an effective way to recharge. The theory was the interplay of auras acted to reinforce each other, along with the positive effect of all those hormones on the brain. There was a saying in Arc circles: *Nothing charges like a good orgasm.*

Evidently taking mercy on her blush, he smiled faintly. "What you need is food. How does a sandwich sound?"

Dave looked up. "Not as good as ten pounds of cow."

"I'll get you your cow in a minute." To Gen he continued, "Sandwiches? Or would you prefer something else?"

She smiled at him, grateful he'd resisted the temptation of innuendo. "Sandwiches sound good."

Ten minutes later, Kurt plunked down the plate in front of her. It held a thick sandwich piled high with ham, cheese, and assorted vegetables between slices of wheat toast. She demolished it while he got a roast out of the refrigerator for Dave -- donated by one of the volunteers -- before fixing his own meal.

"Why don't you go take a nap?" he suggested between bites of ham and cheese. "You're done in."

"That might be a good idea," Gen admitted with a sigh. "What about you?" It hit her after the words were out of her mouth that he could take the question as flirtatious.

Sure enough, Kurt's gaze heated until she felt the impact of that very male intensity clean to her toes.

Then he looked away. "I've got to go to the funeral home, start making arrangements for my dad. Fortunately, I have a pretty good idea what he wanted. It shouldn't be all that tough." Which was, she suspected, an outright lie. "Then I'm going to check with my Feral contacts, see if anyone has heard about any attacks like the one on Dad. After that, I've got an appointment with Sawyer to discuss the case. I just need to get a shower."

"I'll go with you. I need to talk to Sawyer anyway."

Kurt shook his head. "Jake's got the day off. He told me he's going to give me a hand."

"But…"

"Look, you really need to recharge in case we need your magic."

Gen wanted to argue, but she knew better. "You've got a point."

He turned to Dave, but before he could say whatever was on his mind, the tiger looked up from his roast. "I'll keep an eye on her."

"Good." Kurt sighed. "Well, might as well get it over with."

* * *

She dreamed of Kurt. That look in his eyes at the table, so hot and male and hungry. His mouth on her nipple, the swirl of his tongue over her clit. The feel of him, urgent between her thighs, his cock, thick and long, filling her so completely. She spun in the dream's heat, in the images of his big hands and his broad shoulders and his eyes. The feel of muscle rolling under her fingertips as she clung to him…

Something sank claws into her magic and shook

her so hard, her eyes flew open to stare up at the darkened ceiling. She must have slept for hours. "What the…"

The roar of a tiger shattered the night. Dave? *Kurt?* Gen flung herself out of bed and ran for the stairs. Only to stop dead at the door. Clothes. She needed clothes…

Glancing down, she saw she'd gone to sleep in her shorts and a shirt, intending nothing more than a nap. She took off again, racing down the hall and thumping down the stairs, clinging to the banister as she hit every other step in her haste.

Something was trying to get through her wards.

She tried to fling the front door open, but the knob didn't turn. Gen had to fumble with the latch until she managed to flip the deadbolt, then she was out the door, off the porch and bounding into the night, the sound of the tiger's roar in her ears. She had no idea what time it was.

The vibration in her protesting wards set her teeth on edge like the sound of a dentist drill.

Dave's voice rolled out in an inhuman roar. "Get the hell away from our house!"

Genevieve almost ran headlong into a tree in the dark. She caught herself against the trunk at the last moment and stopped, panting, listening.

A female voice spoke, one she didn't recognize. "You shouldn't be involved in this mess, cat. The witch interferes where she has no business and does more damage than she knows."

"*She* does more damage? You murdered Fred Briggs! You shot my friend and forced him to meld before his time. And I'm going to kill you for it." His voice dropped into a ripping snarl that chilled even Gen.

She laughed. "You have about as much chance against us as Briggs did." Even as she spoke, the witch probed Gen's ward with licking tongues of magic, searching for weakness.

Genevieve set her teeth against the pressure and poured more power into her spell as she edged closer, following the sound of their voices.

"You're not a fool," the woman continued in that chilling, oh-so-reasonable voice. "Do you really want to have to register in that damned NTRA database so they can conveniently track us down, imprison us, kill us? Whenever they want? You've seen the demonstrations, you've felt the bigotry. Hell, they've got you spending your life in a cage! You, a war hero!"

"The world is full of assholes, lady. I'm looking at two of them right now."

Genevieve closed her eyes and looked with magical senses, without the distraction of sight. A woman's glowing form faced him on the other side of the revolving wall of symbols that was the ward.

Yeah, that's the Arc, wearing a Spook Suit. And she'd brought a friend.

The polar bear stood behind her, massive and terrifying, with a bullet-shaped head that looked tiny in proportion to his thick, powerful body. Even on all fours, the Feral was huge. The top of the woman's head barely came to his shoulder. He glowed incredibly bright -- brighter than the woman, brighter even than Dave. The glow seemed to throb against Gen's eyelids.

Power streamed from the woman's fingers as she held her hands bare inches from the ward. Raking downward, she sent magic streaming from her fingertips to claw at the sigil wall.

"We regret Briggs' death, but it was necessary," the bear rumbled. "A sacrifice is no sacrifice if doesn't hurt, and killing him did."

"My heart bleeds for you, dickhead. So why the fuck kill him? Exactly what are you trying to do?"

"Free our people," the witch spat. "Keep them safe from the Norms who'd strip us of our rights and deny us the opportunities we've bled and died for. The president and his Congress of bigots piss all over the Constitution they vowed to defend. They deserve…" She broke off.

Dave said exactly what Gen was thinking. "That's why you're doing this. It's a fucking mass assassination attempt!"

"It's more than an attempt, cat. We're going to do it."

"You idiot, killing them would just validate their argument that Talents are dangerous. Even if you pull it off, more bigots will take their place. We won't have a prayer of avoiding the camps you're so worried about, because you'll have turned even the decent Norms against us. You murdered Fred for nothing!"

"Yes, now," the witch said bitterly. "That stupid Arc cunt broke the spell and wasted his death. Now we'll have to make another sacrifice. Another Feral has to die -- and it's on your head, witch." She raised her voice. "And yes, I know you're there, Reyes. I can sense you hiding in the bushes like a coward."

"You're one to talk about hiding," Genevieve snarled. "You shot Kurt's Familiar from ambush."

"Which I wouldn't have done, if he'd stayed out of it."

Dave sneered. "She doesn't like NTRA, so her solution is to kill enough people to guarantee they lock us all up. She's no different from the Caliphuckers. Same Goddamn psychopathy masquerading as a cause."

"Fred wasn't the only one you killed, was he?" Gen demanded, knowing she was right. "A spell designed to murder five hundred plus would have required more sacrifices. Probably a lot more. That's why I couldn't decipher the spell -- it was part of a larger working."

Dave's tail whipped around his striped flanks. "And they all died for nothing, because Genevieve copied the fragment and gave it to the cops. How long do you think it's going to be before the Secret Service knows exactly who you are?"

"The Feds will track down every sacrifice, every last section of that spell, and break it all," Gen gritted, pouring more power into the casting.

The witch sneered. "I'll activate it long before they get it down."

"You'll never get the chance. You'll either die resisting arrest or spend the rest of your life on death row. Human sacrifice is a capital crime."

"They'll have to catch us first." The Arc flung out a hand, slamming a spell into the ward.

Pain exploded in Gen's body, and she fell to one knee, gasping as she fought to reinforce the barrier and keep the witch out. As she struggled, she heard a low, rumbling growl of anticipation coming from the bear. *If that thing gets through, it's going to rip us both apart.*

Where the heck is Kurt? And why didn't I grab my cell? She'd left it lying on the nightstand, where it did her absolutely no good.

"We're going to gut you, witch." The Arc dug her fingertips in the air just beyond the sigils as if grabbing a fistful of magic. "You used a lot of power casting this. When I break it, the backlash will take out whatever you've got left. We'll kill you, and we'll take our time."

Behind her, the bear stared at Genevieve with vicious anticipation in his eyes.

"You're not through the ward yet," Gen sneered, though her heart pounded in terror.

"Only a matter of time." The woman let go and paced along the perimeter of the circle, studying the sigils, looking for weakness. Her hand flashed out.

Agony raked through Genevieve's skull, so savage it was all she could do not to scream.

Within the ward, a sigil distorted. The Arc froze, staring hard at it with a predatory intensity. "There. You must've been getting tired when you cast that."

Oh fuck.

Another swipe of mystical claws, as if the Arc had manifested an animal form like her partner's. Sinking her fingers into the energy field, she twisted her wrist, ripping at it. Genevieve poured more magic into the ward. Despair rolled over her as she realized she was rapidly running through the energy that food and a nap had given her. The Arcanist was right. She couldn't keep this up much longer. When the ward fell, she and Dave were fucked.

No, Goddamnit. Dad didn't raise me to give up. You never, never, never give up! The longer she could keep them at bay, the greater was the chance that Kurt or a cop or somebody would arrive to drive the killers off. *All I have to do is hold on a little longer.*

Dropping to her knees, Genevieve planted her palms on the lawn. Her heart hammered with anxiety, but she forced herself to ignore the fear. She began to chant, drawing energy from the earth, from the trees, from the magic of the sanctuary all around them.

This was her type of magic. As a healer, she knew how to connect with nature, with the magic generated by all life. It might not be enough given her magical exhaustion, but it was something.

She poured her power into the ground and up into the wards, drawing on the magic, the life, that filled the circle with her.

Dave backed away from the ward, retreating until he stood beside her. Thrusting a glowing human arm from his shoulder, he grabbed her forearm. "Draw on me," he said softly.

She didn't dare look away from the ward she was fighting to reinforce. "But if they break through, you'll need your magic to defend yourself."

"And if they don't break through, I won't. I'd rather keep them the fuck out."

She didn't even bother trying to argue. Thrusting her aura against his, Gen began to draw on his magic just as she'd used her own to reinforce Parvati's life force. But now she drew his magic in, funneling it through her body and sending it out to the wards.

The witch leaped back with a curse as the sigil she'd seized grew brighter again, burning her. "Bitch, you're just postponing the inevitable!" she spat.

"Yeah, yeah," Dave sneered, and went into a flawless imitation of the Wicked Witch of the West. "I'll get you, my pretty! You and your little tiger too!" He added a mocking cackle.

"And we will get you, you striped fucker!" the Arc spat. "Let's see you laugh when my bear rips out your throat."

Dave bared his scimitar fangs. "I'm shaking, Witchypoo."

"You should be." The witch eyed them. "Because what's sauce for the goose… is a pretty good idea." She turned and gestured to the bear. The huge Feral moved up beside her.

Genevieve froze in horror as the Arc sank one

hand into the bear's glowing shoulder, drew back the other, and slashed her hand across the ward.

Pain exploded across her consciousness, blinding, ice-cold, ripping into her very life force. Genevieve screamed.

Dave echoed her, human voice ringing over the tiger's agonized roar.

She had never felt such pain from a magical attack, not even during her mother's merciless magical combat practice sessions. She might have been able to fight off the witch alone, but with the bear reinforcing the Arc's power...

Dave gasped what she was thinking. "We're... fucked!"

Stubborn rebellion surged through her. "Not yet... Not..." Teeth gritted, Genevieve gathered her magic and waited, feeling the witch draw back, preparing another thrust. She had to time this exactly right.

This was an insane gamble. If it didn't work, they'd be helpless. It was also the only real chance either of them had.

The Arc drew back and sliced. As she dug into the ward, Genevieve drew in Dave's power. She added it to her own, along with the power of the ward itself.

And slammed it all into the bitch's hand.

The ward blinked out as the witch went flying with a shriek. She hit the ground in a rolling tumble as the bear roared in anguish. Its manifestation winked out.

Staring through her closed eyes, Genevieve saw the shape of a big man, staggering, clutching his head in pain. He reeled over to the fallen witch, picked her up, and swung her over his shoulder before staggering off into the dark.

Beside her, Dave's glowing form collapsed.

Genevieve's gaze darkened and went black.

* * *

It was 9:30 when Kurt and Jake headed back to the house.

"Fuck of a day," his friend commented from the passenger side.

"Yeah. Thanks for going with me." First had come the funeral arrangements, then a series of calls to his contacts with the American Association for Feral Rights.

Then they'd headed over to the Sheriff's Office for the meeting with Sawyer to tell him what they'd learned. The detective had thanked Kurt for arranging the necropsy -- the vet had delivered the bullet that afternoon. After that came a series of follow up questions.

"How many times am I going to have to answer the exact same questions?" Kurt grumbled to Jake as he took the turn into BFS.

"Probably through the trial."

"What trial?"

"Either the Arc's -- or yours."

Kurt flipped him off.

As he pulled into the drive, his headlights swept over something striped lying in the grass next to a pale body. Kurt's heart convulsed in his chest, and he stomped on the SUV's brakes. "What the fuck? Dave? Gen?"

As Jake swore viciously, Kurt threw open the truck door and closed his eyes to look with magical senses. *Oh, thank God.* A dim glow radiated from the two figures.

"They're alive," Jake grunted and threw the passenger door open even as Kurt leaped out and sprang into a dead run toward the collapsed forms.

Kurt fell to his knees next to Genevieve, who lay on her belly, head turned to the side. Reaching through the cool silk of her hair, he sought the pulse in her throat. He blew out a breath in relief when his fingertips found the strong, even throb.

Next to him, Jake pulled out his phone and started making calls.

"Genevieve! Gen, wake up!" There was no sign of visible injuries, no gunshot or bite wounds. No blood. Her skin felt a little cool, but he couldn't tell if it was shock or just lying on the cool ground.

"She hurt?" Jake knelt by the tiger and started running his hands over the thick fur in the light of his cell phone flashlight app.

"I don't see anything on her back, but I don't want to move her to check her front. Don't smell any blood, though."

"Me neither." Jake breathed deep and grimaced. "Hell of a lot of burned magic, though."

He was right. The air had that post-thunderstorm reek Kurt associated with the aftermath of a powerful spell, but there was no skin-tingling sense of active magic. "What the hell happened to the ward?" Closing his eyes again, he saw no sign of the floating sigils Genevieve had worked all afternoon to cast. "It's fucking gone!"

"The Arc must have destroyed it."

"Where's that ambulance?"

"Five minutes out."

The assassins must have attacked them. But where were they?

And why were Gen and Dave still alive?

He stroked the hair away from Gen's face. Her long lashes fluttered at his touch. "Genevieve, wake up, honey. Come on, Gen…"

To his vast relief, she stirred, frowning, her eyes slitting open. "Kurt?"

"Yeah. Are you hurt anywhere?"

She lifted a shaking hand to her forehead and hissed in pain. "Oh God, my head…"

"Probably backlash. Your wards are gone. What happened? Did they hit you?"

A frown formed between her brows. "I… don't think so. Just… just magic."

"The Arc… and that fucking bear showed up…" Dave rasped, lifting his great furry head. "The Arc tried to break the ward."

"Must have worked. It's down."

"No, that wasn't her. Gen did it herself. Drew on my magic, hers, and the wards, and blew both those assholes across the yard. I don't know what happened after that." He rose on all fours, only to immediately sink back down on his belly. "Oh God, I think I'm going to vomit."

"Don't," Genevieve begged. "If you start, I'll go too."

"So you're both suffering from backlash?" Kurt demanded. "You weren't otherwise hurt?"

"Nothing's bleeding, if that's what you mean." Dave's glowing eyes slid shut. "No inconvenient holes anywhere."

Jake rose to his feet. "Then I'm going to see if I can find a magic trail." His lion manifested in an explosion of golden light as he walked off, maned head lowered to the ground. Cats weren't bloodhounds by any means, but Ferals could still sense magic.

"Kurt, we're in trouble," Gen said over the cycling wail of approaching sirens.

"Yeah, I noticed that."

"No, I mean more trouble even than we thought there was. The Arc is a woman. This spell of hers is designed to kill the President and every member of Congress."

"*What*?" Kurt stared at her, trying to make sense of it all. "How the hell is a spell supposed to do that?"

"I have no idea. Even if she blew up the White House and the Capitol Building with Congress in session, there are safeguards in place to keep the federal government from collapsing. It just wouldn't work." Her pretty mouth set in a hard line. "But what it would be guaranteed to do is turn three hundred million people against every Talent in the country."

Dave's tail flipped back and forth. "They'd roast us and the marshmallows over the same bonfire."

Chapter Twelve

Kurt sat back on his heels and raked his hands through his hair with a grunt. "Sawyer and I were afraid it was something nasty, given the number of people my AAFR contact thinks they may have murdered. But we had no idea it was this bad."

She lifted her head and studied him with wide blue eyes. "What did you find out? And how?"

"I spoke to Yvonne Carson with the American Association for Feral Rights after I left the funeral home this afternoon. I told her about your theory that the spell on Dad was part of a larger working. Bad news is, she said there weren't any cases of Ferals killed with an Arcanist spell anyone has been able to detect. But there *have* been six murders of Ferals by other Ferals in the past year. In every case, the cops have charged somebody with the crime, even though the bite wounds are totally inconsistent with that particular manifestation's bite. All of the wounds look like some kind of bear."

"They charged the wrong Ferals anyway?"

"Yeah. AAFR's lawyers pointed out that the manifestation is obviously a bear, but no dice. The cops and prosecutors are all convinced the cases are unrelated, and they've accused AAFR of trying to cover for the Ferals who've been charged. Never mind that the victims are Ferals too. Even the judges refuse to listen. The Ferals can't even get out on bail."

Genevieve sat up, moving as if she was afraid her head was going to fall off. Kurt steadied her with a hand on her lean forearm. "That sounds like some kind of spell."

"Pretty much. I have a feeling that if you hadn't been there, I'd be sitting in jail right now waiting to go on trial for Dad's murder."

"There's no way you would've been convicted. Any half-decent defense attorney would have been able to argue it wasn't a tiger that killed Fred."

"Maybe getting people convicted isn't the point. What if the idea is to delay the investigation until they can finish killing everybody and complete all the sections of this assassination spell?"

"That does make sense. The question is, how close are they to completing the..." Gen broke off. "How many people did you say were dead?"

"Six."

"And your Dad makes seven." Her voice dropped to a mutter. "No wonder the Arc was so pissed."

"Yeah, that occurred to me too." Seven had been considered a magical number going back all the way to ancient Babylon. "You think Fred was supposed to be the final sacrifice? That the spell you broke was the last piece?"

"I can't say for sure, but it does sound that way." Gen hesitated. "Kurt, she said they're going to have to kill another Feral. That the sacrifice will be on my head. What if they go after you?"

"If that bitch thinks it'll be that easy, she's got another think coming. They were only able to kill Dad because they ambushed him. I know they're coming, and I'm going to kick their asses."

Dave bared his teeth, whiskers bristling. "And we'll help him."

Gen smiled. "So will I."

"You already have," Kurt told her. "Hundreds of people would already be dead if you hadn't insisted on breaking that spell."

"My Mom would have killed me if I'd been

dumb enough to leave it active, especially since it used a human sacrifice as fuel."

"You know more about Arc magic than I do. What do we do now -- other than keep them from killing us?"

"Get in touch with the Feds, have them send government Arcanists to all the other crime scenes to break all the sections of the spell. Now. Tonight, because if that bitch manages to finish it, it's going to activate and the President and Congress will die."

"Followed by a hell of a lot of innocent Talents," Dave growled. "It'd just take them longer."

It hit Kurt suddenly that Genevieve and Dave had almost been among those innocents. He looked at her, taking in the curves of her features in the moonlight, the gleam of those big blue eyes.

Before he could think better of it, Kurt leaned forward and took her mouth gently, tenderly. She opened to him. Her lips felt so deliciously soft and yielding as she seemed to melt into his arms. Kissing him back, tongue swirling, her hands clenching in the fabric of his knit shirt.

In the back of his mind, he was aware of Dave rising to his feet and padding off deeper into surrounding trees, as if to give them a little privacy.

His buddy always had been a damn good wingman.

Judging by the sirens, they wouldn't have long before they were ass deep in cops. Kurt wasn't sure he cared.

He pulled back just far enough to whisper, "I almost lost you tonight."

"We barely know each other," she pointed out, though there was a yearning note to her voice.

He sank back on his knees, drawing her tighter

against him as he stared into her lovely eyes. "Does it matter?"

"It should. I keep telling myself we shouldn't keep acting on this attraction -- that it's just a product of a traumatic situation, hormones, and anxiety driving us to do something dumb. And all that's true."

Kurt smoothed her silken curls back from her face. "Yeah, it's a pretty extreme situation." Stroking his fingertips over the line of her jaw, he kissed her softly. "Maybe it is just hormones and tragedy. But what if it's more?"

"It probably isn't."

"Maybe. But right now, it feels pretty damn amazing. And I've got to admit, I'd like to find something in this fucking nightmare that doesn't feel like the end of the world as I know it. I…"

"Jesus H Christ!" Sawyer snarled, suddenly looming out of the darkness. "Did you get me out of bed to watch you two make out?"

"Ahh!" Genevieve jerked so violently, she almost fell on her ass.

Stoli's fury heated Kurt's blood as he steadied her. He glared at the man. "No, Goddamnit, I found her lying here in a heap. I thought she was dead."

The anger faded from Sawyer's face as his gaze softened into something like sympathy. "I guess I can see that. What happened?"

"Can we go inside?" Genevieve interrupted. "My head feels like it's about to explode."

* * *

Half an hour later, Gen, Kurt, Sawyer and Jake sat around the kitchen table over cups of coffee. Dave sat on his haunches at the table's other end, golden eyes alert and glowing.

They'd briefed the detective as the crime scene

team worked the yard. And the cop wasn't happy about what he'd heard. Now he grimaced. "I've got to call the sheriff, get him to bring the FBI and Secret Service in on this."

Genevieve nodded. "Mom says the Feds have a pretty good Arc squad."

Sawyer frowned deeply. "I don't get how these spells would still be working, when at least one of them is a year old or better. How the hell is that even possible?"

Gen considered the question. "From what Kurt said, all the involved jurisdictions have really small departments. Too small to have an Arcanist, because a good Arc would have detected the spell."

"If they knew to look for it."

"Since standard procedure is to scan the scene in any case involving magic, they'd have seen it. Spells like the one I broke last night are hard to miss."

Sawyer shook his head. "But even so, they would have had to draw a spell on the ground and kill the sacrifice inside the circle, right? How did the detectives not notice that?"

"Probably used some kind of paint you can't see in visible light. Ultraviolet or something. Point is, if they didn't physically erase the spell, it would still be running, given the sacrifice used to power it. Which is why the Feds need to get people there to break those spells now."

He sighed and rose to his feet, pulling the phone out of his pocket. "Guess it's time to start waking people up before that fucking spell goes off." Sawyer walked into the hall. "Sheriff? Sawyer. We've got a problem…"

"That," Dave muttered, "is putting it mildly."

* * *

Genevieve and Kurt sat on the couch in the living room, nursing glasses of wine. Sawyer had left with his notebook full of scribbled notes. He'd already been on the phone with the local FBI Special Agent in Charge.

The SAC seemed to be taking the situation seriously, thank God. She said she'd be calling her bosses to arrange to have FBI Arcanists visit the six other scenes to investigate and break any spells they found there. In the meantime, the Feds would get all those officials out of Washington to make them harder to target.

Jake had headed off to bed in what had been Fred's room; he planned to stay with them for the next couple days to help protect Genevieve. Tonight's attack had proved just how necessary that was.

Gen sipped her Riesling, savoring the cool, crisp taste. Overhead, water rushed through pipes as Jake took a shower.

Dave padded through on his way out the front door. "I'll take the first watch."

Kurt looked around at him. "I'll be out to spell you at three."

"I'll take another shot at those wards in the morning," Genevieve told them both. "Hopefully tomorrow night we'll all be able to get some sleep."

The tiger sighed. "Let's hope so." A moment later, they heard the door open and close behind him.

Genevieve listened to the rush of water through the pipes with longing. "I am in desperate need of a shower."

"So am I." Kurt's golden gaze flicked to hers and heated at the implications. His voice dropped to a deep, low purr. "We could always conserve water."

Genevieve had to smile at that. "I'm all for being green."

He stood, caught her around the waist, and pulled her toward him as he sank back down again, tugging her down on his lap. Gen let herself sink against him, enjoying the hard strength she found in the warm circle of his arms. The feel of him gave her a desperately needed sense of safety after the stark fear of tonight and the unsettling realization of how much rode on what they did next.

Kurt kissed her, brushing his lips back and forth over hers, slipping his tongue into her mouth to circle and stroke. He tasted of Riesling, sweet and fruity, and the cool tingle of magic. His arms tightened around her waist, and one big hand sliding down over her body, stroking over the curve of her hip, then up again, running up under the hem of her T-shirt, playing over the flesh of her waist to find her breasts.

She expected him to pull the cup up and bare her flesh, but instead he let his fingertips dwell on the full curve through the fine lace. His thumb slid back and forth over the nipple, making her breath speed. He went on kissing her, slow and searching, lazy, thorough, tongue moving over and around hers in dancing velvet strokes.

Genevieve groaned in soft pleasure, reaching up a hand to explore the angles and hollows of his face, feeling the faint bristle of the five o'clock shadow against her fingertips.

Beneath her ass, the thick ridge of his erection began to grow, hardening and lengthening under her weight. He rumbled against her mouth, a sound less human than tiger. This time it didn't alarm her as it had the last time they'd made love. He hadn't lost control then, and she doubted he would now.

Even so, she could feel his magic swirling around her like currents in warm water, surrounding her with liquid pleasure. It added another layer of delicious sensation to those he created with mouth and hands and the pressure of that thick cock under her ass.

When he drew back again, they were both breathing hard. Kurt rested his forehead against her cheek. "When I saw you lying in the yard today, it scared the fuck out of me. I was terrified you'd been clawed open like Dad. All I could think was, 'I just found her. The bastards can't have taken her already.'"

She stroked a hand through the dark silk of his hair, so cool and soft under her fingers. "But they didn't. Though they certainly gave it their best shot."

"They'll try again."

"Maybe not. Maybe they'll back off when the FBI breaks the spells. There won't be any point in trying to kill us anymore."

"Let's not think about that right now." His hand tightened on her breast, thumb stroking hard along her nipple. "Think about this."

Genevieve gasped at the rough, erotic pressure. Her eyes drifted closed, as she sank into the sweet sensuality of making love to Kurt.

He growled softly, his free hand moving around her thigh to find the seam of her shorts. The tips of his fingers stroked up and down over the ridge of fabric in a tease of sensation, a promise of pleasure. Genevieve shivered in delight, conscious of the jut of his cock against her pussy. Unable to resist, she rolled her hips over his length, stimulating both of them ruthlessly.

"Minx," he rumbled, gold eyes glowing. "You're asking for trouble."

Upstairs the shower cut off.

His fingers tightened between her thighs, rubbing back and forth, slipping between her vaginal lips, to press the seam of the shorts between them. She panted, head tipping back, eyes sliding closed. For a moment, she let herself swim in the lush pleasure before looking down at him again. Kurt stared up into her face, brushing his fingers back and forth as he stared up at her, his gaze hot with sensual demand.

Her breath came faster, and she shivered in need. He reached up with his free hand, combing his fingers through her disordered red curls. "I love your hair."

"I love your eyes -- among other things." She smiled, as the colors of his gaze snared her again. "I never realized how beautiful Feral eyes were before. So many colors, umber around your irises, autumn gold, lemon yellow. And when they start to glow, they're like flame. Hypnotic. I know I'll never be able to capture it, but I'd love to try."

They kissed again, tongues dancing in mutual seduction. By the time he pulled back, her heart was pounding, her nipples even harder.

"The guest room door just closed," he murmured. "I think the coast is clear." His lips curled into a very male smile.

Gen smiled back. "Good. I'm feeling a little… dirty."

He chuckled and gave her a swat on the ass. "Then let's go clean you up."

* * *

Kurt watched Genevieve strip, revealing that long, graceful body of hers. He loved that creamy redhead's complexion, with its dusting of freckles across the shoulders. The sweet curves of her breasts hung full and round, tipped by blushing pink nipples drawn into hard points.

Her long fingers flicked open the snap of her shorts, slid them down over her hips. She didn't shave between those long, pretty legs, though the hair was neatly trimmed, its color the same bright copper as her hair. Her legs curved with long runner's muscle, like her lean arms.

Genevieve propped a fist on one hip and eyed him. "Are you going to get undressed, or just drool?" Her mouth curved in a wicked little smile.

"But drooling's so much fun."

With an exaggerated sigh, she stepped forward, caught the hem of his T-shirt, and pulled it off over his head. Now it was her turn to stare, blue eyes going wide, darkening to cobalt as she scanned the width of his chest. "You must spend a lot of time in the gym."

He shrugged. "Sometimes I have to help pick up unconscious six-hundred-pound cats. And since I work with a lot of retired volunteers, I need to bring as much muscle as possible to the job."

"Either way, I approve." She reached out and brushed her fingertip over one nipple. Kurt had never considered his nipples particularly sensitive, but there was magic in Genevieve's touch.

The swirl of sensation vibrating through him made his cock harden even more. His hands shook as he unzipped his jeans and skinned them down his hips. His erection sprang free, long and dark and hungry.

A mischievous female hand darted out and curled around it in a teasing silken brush of fingertips.

Lust weighted his balls with heat. Kurt reached in to turn on the spray, then adjusted its temperature. He had no interest in a cold shower.

Genevieve stepped up behind him to press a kiss between his shoulder blades, and rake her teeth over his skin. Her fingers danced over his shoulders in teasing strokes that made him groan in delight.

His cock jerked, dancing upward in lust. Kurt

swept the shower curtain aside and made an "after-you" gesture.

Genevieve stepped inside, and he took the opportunity to brush his fingertips across the curve of her ass. She jumped a little and grinned back at him.

He faked innocence he was far from feeling as he stepped under the warm spray with her. "What?"

"You are a bad, bad man."

Kurt gave her an exaggerated leer. "You have no idea."

"Actually, I'm getting a better idea all the time." She stepped against him, wrapping her arms around his neck, kissing him hungrily. Water pounded down on their shoulders in a liquid caress, thin streams snaking over their skin, droplets beading and rolling.

Kurt reached past her to pick up the bottle of shampoo. He squirted it into his palm, then started working it through her long hair, enjoying the slippery sensation of lather and thick silken curls.

Genevieve picked up a bar of soap and rolled it between her own palms before running it slowly over his chest in long, swirling caresses. His eyes drifted shut and he caught his breath. They stroked each other, using the shampoo and the soap and the slippery lather as another path to pleasure, another addition to the sensation. Magic added a deeper layer of pleasure, as their auras interacted.

In the depths of Kurt's mind, Stoli rumbled softly, hungry and possessive. Wanting more of her, wanting to claim her as mate, just as Kurt did. It didn't seem to matter how long he had known her -- or how long he hadn't. All he cared about was the need for her, the need of her touch, her hands, her mouth.

Her. She sank to her knees in the tub and reached for him. Kurt froze, his breath catching, as she wrapped the long fingers of one hand around his cock, cupping his balls in the other. Her mouth swooped down over him, taking him on an incredible wet, silken slide into pleasure that damn near made his eyes cross. She couldn't quite swallow his entire length, but it was still enough to make his head drop back into a helpless moan. "Gen... God, Genevieve..."

He started to tell her to stop, that he wouldn't last if she kept that up, but then she pulled back and started swirling her tongue over the head of his cock. Stoli rumbled, deep and wild, the sound not human at all.

He found himself gripping a fistful of wet red hair and forced his hand to loosen. He didn't want to hurt her.

She drew off him, pushing his cock up, and licked up the thick vein that ran up the underside of his shaft. Sucked his balls into her mouth, first one and then the other.

Pleasure roared along his nerves, so intense his thighs shook.

"Enough!" Kurt gasped, unable to take anymore. Before his body could talk him out of it, he reached down, caught her arms, and pulled her to her feet. Turning her so she faced the tiled rear wall, he stepped up behind her until his cock pressed up against her luscious little ass.

He filled his hands with her -- one hand cupping the lovely curve of a breast, the other slipping between her thighs.

Now it was her turn to moan. He and Stoli shared a tiger's smile.

* * *

Genevieve quivered as Kurt began to tease her, soapy fingers milking one nipple as his other hand slid down to stroke her clit in swirling loops and figure eights. A forefinger slid into her pussy, already slick and swollen from his teasing. Each tiny caress sent another perfect pearl of delight sliding through her mind. Her need rose, hot and sweet.

She craved him. Craved the thick thrust of the cock she felt pressed against her ass. It felt so delicious, being surrounded by him, by his thick muscle and sheer size. By the hot tingle of his magic surging and swirling against hers.

She had to have him. "Kurt." Her voice sounded guttural, more like his own animal growl. "Kurt, now."

But he went on playing with her, teasing nipples and clit and cunt, stroking and squeezing. "I don't think so."

"I do. *Now*!" She rolled her ass back against his shaft, turning the motion into a teasing caress of her own.

Stoli made that rumbling sound, hot with anticipation. Gen knew how to break his self-control. She bent, bracing her palms against the tile wall, pushing backward, lifting her ass like a tigress demanding to be mounted.

The tiger growled in Kurt's voice. He released her breasts, her sex, and grabbed her hips in one hand. A moment later she felt the press of his cock's smooth head against her vaginal lips. He probed, found the opening. And thrust, hard, deep, ruthless. Filling her, pushing deep, deeper, sliding right to the balls in a storm of lush sensation. Both of them cried out.

"Genevieve!" He drew out and shoved in, the thrust deep and grinding and exactly what she needed. He slid a hand around, finding her clit again, stroking, circling, as he began to pump.

In and out and in, and God, it was so sweet, so

blinding. Bodies and magic grinding together until sparks of sensation danced over her skin, and she could no longer tell mystical sensation from physical. And it didn't matter, because it was all overwhelming, a psychic storm that shook her brain in her skull.

The climax went off between her thighs like a bomb, ripping a raw scream from her lips. Shaking, she collapsed against the wall, would have fallen if not for the grip of his big hands as he shafted her.

"Genevieve!" Kurt bellowed, the sound so amplified by his magic that it made her ears ring.

He stiffened, pulling her up off her feet as he came, bowing into her.

Stoli roared.

Kurt put her down on her feet again, leaning into her, pressing her against the shower wall. For a long moment all either of them could do was pant. She could feel him shake against her, and felt a certain satisfaction. At least she wasn't the only one knocked off her axis.

"God," he muttered. "That was..."

"Yeah." Her voice rasped, and she had to stop to clear it. "That's putting it mildly." A smile curved her mouth. "Thanks."

His powerful chest vibrated against hers in a chuckle. "Believe me, it's mutual."

And probably a very bad idea, the voice of common sense told her. She ignored it. Again.

* * *

Early the next morning, Jake headed off for his shift, telling Kurt not to get killed while he was gone. Soon the house filled with volunteers bearing covered dishes that filled the place with the scents of roast, fried chicken, assorted casseroles, and a bakery's worth of desserts. All their way of demonstrating their support and sympathy.

Genevieve would have preferred to start work on casting the wards yet again. Kurt vetoed that, telling her he needed to tend to his cats and bury Stoli, and he wanted to make sure she was protected during the casting.

Given what had happened the day before, she couldn't really protest.

After breakfast, Kurt, Gen, Dave, and the volunteers gathered on a hillside beside the man-made lake. It was a pretty, grassy spot, sheltered by oaks and maples ringed by azalea bushes, a favored location for picnics.

It was also the BFS cemetery. Stone pavers engraved with the cats' names marked the graves, except for a few bronze markers that denoted the plots of Familiars.

Kurt had used a Bobcat skid-steer loader -- a small earthmover similar to a bulldozer -- to dig a grave for the tiger.

As Gen watched, he used the Bobcat's bucket to lower the enormous cat into it. Her heart ached for him as she watched him work, his face set in lines more rigid than the pavers.

His volunteers showed all the grief he fought to hide. They cried without shame, some silently, others sobbing aloud.

Gen found herself wiping away her own tears.

"I know Stoli's still alive in Kurt," Karla Morgen told her, tears flowing down her cheeks. A graying, motherly woman, she served as the volunteer coordinator for BFS. "But we'll never see him again."

Gen could only nod. "I know what you mean."

One at a time, volunteers came forward to talk about Stoli. All tigers could be unpredictable and aggressive, but Kurt's Familiar had evidently had a goofy, affectionate streak.

Dave went last. "I'm gonna miss you, Tigger." His voice sounded ragged.

Kurt stepped up to the side of the grave and opened his mouth to speak. Then he shook his head and got back in the Bobcat.

The low notes of "Taps" began to sound. Gen looked around, confused -- there was no sign of a musician or sound system.

Then her gaze fell on Dave, standing by the grave in his vest with his tail and whiskers drooping.

Oh.

As she watched Kurt push the pile of red soil over his Familiar, she felt a knot of hot rage gather in the center of her chest. *Those bastards need to pay for this. For Stoli. For Fred. And most of all, for Kurt.*

She was going to do everything she possibly could to make the terrorists pay for every drop of blood they'd shed.

When the grave was covered, Kurt parked the Bobcat and swung down off the little machine to join her. "Let's go check on Parvati," he said. He forced a smile, though it didn't reach his eyes.

She forced one of her own, aching. "Sure."

* * *

The tigress looked so bright-eyed and healthy, Gen was cheered.

Even Kurt's smile looked a little less forced. "Think she's ready to go back to her enclosure?"

Genevieve closed her eyes and touched her aura to the cat's. Parvati's magical field was much brighter, and many of the red nodes that signified cancer had vanished. "I think we need to give her a little more time close to the sketch. A couple of days, maybe."

He blew out a relieved breath. "Now if only the rest of us can get through this." He took her hand in strong, warm fingers. "Want to help feed the cats?"

Chapter Thirteen

Turned out there was a reason for all the different T-shirt colors. They indicated the size cat you were qualified to feed. The eighty volunteers formed teams of five to feed the animals on their assigned routes.

"We have to train the hell out of people," Kurt told Gen as the volunteers loaded big hand-pulled carts full of buckets and plastic containers of food. "First, feeding these animals can be dangerous, and if you don't pay attention to what you're doing, you can get seriously hurt. Second, feeding time is our best opportunity to observe the cats to see if any are injured or not eating properly."

It was one of those bright sunny mornings, as the volunteers fanned out across the park, each wearing rubber gloves and carrying sticks for use in feeding especially finicky cats. They'd skewer chunks of meat, extend it through the enclosure fence, and let the beast nip the food off the rounded end.

Gen studied the enclosures with interest. A small square cage was attached to one end of each, just big enough for a cat to step inside. A big bowl of water was secured to one of the galvanized wire panels above a square cement pad. She gestured at one. "What are those little cages?"

"We call them lockouts. We feed the cats in them so we don't end up with rotting meat scattered everywhere. The larger enclosures are constructed in two sections so we can close a cat in one half while we clean the other. That way we can make things safer for our volunteers, though they still have to be careful."

Gen followed Kurt to the enclosure that housed one of the BFS tigers. The cat, whose name was Shiva, paced hungrily outside her lockout.

"Stay back," Kurt warned Gen. "You don't want to get too close. All these cats can move fast, and some of them have paws small enough to fit through the fencing."

As she watched, Kurt loaded the square feeding stone with softball-sized chunks of something called mush -- ground meat that was a combination of intestines and organ meat mixed with vitamins. He added a quartered chicken and a hunk of beef for a total of fifteen pounds of protein.

Kurt stood up, grabbed the rope, and moved well back from the lockout. He pulled to raise the guillotine door.

With a roar that made Genevieve jump, Shiva exploded into the lockout and fell on the food. The tigress paused between ravenous bites to snarl up at them.

Gen found herself stepping back, eyes wide. "Damn."

"Don't be fooled by Stoli and Dave," Kurt told her quietly as he picked up a clipboard and started moving around the lockout, watching the way Shiva moved and making notes. "Given the chance, these cats would kill us. None of us -- not even me -- can ever forget that. A moment's inattention could be fatal."

"And yet you and your father and your volunteers have dedicated yourselves to protecting them."

"Well, yeah." He shrugged. "We owe them."

* * *

Kurt was finishing up his route when she got a text message. Gen excused herself to answer it.

"There is one piece of good news," she said when

she came back. "Sawyer just called. He spoke to the Charlotte FBI Special Agent in Charge this morning. The Feds have mobilized teams to the various scenes. We were right about those murders -- they were definitely human sacrifices, and they all had spells still active."

Some of the tension left Kurt's shoulders. "Once the FBI Arcanists start breaking those spells, the witch won't be doing anything except nursing a headache."

"It may not be that easy. The Feds are having trouble finding weak points they can exploit to destroy the spells. They're trying to document the sigils so they can figure out what's going on."

Unfortunately, you couldn't use a camera for that kind of documentation. An Arcanist had to look at the sigils and copy them precisely as Gen had.

Kurt grimaced. "They'd better get it figured out fast, or we're all screwed."

His immediate duties finished, they returned to the office, where Kurt learned the coroner had released Fred's body to the mortuary. He started finalizing plans for the visitation and funeral, wrote his father's obituary, sent it to the funeral home for publication, and posted it on the BFS website and Facebook page.

Genevieve spent the rest of the morning in meditation sessions designed to recharge her magical batteries. That went better than she expected, in part because they'd made love. She'd heard sex between Talents was supposed to be good for that, but she'd never experienced it herself until now.

Evidently they were compatible in more than one sense of the word.

When they sat down to lunch, Genevieve found herself studying the work and play of his biceps and muscular forearms. An image flashed through her mind, Kurt, water rolling across his skin and down his chest, the feel of his big hands on her breasts. Heat flashed over her, and she forced herself to apply herself to her meal.

Her cell rang. Gen scooped it out of a pocket, recognized the number, and answered with a smile. "Hey, Sawyer. Please tell me the Feds broke one of those spe…"

The sound of screaming cut her off. She froze, eyes flying wide. Kurt stiffened, staring at her in horror.

"Genevieve," Sawyer shouted over the bedlam. "The fucking polar bear and the Arc sniper are killing people in the Faraday Square. We need you here now!"

"Shit," Kurt snarled. Dave stuck his head around the kitchen door and stared, his ears flattened. The Ferals could probably hear Sawyer as clearly as she did with the phone to her ear.

"What happened?" Gen demanded.

"The damned bear just appeared in the park fifteen minutes ago and attacked a guy having lunch on a bench. Literally bit his head off. When a city cop tried to intervene, the Arcanist shot him."

"They've set up another spell," Genevieve breathed in sick horror. "They realized they were out of time and they're trying to finish the spell *now*. I've got to break it!"

"Why in the hell do you think I'm calling you… Motherfucker! Bullet just whined past my head!"

"We're on the way." Genevieve sprang to her feet and sprinted for the door, Dave galloping ahead of her, Kurt at their heels.

The tiger skidded to a halt. "Where's my safety vest?"

Kurt swore and dove into the closet to grab the

orange vest Dave had worn to the press conference. They all banged out the front door without stopping to lock it.

"What car are you using?" Sawyer yelled over the phone as they clattered down the porch steps. "I'll have a cop give you an escort. Damn it!" Gunfire sounded in the background.

"Tell him we'll be taking one of the BFS SUVs," Kurt snapped.

She repeated it.

"Let me get somebody on the way." Sawyer hung up.

Kurt thumbed his key fob as they raced across the yard. The SUV's back hatch popped open and Dave leaped in, making the truck rock on its wheels. Gen scrambled in on the passenger side as Kurt slid in, threw the vest to Dave, and started the engine. He backed up so fast, the tires squealed on the paved drive.

Dave cursed in the back. Gen glanced back to see he'd manifested arms and was struggling to fasten the vest.

The cell rang. Sawyer was already talking by the time Gen lifted it to her ear. "Nolan's fighting the bear, and our SWAT team is exchanging fire with the shooter. The bitch is invisible, and we can't see where to shoot. And that fucking bear is trying to tear Nolan apart. We got four civilians and two cops down that we can't get to, and we're still trying to get civilians out of the line of fire. Where are you?"

"Tell him we'll be there in ten," Kurt told her.

"We're all on the way, including Dave. He'll be able to pinpoint where the Arc is for you while Kurt reinforces Jake, and I try to break that spell."

"Good. I'll round up some body armor for you,

or the bitch will shoot your ass."

The line went dead. Genevieve stared down at the red END phone icon, feeling sick. As tough as last night's magical battle had been, nobody had been shooting at her.

She just prayed she didn't freak out and screw up. Entirely too many lives were riding on this -- and not just theirs. God knew how many people were going to die if she didn't get that spell broken in time.

"You do realize this may be a trap for Genevieve," Dave said from the back.

"Which is why you're going to stay with her," Kurt growled in a vibrating Stoli rumble. "If you can create a protective manifestation around her, it'll give her more time to break that spell." He flicked her a grim glance. "How close do you have to get?"

"Right up on it. The Arc would have added wards to her spell to make it harder to break. The only reason I was able to do it so easily the last time is because she had no idea I'd get involved." She clutched the door handle as they rounded a corner, then passed a sports car in a blur. "But I'm not the only one they're after. She wants to sacrifice another Feral."

"Sounds like she's trying to use Jake. I just hope they don't kill him before we get there and break that spell." A muscle in his jaw rolled. "I don't want to lose him too."

"We're not going to lose anyone," Dave growled. "We're going to kill those fuckers."

Kurt drove through town as fast as he could and still maintain control. "Where in the hell is that cop?"

"Judging by the siren, coming up behind us," Dave said.

Gen couldn't hear a damn thing, but Kurt nodded. "Yeah, there he is." He slowed fractionally.

A moment later, she finally heard the siren wailing closer. The deputy passed in a black and white blur.

Kurt floored it again as the cop took the lead on a wild route up and down side streets to bypass Laurelton PD roadblocks. Heart hammering, Genevieve braced herself as the SUV shot toward Faraday Square.

And tried not to wonder if they'd all be alive in an hour.

* * *

Kurt was distantly aware of faces staring at them wide-eyed, as news and police helicopters circled overhead and television cameras swung to track them. He ignored them all as he followed the cop down the side street that ran parallel to Faraday Square. What looked like every police car in the city was parked up and down the road, blue lights whirling. Tense cops in body armor strode along carrying assault rifles and shotguns.

He parked behind a line of cop cars, keyed the hatch open for Dave, and jumped out. Several of the cops turned and stared at the tiger in his orange DAVE vest. He ignored them and trotted after Gen and Kurt as they headed for the waiting deputy.

"The brass is this way," the officer told them, his tone clipped, his face white and tense. He headed off down the brick walkway that led between the shops of the square.

A cluster of cops in body armor crouched in the shelter of the wall, several of them popping off measured shots around the corner.

They were answered by a rolling burst of automatic fire that made all of them duck.

Sawyer saw them coming and moved toward

them carrying a Kevlar vest and a helmet. "I don't need that," Gen told him. "Dave's going to manifest…"

"Let them put the gear on you," the tiger interrupted. "You need all the protection you can get."

Kurt closed his eyes and let Stoli surge to the surface. The tiger manifested in a brilliant tingling explosion of magic, forming a solid shell of energy that would hopefully protect him against sniper fire.

Around him, cops jerked back, staring wide-eyed as he headed for the opening of the alley. A cluster of armored officers stood holding automatic rifles and looking frustrated.

A short, muscular man in body armor turned to look at him. The front of his bulletproof vest read SWAT, with "LT. GALLOWAY" lettered in smaller white letters over his left breast. "You're the Feral?"

"Yeah." *What, the glowing tiger doesn't give me away*?

"Can you see where that invisible bitch is?"

"I can try." Closing his eyes, Kurt scanned the scene with his magical senses. Faintly glowing shapes milled around him -- the auras of the surrounding cops.

Beyond that lay Faraday Square, a long, narrow park that lay like an island between two streets running between the shops. An avenue of dimly shining trees marched on either side of the strip of green.

Behind one of those trees stood a brightly glowing figure, arms positioned as if holding an invisible rifle; the weapon was non-magical.

Kurt pointed toward the figure and opened his eyes. "She's there, behind the fourth tree."

"Thanks!" The SWAT team commander bared his teeth in something that definitely wasn't a smile.

Turning, he lifted his AR-15 and brought it to bear with a growl that could have come from a Feral. "Light her up, boys."

The entire team opened fire a thundering fusillade.

Finally Galloway gestured, and the firing stopped. "Did we get her?"

But when Kurt shut his eyes again, the figure was still there, though crouching behind a different tree. "She's behind the fifth tree now…" But then he spotted two huge, glowing shapes struggling through the cluster of trees. "Fuck, hold your fire. I've got to get to Jake."

Galloway swore. "Go!"

But Kurt paused. "Have you tried concentrating your fire on the bear? If you beat on a manifestation long enough, hard enough, it'll collapse when he runs out of magic."

The lieutenant shook his head. "We tried that when this started. The bastard kept disappearing and grabbing cops until we had to send Nolan in. We can't shoot at the fucker now without hitting our officer."

"Fine. Jake and I will just have to get that manifestation down the hard way." He stared up the brick walkway between the avenue of trees that led to the Colton Faraday statue in the square's center. Just beyond that lay a wide empty circle of grass where the city set up a portable skating rink during the winter.

And that, Kurt thought grimly, *is probably where the bitch laid her spell circle.*

They must not consider mere Norms suitable sacrifices, or they'd have already killed someone in it. Jake, on the other hand, might be just what they had in mind.

Nolan and the bear stalked one another around

the base of the statue, snarling like a pair of chainsaws.

Kurt threw his head back and roared before leaping into a gallop, racing across the road that ran beside the park. People shouted and cursed. Someone fired -- probably the sniper -- but the manifestation carried his body forward so fast, she missed.

The bear saw him coming, wheeled, and ran up the brick walk toward the grass circle. Kurt raced after him, aware of Jake charging after the bear just ahead of him. The lion manifestation still looked solid, except for a dimmer patch across one shoulder.

It was a good thing Kurt had come when he had, because the bear was probably directing all his attacks at that spot. If the killer could break through, he'd shatter the manifestation the way he had Fred's. Then he'd drag Jake into the circle and kill him.

Unless Kurt got him first.

With an earsplitting roar, the bear reared over Jake, swinging a huge paw that caught the lion on one shoulder. The force of the blow sent him flying to slam into the base of the statue. The cat manifestation flickered and went out, as if Jake had lost consciousness.

The bear charged after him, obviously intending to drag Jake into the circle and kill him. Kurt raced after them and leaped, landing on the bear in an explosion of sparks. He clamped his glowing jaws around the back of the manifestation's thick skull, claws digging into the bear's massive torso.

The Feral roared in rage as the magic of their manifestations clashed with the burning sting of fire ant bites. Kurt ignored the pain, clamping down hard, using all his and Stoli's combined power in a furious effort to crack the magical shell and kill the man beneath.

The bear reared, twisting as he tried to get at the tiger on his back.

Oh no you don't, fucker, Kurt thought, tightening the grip of teeth and claws. *You're going to pay for what you did to my father*. As he ground his jaws, magic blazed in his mouth like he'd crunched down on a live wire. Pain detonated in his jaws, but he refused to let go.

If the bastard got free, he'd drag Jake into that spell and trigger whatever Armageddon the terrorists planned.

Rearing, the terrorist slammed himself into the statue's base again and again, hammering blows that sent electric jolts through Kurt's body. It took all his physical strength and will to hang on, to bite down harder.

Out of the corner of one eye, he saw Jake fight to rise, his manifestation flickering on and off like a light bulb.

Beneath his fangs, he felt something give way. The bear manifestation was beginning to fail. *Got you now, you son of a bitch!*

The bear dropped back onto all fours, ran a few steps back, then threw himself against the base as his magic erupted in a torrent of sparks.

It felt like being hit by a lightning bolt, a crushing impact that sent pain flaring through Kurt. He yelped as his manifestation winked out.

Stoli roared in rage. The manifestation reappeared as the tiger flipped onto his back a heartbeat before the bear landed on him.

Kurt caught the bear manifestation with all four paws and lunged at the bear's muzzle. Electric jolts of pain scraped his magical shell as the bear ripped at him. They tumbled over the grass, clawing and biting.

It was like being in a car wreck.

Fuck, he's powerful! Where the hell does he get all the juice?

Kurt felt dagger teeth clamp down on his manifestation's throat, digging deep, trying to punch through his shell. Cursing, he ripped at the bear's ribs with three-inch glowing claws.

As the bear's fangs dug in, something gave. *Fuck, my manifestation's weakening…*

A lion's roar shattered the air. Jake fell out of nowhere to slam down on the bear, sinking his fangs into the back of the Feral's skull, going for the same vulnerability Kurt had been trying to punch through.

Yes! Kurt dug in his claws into the bear's ribs as his friend tore at the terrorist, trying to shatter the energy shell.

Longer, just a little longer and we'll have the fucker…

Except… Jake's lion looked much dimmer than he'd ever seen it, as if the beating he'd taken had weakened him. *Hang on!*

The bear rolled onto his side… and vanished from between them, leaving them both clutching empty air. The terrorist had dropped his manifestation so he could escape paws suddenly too far apart to hold him. The Spook-Suited human bounded up and leaped away before they could grab him again.

"Damn it!" Kurt spat, only to see the bear reappear behind his friend. "Jake!"

The cop's eyes widened through the glow of his manifestation just as the bear's huge paws seized him and fanged jaws clamped down on his shoulder.

The lion manifestation popped like a soap bubble. Jake screamed in agony as the bear began to drag him backward toward the spell circle.

"Oh, no you don't!" Kurt leaped on the bear,

diving for that same neck wound they'd both targeted before. He dug all four sets of claws into the bear's sides, ripping until the terrorist dropped Jake to land in a broken heap.

Kurt didn't even have time to wonder if his friend was still alive as the bear twisted and rolled, raking at him in an explosion of magic and agony. He bit down, trying to keep the bear from tearing free, refusing to give in to the pain. *I'm going to kill him for you, Dad…*

Magic exploded around him, an electric jolt that clicked his teeth together and made him see stars. The bear had rolled him right into a spell.

Oh fuck. He closed his eyes, spotting sigils spinning around them. Kurt fought to maintain his hold, but the sigils rotated faster as the magic tightened its sickening grip. A sensation of evil slid over him, lifting the hair on the back of his neck. His stomach roiled as if he'd sucked in a mouthful of raw sewage.

That moment of distraction cost him. The bear ripped out of his grip.

Just beyond it, he spotted Genevieve at the edge of the spell circle. Dave's human manifestation glowed around her, stretched and distorted as he tried to cover both her and his own tiger form.

There was no way in hell he'd be able to hold it for very long, and if it went down before Genevieve was finished with that spell, they were all screwed…

"Now, you little motherfucker!" The bear reared, lips peeled off glowing teeth, about to plunge down on Kurt…

CRACK! CRACKCRACKCRACK!

Bullets sparked and whined off Dave's manifestation as the Arcanist sniper fired at them. A thunderous fusillade answered as the cops returned fire, trying to triangulate on the invisible witch.

"Arhhh!" A woman's scream, sharp and high with pain.

The bear's huge head jerked around, and he spun toward the sound. "Indigo!" The Feral leaped away. The cops opened up on him in a thunderous explosion of gunfire, but the terrorist kept going, racing in the direction of the female cry.

Kurt scrambled to his feet, about to throw himself after the killers. From the corner of one eye, he saw Gen gesture, chanting.

Magic rolled across the circle, foaming over his skin. Closing his eyes, he saw a wave of glittering sparks spilling over the sigils that ringed him. Wherever it touched, the terrorist's magic winked out. *She's done it*!

But there was no time to gloat. The bear paused for a heartbeat between the trees, magic wavering around him as the terrorist bent to pick something up off the ground. *The Arcanist*?

Then the killer was off and running again. Even as the cops blasted away at him, he disappeared down a side street.

With a massive roar of rage, the cops charged after him. Dave sprang into pursuit, muscles rolling under his thick, gleaming fur.

Kurt paused just long enough to reinforce his manifestation and repair the damage from the bear's claws. Then he raced after Dave as his friend easily outpaced the cops.

They couldn't let the terrorist get away, or they'd be right back where they started.

* * *

Her heart in her throat, Genevieve ran to Jake. He lay in a wide splatter of blood just beyond the boundaries of the terrorist spell. He looked far too much like Fred, lying just like that in the arena, the victim of the same claws and fangs.

She fell to her knees beside the cop. "Jake! Jake, are you okay?"

Stupid question.

Jake stared up at her with dazed, uncomprehending eyes. Blood covered his upper chest from two huge puncture wounds in his shoulder where the bear had ripped into him. And there was absolutely no way she could heal him. She didn't have her pastels or paper, and even if she'd had them, Jake would bleed to death long before she could cast anything useful.

"Medic!" she shouted, glancing around wildly. Now that the terrorists were gone, EMTs were swarming over the scene, checking people, loading those who were most injured onto stretchers and wheeling them to the ambulances that were now emerging from side streets "This man is dying!"

"He's not the only one!" an EMT shouted back.

"Fuck," she muttered. Maybe she could stop the bleeding long enough for one of the paramedics to get to him.

Clamping a hand over the puncture, she winced at his cry of pain. "Listen to me, Jake," she told him in a low, fierce voice. "You're losing too much blood. You've got to create a manifestation to block the wound. You know how to do that. They teach it in Basic."

Jake blinked slowly. "Can't... Can't manifest... Don't have..."

"I can reinforce your magic, but you've got to create the initial form. If you can start it, I can keep it running."

"Okay. I'll... I'll try..." He coughed, the sound wet. His golden eyes drifted close, and for a moment she thought he'd lost consciousness. Her heart sank.

Magic bloomed hot under her hand -- a tingling shell of the same kind of force Ferals used to create their beasts, just wide enough to block the wound. Dave had done the same thing when Fred was bleeding.

"Yes! That's it! Hold it, Jake!" Gen poured power through her aura into his, strengthening the manifestation, sealing the wound closed. The bleeding slowed, stopped.

"Stay with me, Jake," she told him, concentrating fiercely. "If you go out, I'm not sure I'll be able to maintain it."

"You can... do it." His mouth moved in the twitch of a smile. "You're... A keeper..."

She had to keep him talking, had to keep him conscious. "What do you mean?"

He grunted. His face was paper-pale, and his skin felt cold under her palm. Gen wondered uneasily just how much blood he lost. He coughed, and the sound rattled. Had the bite hit his lung?

Frowning, she probed with her magical senses. No, the bear's fangs had missed the right lung by a fraction, but the collarbone and shoulder blade were shattered. There was also a hell of a lot of damage to the surrounding muscle. He was going to need surgery, assuming she could get him through this.

"Kurt's a lucky... bastard," he wheezed, his lips twitching in a labored smile. "If you two... don't work out... I'm here."

Before she could answer, his eyes fluttered shut. Beneath her fingers, his manifestation softened, on the verge of winking out.

Gen cursed. Despite its alien magic, she grabbed the structure and poured all her remaining power into it. It hardened again under her hand. If she lost it, Jake would be dead in minutes. Throwing back her head, she shouted, "I need a paramedic or this man is dead!"

"We're coming, damn it!" A team raced toward her, pulling a stretcher after them.

She blew out a relieved breath and began briefing the pair as they checked Jake's vitals. Five minutes later, they were loading him onto the stretcher and heading for the nearest ambulance, Gen trotting alongside, one hand still clamped over the wound.

As she crawled into the ambulance, she looked back over her shoulder in the direction Kurt, Dave and the cops had gone. *Live, boys. Find those bastards and stop them, but live!*

Chapter Fourteen

Kurt walked into Jake's hospital room carrying Genevieve's sketchpad and pastel box, which she'd asked him to pick up on his way over. Before he'd left, he'd sent the volunteers home, worried that the killers would decide to target them next.

Which unfortunately left Dave to keep an eye on BFS, since Kurt couldn't take the cat to the hospital. At least the Sheriff had agreed to assign a couple of cops to help.

Close. They'd come so close to catching the bastards. So close to being done with this. Stoli paced in his mind, growling in a frustration that echoed his.

Jake looked around as he entered, his gaze a little vague. "Kurt. Hey, dude." His voice sounded slurred, probably from fully-justified painkillers. He looked pale and a little dazed. Which wasn't surprising, considering the bandages that swathed his right shoulder where the bear had mauled him. An IV stand stood next to the bed, a unit of blood hanging from it.

"Hey, buddy. How're you feeling?"

"Like I lost a fight with a polar bear." He grimaced. "I'm gonna get PTSD flashbacks from those polar bear Christmas commercials. I may never drink another Coke as long as I live."

Kurt grinned, but the expression faded when his gaze fell on Genevieve, who sat in a recliner next to his friend's bed.

Stoli rumbled in displeasure.

Cut it out. She's just keeping him company, you jealous bastard. Though he was talking as much to himself as the cat.

A smile dawned on her face, radiant and lovely. "Kurt! God, I'm glad you're back safe!" Gen walked around the bed and met him at the door, wrapping her slender arms around his neck. Rising up on her tiptoes, she found his mouth. Her lips stroked over his, soft as peaches and tasting vaguely of apples.

Though it wasn't a particularly passionate kiss, desire rose in him anyway, hot and fast and dark. He wrapped his arms around her and just held her, enjoying the solid feel of her in his arms.

She could have died today. Again. He tightened his hold, pulling her close, drinking her in.

"Damn, you're a lucky bastard," Jake said with a sound halfway between a sigh and a laugh. "A cruel, selfish bastard, but lucky. I don't suppose you'd share?"

Kurt pulled back with a snarl on his mouth, only to pause at the smile his friend was wearing. It was that joking, *just-giving-you-shit* expression he knew so well.

Jake blinked in surprise, his smile fading, obviously reading Kurt's anger. "Hey, man. Just kidding. Damn, you're in a bad mood. I gather the hunt didn't go well."

"Not really, no." He released Genevieve, giving her a quick stroke on the cheek. She frowned at him, looking troubled, though he wasn't sure why.

Kurt picked up a straight-backed chair, carried it around the room, and put it down next to Gen's recliner. He collapsed into it as she returned to her seat, studying him with a frown.

"We spent almost two hours looking for those bastards," Kurt told them. "We followed them a couple of miles while that damned bear ducked between buildings and backtracked and generally did everything he could to muddy his trail. Luckily, hot pavement takes scent pretty well, and I could feel the bastard's magic on top of that." His fists clenched. "But then the trail just vanished."

Jake frowned. "They got in a car."

Kurt nodded. "Looks like. Finally Sawyer told me to break it off and head home. I think I was making him nervous."

"I can't imagine why," Jake said dryly. "You do realize you flashed your manifestation twice in the past five minutes?"

Kurt stared at him. "What?"

"You didn't know? That's not like you."

"I'm just tired. How're you feeling?"

Jake gave him a crooked grin. "I would definitely not pass the department drug test."

"Given that you just had surgery to keep you from bleeding to death, I don't think anybody's going to have a problem with a little Demerol." One corner of Gen's lush mouth kicked up in a half smile.

Something in that smile made Stoli grumble. What had they been doing while Kurt was out chasing killers?

Don't be an idiot. The man was in surgery, and Genevieve isn't the type to cheat. Though they barely knew each other. How did Kurt know what type she was? After all, she'd fallen into *his* arms quickly enough.

And she's a witch. Like Mom.

Gen pulled out a pencil and started sketching, in preparation for the healing spell she was planning to cast.

"Is that a good idea?" Jake asked, concerned. "You just broke the terrorists' spell and kept me from bleeding to death. You sure you have enough juice left?"

She shrugged. "While you were in surgery, I did

some meditating to recharge. Besides, you aren't dying, at least not now. You've got some broken bones and muscle damage. All I'm going to be doing is accelerating the natural healing process."

"I appreciate anything you can do," Jake said with a sigh. "Otherwise the doctor says it's going to take me at least six weeks to heal all this. I'd go stir crazy long before then."

Kurt grinned. "You *are* one ADD pussy."

"Bite my furry balls."

"Ewww. No."

Jake laughed. They all fell silent, letting Genevieve get to work.

Kurt watched her, the clean, lovely profile, the full lips set in concentration as she worked. Jake began to snore softly, and the sound made Genevieve smile. "Those must be good drugs."

He smiled back despite his bad mood. There was something about the sweet curve of her mouth that he simply could not resist.

So he sat there, watching her, admiring the fine, clean gestures of her slim hands as she drew, the way she stared at Jake so intently every time she looked up. Magic rose around her, making his skin tingle.

It wasn't the aggressive, ugly magic of the bear and the Arcanist assassin. Gen's was far sweeter, and yet somehow it still made every hair on his body stand up. When he closed his eyes, he could see her glowing against the darkness of his lids as she stared at the sleeping lion that was Jake's magic.

She shouldn't be staring at him. She should be staring at me.

It was an irrational, unworthy thought. He needed to get Stoli to calm down -- assuming it had been Stoli. Kurt wasn't entirely sure. The sullen jealousy curling through him could have come from either of them.

I need to get this under control. He squeezed his eyes closed and turned his face to start combat breathing.

Still, images kept appearing behind his closed lids: Genevieve in the shower last night, lather rolling along her curves. The full curve of her breast, the flushed peak of a sweet nipple.

The feel of her sex as he slid into her, so wet and hot and tight.

Kurt's hunger rose even as he fought the memories that threatened to tease his arousal into a roar.

His cock felt as hard as a gun butt behind his zipper.

Arousal might be safer than rage, but not by much. Especially when Genevieve was trying to heal his best friend's injuries. Injuries Jake had suffered trying to save Kurt's life.

And Kurt hadn't even thanked him.

This is unacceptable. A Feral who can't control himself is nothing but a menace.

He forced himself to concentrate on his breathing. In through his mouth, forcing his rib cage to expand to a five count, then breathing out through his nose in a long, slow stream.

In. Out. In…

But even as he worked, he was all too conscious of Genevieve's magic swirling over him like a caress. Like the sensation of her hands on his skin…

He wanted to snatch that drawing pad out of her hands and drag her into his arms. *I can't interrupt the spell*, he reminded his rebellious cat. *She'd have to start over. We need Jake's help to protect her.*

He's a handsome bastard, another voice hissed in the depths of his brain. *I don't want him anywhere around her. I can protect her.*

The way you protected her today? If it hadn't been for Jake, the bear would've had us. Dave couldn't have helped. He was too busy trying to keep her from getting shot.

All of that was perfectly true -- and made not one damn bit of difference to his steaming jealousy. He sucked in another deep breath and made himself think *nothing*. Forced himself to concentrate, to envision a Caribbean beach with turquoise shallows and a salty breeze carrying the screech of seagulls.

Concentrating on the imagined scene, he visualized every detail until he could see himself sitting cross-legged on the beach. The sand felt warm against his skin as the sun beat down on his bare shoulders...

And then Genevieve was there, standing right in front of him on the sand, gloriously naked, her nipples hard and pink, the neat red triangle of her bush bright in the sunlight. The wind whipped her long curls into a swirl around her shoulders. Her blue eyes were more vivid than the sea behind her, lit by sparks of magic. He grew even harder.

Well, that's not going to work.

Gritting his teeth, Kurt took a deep breath and imagined the mountains in winter, snow drifting silently around him as he stood staring up at the gray sky...

* * *

Genevieve added the final stroke to the sketch and studied it with satisfaction. She'd always been good at capturing a likeness. That was one reason her magic was so effective; the concentration it took helped her focus her talent.

Her gaze flicked from the page to Jake's face. He lay with his handsome head turned toward her on the pillow.

She frowned, eying the image. It had come out a little more suggestive than she'd intended. The way his head lay on that pillow was a little suggestive, as if he were gazing at a lover in bed. It wasn't an effect she'd ever had to worry about before, since the people she drew in hospital settings were generally children rather than handsome men.

Still, it was a good likeness...

Magic crackled against her senses, hot and more than a little aggressive. Startled, Gen turned. Kurt stared at the drawing, naked fury on his face. His hard, golden gaze flicked up to meet hers. "You did a good job of capturing him." There was nothing whatsoever complimentary about his tone, especially given the gravely, growling note to his voice.

An image flashed through her mind. Kurt, his tiger fully manifested, landing on that bear, sinking claws and fangs into the Feral's glowing body in an explosion of rage and animal aggression.

Gen was an Arcane Corps brat; she'd seen Ferals train. Yet a training session was entirely different from all out combat. If she'd learned anything from the past couple of days, one thing was painfully clear: *Kurt could rip me apart without breaking a sweat*.

Ice slid through her veins as she met those blazing gold eyes. His magic stung her senses with an alien crackle.

Gen was on her feet before she even thought about standing, her gaze flicking to Jake's unconscious face. Unfortunately, he was nowhere near healed enough to help her. In fact, if he tried, it would probably send Kurt completely over the edge.

"Don't look at him when I'm talking to you," Kurt growled, his voice deep and grating.

Genevieve took a step back as he rose from his chair, his gold eyes glowing hot in his set face.

Never show fear to Ferals, her mother had told her when she was only a child. *Don't meet their eyes dead on, but don't cringe either.*

So when Kurt started toward her, Gen forced herself to hold fast despite the pulse pounding in her ears. She had to help him reestablish control, or they were all screwed. "Kurt, you need to take a deep breath and get a handle on Stoli," she said in a cool, careful voice. "You're losing it."

He bared his teeth and stepped right up to her, invading her personal space until it was all she could do not to jump back. "Stoli's not the problem," he gritted. "*You* are the problem. Have you got some kind of thing for Ferals? Some kind of kink?"

Gen stared, so startled that for a moment she forgot to be afraid. *That doesn't sound like him at all.* She'd seen Kurt get possessive before. Hell, in the arena, she'd been afraid he was going to jump Sawyer.

But he'd never turned that anger on her. She hadn't even thought he was capable of it.

A chilling, alien magic rose, swirling around him, feeling... wrong. Greasy, like something half-rotten...

Heart leaping into her throat, Gen closed her eyes. And saw, revolving through his aura, a set of glowing sigils. "Kurt, you're under a spell!"

His lips pulled back from straight white teeth. "Yeah, yours. I'm not going to let you make me dance like a puppet." Big hands snapped out and closed around her shoulders. Rage made his eyes blaze. "You think you can get away with that after what my mother did to me?"

Genevieve forced herself to meet his savage gaze. Gathering her courage, she planted her hands on his chest, rose on her toes and kissed him. He froze, startled.

And she sank her aura into his, wrapped her power around the alien sigils, and clamped down hard. The first of the sigils winked out.

Eyes widening, Kurt stiffened and tried to pull away.

Gen held on, grabbing the alien sigils to drown them in power one by one.

She'd thought when she'd kissed him the first time there had been something strange about the feel of his magic, but she hadn't realized just how *wrong* it was. If she'd closed her eyes during that hello kiss, she probably would have spotted it, but she'd intended nothing more than a peck. She'd thought the feeling was just the residue of the fight, but it had been a hell of a lot more than that.

Setting her teeth, she ground down hard on the spell's final sigil. It exploded in a rain of red sparks.

Kurt staggered back and would've fallen, but she grabbed his arms, managed to steady him. "Shit!" he muttered, looking whiter than Jake even after all his blood loss. "They tried to make me kill you."

"Yeah, they did."

He gave her a look of raw anguish. "God, Gen, I'm so sorry! I would never…"

She blew out a relieved breath and gave him a smile. "I know that, Kurt. That's how I knew you were under a spell -- what you were saying was so completely out of character."

He dropped into a chair, looking as shaken as a man who'd almost walked into a buzz saw. "But I thought you broke the spell! How could it still be active?"

"Maybe they laid more than one."

Leaning forward, he braced his elbows on his knees and scrubbed his hands over his face. "I remember feeling some kind of nasty magic hit me. I thought the bear had just rolled me into that circle of theirs, but what if that wasn't it?" He looked up at her, frowning. "Where was the Faraday Square spell?"

"About three feet inside the grass circle where they put up the skating rink at Christmas."

"Then that wasn't what I felt. I was well outside that circle." He leaned back in his seat and stared up at her, shaken. "Why cast a spell to make me kill you if they intended to sacrifice me before I ever got the chance?"

"Maybe it was a contingency plan. If I succeeded in breaking the spell before the bear killed you, they were done. The FBI would eventually break the other spells, given enough time." Gen nibbled gently on her lower lip and dropped into the recliner. "The Arc did tell me I was going to pay for getting involved."

"So it was a twofer," Kurt said. "Revenge on you, and revenge on me for surviving their spell." He stood up in a rush and began to pace, his big hands curling into fists. "I want to tell you to get out of here, to get as far away from me as you possibly can. What if they try this again? What if it works next time because I'm a fuckin' idiot and don't realize what's going on?"

"I didn't spot it either at first. It was a subtle piece of work, designed to build and build gradually until you snapped. If it had been strong enough to make you jump me when you walked in the door, there was too great a chance I'd break the spell before you managed to kill me. If you got angry naturally and the spell just amplified what you were feeling, they figured I'd be a lot less likely to realize what was happening and break it. Or you might have caught on and regained control."

"I should have sent you home after Dad died. Told you to leave town."

"If I'd been at home alone when they came after me, they'd have penetrated my wards and killed me. It took Dave and me working together to drive them off."

Gen stood up and stepped into his path, blocking his restless pacing. She rested a hand on his cheek to bring his golden gaze to hers. "We need each other, Kurt. It's the only way any of us are going to get through this. Two civilians and a cop are dead, five more civilians and another pair of cops injured. We have to work together or the death toll is going to go even higher."

Sawyer spoke from the doorway of the hospital room. "It's two cops dead now. Jenkins died in surgery." He walked in looking grimmer than Genevieve had ever seen him. "The Feds think they've identified the terrorists -- there aren't a hell of a lot of teams with a polar bear Feral and a female Arcanist. Indigo and Virgil Ford are a former CIA wetworks team."

"So not Caliphate terrorists," Kurt said.

"Nope. The Fords were forced into retirement a year ago. Seems they'd been saying a lot of bigoted, violent shit about Norms running the US."

Gen glowered. "And the CIA ignored that?"

"Apparently they also had some friends a lot higher up the food chain who thought they were just running their mouths and wouldn't really do the crap they were threatening."

"Oops," Genevieve said.

"Yeah. Oops."

"Have the Fed Arcanists at least broken any of the assassination spell?"

Sawyer blew out a breath and shook his head. "They've tried, but they haven't been able to pull it off. At least not yet."

Gen frowned. "Until they do, we're in a seriously precarious situation."

"No shit. They're assembling the most powerful team they can. The SAC seems pretty confident that if they all work together, they can break it. Once they figure out how to drop the first one, the others should be a little easier."

Kurt hooked a thumb at Genevieve. "Gen was able to do it all by herself."

"They think that could be because she took it apart within minutes of Fred's death. If she hadn't acted so fast, she wouldn't have been able to break the damn thing."

Genevieve considered the question. "Makes sense. Have they figured out what the spell actually does?"

"Based on the sigils they've been able to decipher, they think the spell is aimed at the individual officials themselves. They're putting them all under the protection of at least one Arcanist who will erect wards to protect them." Sawyer looked at her. "I think you'd be well advised to stick with Dave and Kurt."

Kurt just grunted.

"You guys did a hell of a job today. You kept a really ugly situation from becoming a hell of a lot worse."

"Between fucking up. The bastards almost made me kill Genevieve just now."

"Wait, what?" Sawyer straightened in alarm. "What the hell happened?"

Gen sighed and told the detective what had just happened. "He's beating himself up about not fighting the spell off."

"He does that," Jake said from the bed, sounding a little groggy. "His daddy raised him to be such a Boy Scout, it's like being friends with Clark fucking Kent."

"Pot, kettle, Bruce Wayne," Kurt shot back.

Sawyer snorted. "Considering the way you saved everybody today -- including the President of the United States -- you might as well be wearing capes. I hope you three are ready to become national heroes, because that's exactly what you're going to be. I'd bet money there are assorted medals in your future."

Kurt glowered, obviously uncomfortable with the idea. "They can keep the damn medals. I just want them to approve the federal grant I submitted to expand BFS."

Jake looked at Sawyer. "If you squint, you can almost see the big red S on his chest. Let's just hope that fucking Arc doesn't have a stash of Kryptonite."

"Funny, funny guy," Kurt growled.

"If it makes you feel any better, the Feds are sending a team of Feral agents and a pair of Arcs to help with security. They're due to fly in in a couple of hours. In the meantime, we've got deputies on guard at BFS."

"Why don't they just put Gen in a safe house? The Feds have places with wards so strong even that Arc couldn't get through."

Sawyer frowned. "That's... a pretty good question."

"Maybe they're planning to use her as bait." The cynical twist of Jake's mouth was definitely not a smile.

"Fuck that."

"Gotta agree with you there." Sawyer turned to Genevieve. "You need every Feral bodyguard we can find. There's no telling how long it's going to take them to get those spells down, or to catch those bastards. You're going to be in danger every minute they're still running free."

"So I need you." Genevieve moved over and dropped to her knees until she could meet Kurt's glowing gaze. "Don't try to send me away again, because I'm not going to leave. You need me too."

Jake eyed them both. "Kurt, buddy, if you don't hold onto this girl with both hands, you're an idiot." For once, there was no humor at all in his voice.

"No," Kurt said hoarsely. His eyes locked on hers, hungry and intense. "I'm not going to send her away."

The tension in her neck relaxed for the first time since she'd realized he was under that spell.

* * *

Later that afternoon, Genevieve made a Skype call to her parents. Her mother had identified most of the sigils, but there were a few in the innermost ring of the spell neither Diane nor Gen's father had ever seen before.

Genevieve told them about the Feds' problem with breaking the spell -- and that Kurt, Dave and Jake remained in danger of becoming that final sacrifice. The cops had put BFS under surveillance in case the terrorists showed up.

"What about the President and Congress?" her mother asked. "They're in the bull's eye too."

"They've all got Arcanist bodyguards."

"Which is really ironic considering these are the same people who want to make us all register."

"This kind of crap is *why* they want us all to

register," Dad said. His voice dropped to a growl. "Fuckin' terrorists."

"Which is why we need to kill these idiots before they hit their targets."

"You need to turn the tables on this little bitch," her father said. "She's so fond of traps? I think it's time you set one for her."

Which sounded like a damn good idea to Genevieve. She and her folks spent the next hour brainstorming ideas. Finally they ended the call so each could work on the separate layers of the spell they had in mind.

Kurt returned from transferring Parvati to a larger cage, and headed upstairs to take a shower. Genevieve, absorbed in her spell, barely noticed the sound of the water rushing through the pipes overhead. The water cut off again as she studied the four sigils none of them had been able to identify.

What the hell do they do?

Chapter Fifteen

Dave padded into the living room where Gen sat with her sketchpad. Out of the corner of one eye, she saw him manifest a human arm to pick up the remote and turn the television on. He channel surfed for a few moments, only to stop on CNN. "Hey, Gen, both houses of Congress just declared an unscheduled recess. And the President is going golfing. Sounds like they're all getting the hell out of D.C. before our terrorist buddies get a chance to nuke 'em."

Gen snorted. "At least they have a keen sense of self-preservation."

"Can't get reelected if you're dead."

BFS, too, was under guard. A pair of FBI agents and a deputy were patrolling the park now. The two feds had dropped by earlier in the afternoon.

Dave fell silent as she concentrated on her work. A moment later he swore. "Oh, hell, we're famous again."

Genevieve looked up and cursed softly. Evidently one of the helicopters she'd heard overhead that afternoon had gotten video of the fight.

The image dissolved to a split screen. On one side was a pretty, dark-haired anchor Genevieve didn't recognize. "So what did you think when you realized it was your son fighting the bear Feral?"

On the other side of the screen, a woman wiped her eyes. A caption below her face read "Melody Anderson, mother of Feral hero." She appeared to be middle-aged, judging from the graying roots of her dark hair and the lines that bracketed her wide mouth. Something about the shape of her face looked vaguely familiar. "I was absolutely horrified." She had a beautiful voice, surprisingly deep for a woman's, with a purring note that made every word sound like the lyrics of a song. "I watched with my heart in my throat the entire time. I just knew my baby was going to get killed right in front of me. It was bad enough finding out about Fred's death from the news -- nobody called me -- but seeing the same vicious killer going after my son, watching him fight for his life…"

"Oh fuck," Dave said, sitting up, his round ears swiveling forward as his whiskers fanned back. "Kurt! Your mom's on television!"

"What?" Feet pounded down the stairs. Kurt stalked in. He stopped dead at the sight of Melody Anderson crying for Fred. "You've got to be kidding me."

"You just have no idea how painful it was, watching that… creature try to tear my son apart!" She wiped her eyes with a wadded tissue.

The anchor looked skeptical. "I thought you said you and Fred Briggs were divorced."

Kurt's mother sniffled. "Well, yes, but I still felt something for him."

"Right," Kurt growled at the TV. "That's why you cheated on him every time his back was turned."

Genevieve winced at the pain and anger in his voice.

The image cut to a wedding photo of a very young Melody and Fred Briggs as the woman talked about how handsome and heroic her husband had been when they met. Next came several photos of Kurt as a child. In one, he was four years old, standing with Melody, Fred and his lion. Lahr appeared to be watching Melody -- and he didn't look friendly. At all. Kurt's mother, for her part, had one shoulder hitched up as she eyed the lion nervously.

"Fred loved his cats," Melody said bitterly.

"More than he ever did me."

"That's a damned lie," Kurt said through gritted teeth. "He loved you, Mom. You just hated the cats, and you were jealous as hell of Lahr." He grabbed the remote off the floor where Dave had left it and muted the television. He pulled out his cell and began to dial it with hard stabs of his thumb.

Genevieve watched a muscle flex in his jaw as he listened to the phone ring. When someone picked up, he didn't even say hello. "You are not using Dad's murder to get free publicity for your band, Melody." His tone was icy with control. He paused, listening. "You gave up the right to be called 'mother' when you walked out on us."

As Gen watched, he began to pace, striding back and forth. "Here's a question, Mother of the Year: When's my birthday?… That's what I thought."

Dave looked away, squeezing his eyes shut.

"You had better by God think twice about talking to another reporter. Stoli just died. I seriously doubt you want a visit from me."

He hung up and lifted his phone as if seriously considering hurling it across the room. Instead he threw himself down on the couch, flipped the cell onto the coffee table, and buried his face in his hands.

Genevieve closed her eyes and studied his aura.

"No, Goddamnit, I am not under another spell."

"I'm sorry, it's just…"

"That I sound like a crazy man."

"No," Gen said quietly. "More like a man who's been badly wounded by the one person he should have been able to trust."

"Yeah. Not only did my mother cheat on Dad, she used her Talent on both of us."

Gen stared at him, appalled. "Her own family?"

"Yeah. Melody is a Bard. Not a particularly powerful Bard -- she was only able to use her magic on people who were in the room with her. Her singing ability wasn't all that great either, so she never had the recording career she dreamed of."

A really powerful Bard could affect their listeners even through a recording, but that was relatively rare. The best had both magical ability and a great singing voice.

"Dad met her when her country band played at a bar in Virginia Beach, near Norfolk, where he was stationed." Kurt sounded less furious than weary now. "They started dating."

Gen thought of the wedding photo. "She was pretty when she was younger."

"Yeah. Yeah, she really was. And Dad was completely gone on her. Which is why when she got pregnant with me, he talked her into marrying him. Apparently she'd considered ending the pregnancy."

Genevieve winced. "Ow."

"So they got married, and I came along. Unfortunately, Dad was gone a lot on Arcane Corps missions, and it didn't take Melody long to realize a little kid and a musical career don't mesh. She started pushing Dad to quit the Corps. Since the military was downsizing at that point, Dad agreed to get out. That was when he decided to open BFS."

"I gather things didn't improve."

"No. Running BFS involves almost as much travel as the Corps. He was always driving somewhere to pick up a cat or take one somewhere else for medical treatment. That suited Melody just fine, because she'd started having an affair with her new lead guitarist."

"With you there?"

"Yeah."

"How the hell did she get away with that?" Dave asked, the tip of his tail flicking. "Fred would have smelled the guy on her."

"Plus, how did she know you wouldn't let the cat out of the bag?" Gen asked.

This time there was no rimshot, nor was there humor in Kurt's twisted smile. "She was a Bard."

Genevieve stared at him. "She cast spells on you to keep you from talking?"

"Got it in one."

"Christ, what a bitch."

"With a beautiful voice, though." He sounded almost wistful now. "She'd sing me to sleep every night -- especially when Dad was out of town and her boyfriend was over."

"Jesus," Dave muttered.

"Dad told me whenever he got suspicious of her, she'd sing him a love song, and he'd start thinking he was being paranoid."

"And he didn't kill her when he found out?" Dave flicked an ear. "The man's self-control was a hell of a lot better than mine would have been."

"Mine too," Kurt admitted. "In retrospect, it's surprising they lasted as long as they did. But when Lahr got testicular cancer and died, the whole fucking situation just imploded."

"Because Fred melded with Lahr and she couldn't deal," Dave guessed.

"Not to mention she'd just turned thirty, and she thought she needed to start touring a lot more. Dad told her I was too young for her to disappear for months at a time."

"Bet she loved that."

"Yep. She and Fred started fighting. The meld with Lahr gave Dad more resistance to Melody's magic, and he realized she'd been using her powers on both of us. He was furious."

Gen shook her head, unable to imagine doing something like that to her own family. "I don't blame him."

"One day Fred left to pick up an abused lion, and Melody saw her chance. No sooner was he out the door than she started packing to leave. She told me I was going to be staying overnight with Jake and Bobby while Dad was gone, because she was leaving."

"Without taking you?"

"Of course without me. I was the albatross around her neck. She told me she loved me, but she had to pursue her dream." He sounded so controlled, almost emotionless, despite the pain of his words. "I cried. I begged her to stay. But she said she had to leave before Dad got back, or he'd kill her. She said that's why she couldn't take me with her -- because he'd never let her go if she did. Which was true."

"That bitch is lucky to be alive," Dave growled.

"Especially since Dad turned around and caught her on the way out."

"He suspected she was leaving him?"

"Actually, he told me later he just had a bad feeling. Called his USDA contact and told him he'd be a little late. He drove up just as she was loading me in the car to take me to the Nolan's."

Dave made a rumbling sound of sympathy.

"I ran to him and threw my arms around him and told him she was leaving us, that she didn't want me anymore." He shook his head. "Dad lost it. Not so much because she was leaving as that she'd hurt me. He manifested his lion. She pulled a gun."

Gen stared at him in horror. "With you with your arms around him?"

"Yeah. Dad realized if he got anywhere near her, he'd kill her. He told her to get the fuck out, and she did. He told me he could have forgiven her cheating, but not the way she'd used her magic on me."

"Hell, I don't blame him," Dave said.

"I've seen her maybe three times since then. She sent birthday and Christmas presents for a while, then just cards. Then I got a card talking about my birthday being on July twenty-first -- my birthday's on the twenty-fifth."

Genevieve flinched.

"So after she dumped you, did her career ever take off?" Dave asked.

Kurt shook his head. "Never even made it to one-hit-wonder."

"Serves the bitch right," Gen growled. "I'm seriously tempted to sit down and draw her portrait." When they stared at her, puzzled, she bared her teeth. "Bald. She wouldn't have a single dyed hair left on her head by the time I got done with her."

Kurt laughed. "You're not a nice woman."

"Neither is she." What must it have been like for him, knowing that his own mother had turned her magic against him? Suddenly she remembered what he'd said at the hospital when the spell had had him in its grip. *"I'm not going to let you make me dance like a puppet. You think you can get away with that after what my mother did to me?"*

Oh, hell. Gen had known he was wary of Arcanists, but she'd assumed that distrust had been born from his experiences fighting the Caliphate. But Kurt's mother had inflicted psychic wounds far deeper than Gen had ever imagined.

What must it have been like, being raised by a man who'd been so thoroughly betrayed? What must it be like to know even your mother's lullabies had been an act of manipulation?

Melody Briggs had betrayed him and his father in every possible way. She'd even been willing to endanger her son's life to protect herself.

Genevieve's childhood experiences with magic had been completely different. One of her earliest memories was watching her mother cast a spell. The sigils had floated in the air, intricate lines and curves of glowing magic that bobbed around them, rotating slowly, spinning like soap bubbles.

Magic for her had never been anything but positive. Oh, she'd always known that people could kill with it. After all, she'd been ten years old when Caliphate terrorists destroyed the Twin Towers.

But Kurt had been the victim of magic more often than he'd been its beneficiary.

It all made her heart hurt. Not just for him, but for herself. The depth of the pain was so intense it stole her breath.

Genevieve froze, feeling as if someone had just hit her over the head with a frying pan. *Oh, God. I'm in love with Kurt Briggs. And there's no way in hell it's ever going to work.* She was distantly aware Kurt had stalked out of the living room. A moment later, she heard the kitchen door slam as he went outside.

"Are you all right?" Dave asked.

Gen sank down on the couch. For a moment, she just sat there feeling battered.

"Hey." Dave padded over to her and sniffed. He was so big that his head was level with hers. "Are you all right?" he repeated

"Fine."

"You do realize I can smell lies?"

She stared at him helplessly, eyes stinging. "I'm

in love with him."

Dave flicked his ear. "No shit. I don't think I've ever seen anybody fall as fast and as hard as you two."

"There's no such thing as love at first sight."

"Ordinarily I'd agree with you. Every time I've ever fallen for anybody this quick, it was just an acute case of lust. My tenth-grade science teacher... I had it so bad for that woman. It's a good thing I didn't have my cat at that point, or her husband would have been Tender Vittles."

She leaned forward and rubbed her face tiredly. "I'm surprised Fred even let me and my sketchpad inside the door to begin with."

Dave shook his big head. "It was that or put Parvati down."

Suddenly Gen wanted to get the hell out of there instead of hanging around getting her heart ground into hamburger. *Kurt's never going to love me because he'll never be able to trust me.*

Dave extended his big head until she was almost nose to nose with him. She could feel his aura roll across hers in a tingling wash of magic. "Gen, whatever you're feeling isn't unrequited. Yeah, magic users have done a lot of nasty shit to Kurt over the years. But the existence of assholes does not prove the entire human race puckers."

She couldn't help but smile. "Sometimes it does feel that way, though."

"Granted. Look, I won't deny Kurt's got his demons. I'm also not denying he's got reasons for them. And it's certainly true his daddy had a thing about non-Feral women being a bad bet."

"Given his ex, I'm not surprised."

"Got that right." Sighing, Dave sat back on his haunches. "I knew Fred's attitude had something to do with Kurt's mom, but I never realized how bad it was. I don't blame Fred for being paranoid." He lifted a huge paw and put it on her knee. It was twice as big as both her hands put together. "But you're nothing like that bitch, and Kurt knows it. Do you really think Melody Briggs would have run out to help when she heard Fred roaring in pain? Do you think she would've had the guts to break that spell, or that she would have tried to help Kurt regain control the way you did?"

"Considering her fear of Ferals, I don't even understand why she stayed with Fred as long as she did."

"I guess she thought she could use her magic to manipulate him into supporting her indefinitely while she ran around with her boy toy. Kurt is not an idiot -- though I'll admit there have been times lately I've had my doubts. Fact is, though, he's one of the most intelligent, dedicated and courageous men that I've ever known. He will fight for you -- against the Ferals, against the terrorists and against himself if he has to."

"I know," she said softly. "Otherwise it wouldn't hurt so fucking bad."

"Look, Gen, you can make it work. Don't give up." Golden eyes met hers, rich with sympathy. "I would have given anything to have found a woman like you before I got myself killed. Now it's too goddamn late. Unless I meet a woman who's trapped in a tigress' body, I will never have what you and Kurt could. If you throw that away, both of you are idiots."

Her heart ached for the longing in his voice, but she had no idea what to do for him.

"Do me a favor, Gen. Fight for him." The tiger moved away, the floorboards creaking under his weight. "Now, unless I miss my guess, he's out there in Fred's meditation garden tormenting himself. Go out there and kiss him or something. I'm going to play Call of Duty."

Genevieve blinked at him as he walked over to the television and the PlayStation that sat on the entertainment center beneath it. Manifesting two human arms, he turned on the system, picked up the controller and settled back on his haunches as it booted.

Genevieve watched him start shooting zombies, trying to work up her courage.

"Gen?" he said, without looking around.

"What?"

"Go neck. Or whatever." His voice dropped to a mutter. "Lucky bastard."

She laughed and headed into the kitchen, then opened the door into the back yard. As the door closed behind her, Genevieve took a deep breath, savoring the scent of flowers and freshly cut grass.

It was a lovely space, surrounded by a high wooden privacy fence lined with rose bushes and azaleas. A huge magnolia reigned over one corner, limbs spreading wide in a cloud of glossy oval leaves. In the spring, it would be covered in blossoms the size of saucers.

Beneath the great tree stood a lovely little water feature. A spring chuckled its way from a crown of stones, tumbling into a pool occupied by koi and water lilies.

Kurt sat on the ground beside the pool in the lotus position, his hands resting on his knees, palm up. His eyes were closed, his face not so much peaceful as expressionless. She knew it was more mask for his pain than anything else because there was a faint wet sheen on his cheeks.

He'd been crying. She wondered if it was for

Fred or for himself.

Probably Fred. When things went wrong, Kurt's instinctive reaction was to fight instead of whine.

Unlike, apparently, his mother, who'd complained because she'd found out about her ex-husband's death from television news. The woman was an incredibly self-absorbed bitch.

Had she even told Kurt she was sorry his father was dead?

"You know, your mother could've gone to jail for what she did to you. You can get twenty years for felony magical influence."

His eyes didn't even open as he spoke, as if he'd known she was there. With his senses, he probably had. "It's a pretty toothless law, almost impossible to prove."

"Fred still could've brought charges against her."

Finally Kurt opened his eyes. She almost wished he hadn't; there was such pain in them. "She would have claimed he was lying to get back at her because she'd left him. A Bard's magic doesn't leave the kind of evidence an Arcanist's does. No obvious effects on your aura. Besides, Fred would never have admitted he let her do anything like that to him or his child. It shamed him that he hadn't realized what was happening." He smiled slightly. "Dad took that whole King of the Jungle thing seriously."

"I still can't believe she did it. Even aside from FMI being both immoral and a felony, she took a big risk."

"It never occurred to her he'd catch her. Even if he did, she probably figured she could sing her way out of it."

Gen snorted. "Then she was definitely delusional. I'm good, but even I wouldn't play that game."

"You're a hell of a lot smarter than Melody. And you're not a bitch."

"Flatterer."

He looked thoughtful. "You're also far more courageous than she ever was. Which is part of the reason I find you so attractive. Fear tends to bring out a predatory reaction in any cat, even a Feral, which we have to control. That gets incredibly exhausting after a while. But you don't seem to fear me even when you should."

She shrugged. "If anybody can be trusted to control himself, it's you. Everybody has animal impulses, Kurt, including those of us who haven't melded with big cats. One of my boyfriends had zero magic, but he scared me a hell of a lot more than you at your angriest."

His vivid eyes narrowed, taking on a deadly glint. "Who was this asshole?"

"Don't worry, I took care of him. The first time he tried it, I told him he'd never get another erection as long as he lived. I was bluffing -- I'd have gone to jail -- but he didn't want to take the chance."

"Hell, I don't blame him. Still needed his ass kicked."

"And he'd have gotten worse than that if my dad had found out about it. Fortunately, he was a cowardly little jerk, and I never saw him again."

"I'm not surprised." The curl of Kurt's upper lip suggested he'd love to find her idiot ex- and hit him a few times himself.

And a small, unworthy part of Gen would have loved to watch.

Suddenly unable to sit still any longer, she rose to her feet and started wandering around the back yard. Pausing, she studied a neat flowerbed. "Is this a butterfly garden?"

Kurt rose, all muscular feline grace. "Yeah. One of Dad's projects. Whenever he was feeling particularly stressed, he'd come out here and dig in the dirt." He gazed around them, a half smile on his face. "It's funny. BFS was his life's work, but I feel his presence here more than anywhere else in the sanctuary."

"I can see why." Gen inhaled, drinking in the perfume of the flowers and the smell of the falling water. She'd always loved being in nature -- feeling the magic of life, of the ancient earth itself. She let her eyes slip closed to drink it all in.

The feeling was especially intense here, in the heart of BFS, with its plants and cats, with its spring-fed lake bubbling up from deep underground. There was such power here. She'd felt it when she laid the wards around the house. Such old, old magic. Magic she'd drawn on when she'd fought Indigo Ford.

The same magic Indigo drew on to cast that spell in the arena. An idea niggled at Gen's consciousness, and she dropped to her knees on the ground. For a moment she hesitated, picturing those four strange sigils from the terrorist's spell, the ones her mother hadn't been able to identify.

Lips pursed, she sketched one of the four sigils in the rich, dark soil. As her finger moved through the Earth's aura, she felt the turbulence the shape imposed on the magical field. Her heart began to beat faster, and she drew the next sigil in the series.

The sensation of turbulence increased. It reminded her of the feel of a key turning just before the lock clicks open.

Genevieve hesitated a moment, wondering if it was safe to do this.

Only one way to find out. She bit her lip and sketched the final sigil.

The power of the earth surged up through her finger and into her arm, up her spine, to spear into her brain in a blinding rush of magic. Genevieve sucked in a startled breath as the power stormed through her, more intense than anything she'd ever felt.

This is the key. This is how Indigo harnessed the Earth's power. The terrorist had found a way to embed the sigils in the earth's magical field.

Which suggested that the longer the spell was in place, the stronger it would grow as it burned its way into the earth's aura.

Gen stared at the sigils as they rotated slowly in the air behind the darkness behind her closed lids. *Hell, how did I manage to break the arena spell at all*? She thought back to Indigo's first attack on the house, when Gen had drawn on Dave's power to reinforce the wards.

And then there was how making love to Kurt let her recharge her magical batteries.

She went still, soaking in the magic of the sanctuary as it rolled up through her knees. She could feel all the animals and plants around her, but it was more than that.

Lifting her eyes, Gen gazed up at Kurt's house. Five generations of Ferals had lived there, working the land and raising Feral animals in intricate mystical rites.

BFS was a place of power.

Gen closed her eyes and looked at the rotating sigils. Flashes of imagery appeared in her mind, snippets of possibility.

When she opened her eyes again, she found Kurt watching her, frowning. "You just thought of something. I need to know what."

"I think I know how we can turn the tables on the Wicked Bitch of the West." Genevieve sprang to her feet and headed inside.

"You're beginning to irritate me."

She stopped to give him a brilliant smile. "I just figured out how Indigo made her spells so hard to break. What's more, I know how we can put them to use."

"I gathered that. My question is, are you going to share with the class?"

So she did.

Chapter Sixteen

An hour later, the sun was setting, painting the garden in shades of gold and rose. Kurt watched Genevieve as she moved around the garden perimeter, airbrushing sigils in preparation for the spell she'd described.

She looked so graceful, a slender, long-legged figure in shorts and a BFS T-shirt. Her shining mane of red hair curled around her shoulders, emphasizing the feminine strength of her features.

As she bent, the airbrush rumbling in her hand, her shorts drew tight over the smooth, lush curve of her ass.

He was as hard as a 2 x 4, his balls hot and tight, his zipper digging into the thick shaft of his erection. Stoli rumbled eagerly in the depths of his mind. His need only grew as she drew sigil after sigil, encircling them with magic.

Despite the throb of hunger, Kurt frowned, wondering how good an idea this really was. He didn't doubt it was necessary. He'd survived the last fight with the bear only because of Jake. Otherwise they all would've been screwed. His friend had come entirely too close to getting killed as it was.

If the terrorists tried again in the next couple of days, Jake would be in no position to back Kurt up. Genevieve had greatly shortened the healing process, but he'd needed surgery for his shattered shoulder and collarbone. He'd be in the hospital through Wednesday, at least.

Being Jake, he also complained about being bored out of his mind. Kurt planned to pay him a visit in the morning, after he took Fred's suit to Bobo Funeral Home.

The visitation was scheduled for tomorrow night, with the funeral the day after. Both events were likely to be hip deep in reporters and photographers who'd do their best to make a painful situation agonizing.

Genevieve stepped forward a pace, and bent again. He watched, trying to divert his attention from the ache of his grief. *Dad, if this works, I'll be able to avenge you.*

If it worked.

Genevieve painted the last of the sigils on the grass, completing the circle. Turning, she moved to the circle's center, where she'd laid out a BFS quilt one of the volunteers had made. She sank to her knees on the lion logo, as graceful as a geisha.

When she closed her eyes, Kurt felt her magic rise. Curious, he closed his own and saw her glowing softly behind his eyelids, straight and slender and lush.

Rose light gathered at the points of her breasts and between those long, lovely thighs. The color deepened as he watched, as if reacting to arousal. *Glad I'm not the only one.*

Her magic rolled over his skin, bringing every hair on his body to bristling attention. Stoli made a deep sound in his mind, the tiger equivalent of a purr, all rumbling pleasure and rising hunger. The currents of her magic on his skin grew warmer, a flush of heat that made his balls even heavier as his cock lay like a rifle barrel behind his zipper. Kurt moved forward before he had time to think better of it, craving a taste of her.

Her glow brightened. Different shades of pink and rose rolled over her glowing skin, currents swirling through her aura.

He caught a glow from his peripheral vision, and

looked down. Stoli burned around him even without being fully manifested to the human eye.

Kurt swallowed with the hot rise of lust, craving the taste of her silken mouth. Those lush lips glowed as red as a Valentine heart against the pink of her aura.

He fought the impulse to reach for her, knowing it was a bad idea to touch someone when they were working magic. If you distracted them, they could lose control of the spell.

Gen's eyes opened, glowing brilliant blue and turquoise against her aura. She looked up at him. She wanted him to kiss her. He could feel her need as vividly as Stoli's.

Kurt bent, slipping his hand into the cool silk of her hair, the curls sliding over his fingers. He covered that glowing mouth with his own, tasting the hot femininity of hers, the blend of mint and ozone.

Her magic struck him like a blow, flaring through his aura. The sensation startled him, reminding him of the first time he'd touched Stoli's consciousness, when they'd bound him and the cub.

Kurt would've pulled back, but Gen reached up and touched his face. He sucked in a breath against her mouth as her power surrounded him in a shimmering dance of sparks. His eyes flew wide.

Night had fallen in the time he'd had his eyes closed, though it had been twilight when he closed them. Sunset should have taken a good ten or fifteen minutes.

Yet now it was dark, and she glowed.

I lost time. Almost as if her spell did something to me...

The thought sent a knee-jerk bolt of unease through him, but he ignored it. Genevieve was no Melody. She'd never betray him.

Gen leaned into him, licking and suckling his mouth, biting softly at his lips, his tongue. Her taste and scent flooded his consciousness like a storm surge cresting a levee.

He trusted her as he never trusted anyone, even the men he'd fought beside. More than Jake or Dave -- or even his father. As much as Kurt had loved Fred, he'd had a streak of ruthless bastard as wide as the Great Wall of China. Genevieve motivated him with her simple belief in him.

With her love.

She loves me. That thought rocked Kurt back on his heels so hard he would've fallen, but she straightened into him, bracing him with her slim body, arms coiling around his neck.

Her skin felt so hot, he'd have thought she was running a fever, if he hadn't known it was the magic running under her skin. Sweat dewed her body, taking on an opalescent glow in the light of her magic.

She released his mouth, drawing back until she could see his face. "Make love to me." He could feel the movement of her lips against his own, as if she kissed him with her speech.

"I love you." He blurted it, voice hoarse, meaning every word.

The moment the sentence was out of his mouth, something in him panicked, fearing to be vulnerable as he'd been to the last woman he loved -- his mother.

Stoli growled in the depths of his brain. Kurt had no difficulty whatsoever translating the tiger's emotions. *Don't be an idiot.*

And the cat was right.

Genevieve froze, looking up at him in wonder, her full lips parted. "I love you, too."

He could read the truth of that in her aura, the

hot rose glow spinning faster in currents of agitation and desire. He reached down and lifted her to her feet, his mouth covering hers, tongue thrusting, teeth nipping. Magic seemed to explode between them like fireworks against the sky.

In the depths of his brain, Stoli roared in triumph.

* * *

Kurt kissed Genevieve as if she were water and he was dying of thirst, claiming her with none of the hesitation he'd shown a moment before. Magic boiled around them -- hers, his, and Stoli's, swirling together like a whirlwind. Her hair floated upward, borne by those whipping currents.

That's never happened before.

And then she couldn't think anything else at all, because he grabbed the hem of her T-shirt and jerked it up over her head. She didn't see where he threw it. The bra went next, his fingers hooking between her breasts to rip the silk as if it were cooked spaghetti.

One big palm cupped her right breast as he slid the other hand behind her back. Lifting her off her feet, Kurt bent her backward and lowered his dark head to the nipples that had ached since she'd begun casting the spell. His tongue lapped and swirled over and around one peak, as possessive fingers caressed the other.

Genevieve gasped, her knees going weak, shivering in helpless need. She'd never known anything like this blend of magic, pleasure, and desire. The spell seemed to be enhancing the pleasure.

Her need built into a hard blaze that made her shudder. Sweat rolled along her skin as her pussy grew wet.

Kurt was just as affected, judging by the thick

length of him pressing against her belly.

With a feline growl, Gen clawed the hem of his shirt upward. The minute her hand connected with bare flesh, their joined magic leaped like a bonfire sprayed with gasoline. They both gasped.

Growling softly, Kurt helped her drag the shirt off and toss it aside. His body gleamed like golden marble in the spell's shifting light. Gen gathered the surging power and started feeding it to the spell, making the sigils glow even brighter.

He spilled her back onto the blanket, grabbed the snap of her shorts, flicked it open, and tugged down the zipper with a metallic whisper. Gen canted her hips upward so he could strip off her panties and shorts in one ruthless jerk.

Dropping them on the blanket, he fumbled for his belt buckle. She reached to help, her own hands shaking just as hard as his with magic and desire. At last they freed him of the belt, and stripped the briefs and jeans down his thighs, pausing only long enough to toe off his shoes.

Then his hot weight came down on top of her. As he caught himself on powerful arms, the thick muscle stood out in relief, corded shoulders limned in moonlight. He looked down at her, his eyes glowed, hot and bright.

Tiger eyes.

Kurt lowered himself until his muscled chest met her breasts, and the hard jut of his cock brushed her belly. They both gasped as magic burst through them with another hot flash.

He kissed her again, slow and sweet, his tongue entering her mouth in a wave of magic. He groaned at the sensation, and so did she, half blind with delight.

Everywhere they touched, the magic danced in

iridescent flashes she could see even with her eyes open. "Well, the amplification spell is definitely working," she gasped against his mouth.

His only answer was a throaty growl, far too deep for human vocal cords.

Genevieve wrapped her arms and legs around his hard, lean back. That simple contact sent an explosion of magic through her awareness. Her groan of pleasure mixed with his.

A low, growling rumble sounded around them, and she knew it came from Stoli. Kurt drew back a fraction, and the tiger burned in his eyes as he stared down at her. He kissed her, his tongue thrusting deep, then gave her lower lip a gentle tug with his teeth.

As she dug her nails into his back, Kurt kissed along the line of her jaw, taking his time, his tongue tracing sensual sigils over her banging pulse.

Kisses. They were just kisses. And yet somehow he seemed to be touching something much deeper than her skin in an intimacy more profound than anything she'd ever felt.

He paused to nibble her collarbone, and she raised her head and threaded her hands through his hair. "Let me," she gasped. "Let me taste you."

Gold flashed as he looked up at her. His thumb and forefinger closed around a nipple, tugging it upward, sending the magic rolling over her skin. "You are touching me." He grinned. "Everywhere."

"But I want to ride you!"

"No." His smile was slow and taunting. Kurt pushed upward onto hands and knees despite her efforts to cling to him. She watched his great shoulders bunch under his skin as he kissed and licked his way downward. When he reached her breast, his hand tightened, plumping it upward. He extended just the tip of his tongue and licked, a tiny tease of sensation that seemed to strike sparks from her aura like flint and steel.

Need clawed at her, and she rolled her hips upward, grinding against his body, urging him on.

Close. She was so close, already on the verge of orgasm. She squeezed her eyes shut, fighting for control. Behind her lids, she found the tiger watching her -- not a manifestation, but Stoli's magical consciousness.

"Let me touch you," she begged. "Let me taste you." She knew tigers couldn't smile, but it seemed Stoli did.

Kurt yelped in surprise as his body suddenly flipped off hers and onto his back. "What the hell?"

She grinned wickedly. "Thank you, Stoli!" Gen sat up and pounced, swinging a leg over his hips and settling down on top of him.

"That was dirty pool," he gasped.

Her thumbs found his nipples, and she rolled her wet sex across his up and down the length of his shaft. "Do you care?"

He gasped as his eyes went unfocused, reacting to the surge of sex and magic and pleasure. "No."

"I didn't think so," she purred.

It was her turn to nibble her way down the arch of his chest, one thumb playing over his tiny erect nipple, as the other hand reached down to tease the length of his thick cock. A drop of pre-come dewed the slit of the velvet, and she smeared it over him. He fell back with a groan, and Genevieve smiled, enjoying the power his surrender gave her.

She could touch him, just the way she'd always ached to touch him, hands exploring the thick hard muscle beneath his skin, hot with the burn of their blended magic.

Genevieve began to work her way down the lean length of his body, stroking smooth, warm skin over hard muscle, savoring the thick hair that pelted his chest, soft and springy against her fingers.

Each touch, each kiss, sent another delicious swirl of magic through her senses. The pleasure was more intense than anything she'd ever felt this side of orgasm.

Kurt rolled under her, all but writhing. Gen experimented, alternating little brushes of her fingertips with licks and kisses, drinking the taste of him. Everything she did made him shudder in reaction, fingers digging into her skin.

"Genevieve," he gasped. "I'd rather not go off like a bottle rocket. I don't think you'd like that either."

"So use a little of that vaunted Briggs control," she purred. "Let's see how close we both can come without coming." Gen lifted off him onto hands and knees turned around so that she was head down along his torso.

His big hands came up to cup her ass. "I've got to say, I approve of the view."

Genevieve, grinned, eye to eye with his cock. "Looks pretty good from here too." She flicked out her tongue and licked the tip of his shaft. He gasped, digging his fingers into her ass cheeks. Then he grabbed her hips and hauled her backward, forcing her to plant her knees on either side of his head as he gave her a long, juicy lick. His mouth sealed over her clit and he began to suck with a gentle swirl of his tongue around the tight bud.

Not touching. Not quite.

The jolt of delight rolled all the way right up her spine and into the base of her brain. She gasped around the fat head of his cock.

He kept right on licking, sliding his thumb into the opening of her pussy.

Each stroke, each tiny thrust, jolted her with another burst of magic and sensation. The pleasure made her shudder. She swirled her tongue back and forth over the sensitive mushroom head. Between her legs, Kurt echoed the motion precisely, licking and sucking.

Genevieve closed her mouth around the shaft and sucked hard -- and almost screamed as hot, blinding light jolted through her. She heard him curse, felt his desperate effort to maintain control when all he wanted to do was fill her mouth with his come.

I'm feeling what he feels, hearing his thoughts.

Stoli growled. Next came a blaze of raw male lust so intense, she felt it take even Kurt by surprise. It was the tiger's lust. But it was hers too, and his: the furious need to couple.

Strong hands gripped her around the waist and tumbled her off him as he rose onto his knees. He flipped her onto her face and jerked her onto her hands and knees on the blanket.

Gen knew what he wanted even before he grabbed the back of her head, and gently pushed her face to the soft fabric, lifting her ass.

Kurt drove into her, an endless luscious rush. She screamed into the blanket as magic exploded behind her closed eyes. Kneeling behind her, he began to thrust, driving in and out in ruthless digs that should have hurt. Each and every lunge felt delicious, a glorious, gliding delight.

Tiger teeth closed around the back of her skull.

"Stoli, let go!" Kurt snapped, freezing in mid-thrust. "She's not a damn tigress!"

Gen remembered a Nat Geo program she'd seen of a tiger covering a tigress just like this. Gripping her neck to hold her down.

Tiger sex could be violent.

"He's not going to hurt me!" she gasped, knowing it was true. "Just fuck me!"

"Are you sure?"

"Yes!" She howled it.

He began to drive again, deep, digging thrusts that opened her up and raked pleasure along her sensitive sheath. Banging her hard as Stoli gripped her neck in his jaws.

It could have been terrifying, but it wasn't. Instead, she'd never felt such sheer lust, combined with the sense of being united with her partner. Not even Kurt, himself, the previous times they'd made love.

He slid a hand down around her thigh and found her clit, stroking and circling the bud as he gave her fierce, short thrusts.

The magic detonated in an impossible blaze of pleasure that ripped a rolling climax out of her harder than anything she'd ever felt.

Genevieve closed her eyes. Sigils of her spell orbited them, rotating faster and faster, drawing power from the sex.

Binding them.

She caught a wisp of a thought -- *It reminds me of linking with Stoli when he was a cub, only even more intense.* And seeing the memory in his mind, she realized he was right. It did feel the same.

This was Kurt's kind of magic, Feral magic, the ability to bind mind and heart and soul with another life. Yet Ferals had never been able to do it with other humans; human minds resisted being bound that way.

Yet there was some difference from his first Spirit

link with Stoli, though he didn't know exactly what it was, or what it meant. And neither did she.

At last he rolled off her to collapse onto the blanket beside her, boneless and panting. Gen could still feel the clamp of Stoli's teeth in the back of her skull. Then those phantom jaws disappeared.

Kurt looped an arm around her waist and flipped her over on top of him. She lay panting, eyes closed, watching the sigils revolve slowly, still spinning a cocoon of magic around them.

"That was…" Kurt shook his head. "I never felt anything like that."

"Neither have I." She reached out through her magical senses and touched the spell to disrupt it.

It should have died instantly. It didn't. Instead it sank into the earth and went dormant, yet ready to be called up again whenever she wanted.

She smiled in wicked pleasure at the thought of repeating this delicious…

Oh, shit. Gen froze as an icy horror stole over her. Her eyes flew wide.

Kurt stiffened beneath her, jolting out of the lazy afterglow he'd been savoring. "What?" He lifted his head and looked at her, frowning. "What just scared you? You're terrified -- I can feel it. What are you thinking?"

She jumped to her feet and grabbed up her shorts, jerking them on as she looked around for her T-shirt. "Where's my clothes?" Kurt had destroyed her bra, but she had no intention of going inside for a new one. *We might not have that much time.*

Spotting the shirt, Genevieve snatched it up and pulled it on, only to grimace at the sight of the seams. She'd put it on inside out.

Kurt grabbed it, tugged it over her head, turned

it right side out, then put it back on her again. "Would you tell me why you're terrified?"

"I tried to break the spell around us, but it's still there. It only went dormant."

He stared at her for a moment, uncomprehending, before his golden eyes widened. "The arena spell! You think the arena spell went dormant -- that you didn't break it after all?"

"I hope I'm wrong, but I've got to check. Get dressed."

"Hell, yeah, we've got to check." Kurt dove for his own jeans, jerking them on over his hips without bothering with briefs. He zipped up as he stuffed his sockless feet into his running shoes.

Genevieve slipped on her sandals, grabbed her phone to call their FBI guards, and... got no answer. "You're kidding me!" She considered calling 911, but her screaming instincts told her there was no time to waste. "Damn it, let's go."

She sprinted toward the gate, a grim-faced Kurt on her heels.

An orange and black shape lifted his head as they ran past the porch -- Dave, evidently keeping watch. "Where are you going?" The tiger leaped up to follow.

They didn't stop to explain.

Kurt and Dave at her heels, Genevieve raced for the arena, praying she was wrong even as her stomach twisted with the fear she was right. She gestured for Kurt to open the locked arena gate.

"Would somebody please tell me what the fuck is going on?" Dave demanded as Kurt pulled out his keys.

"Genevieve's afraid she didn't actually break the spell Indigo cast on the arena," Kurt explained as he unlocked the gate.

"I'm worried it just went dormant."

Dave's eyes widened. "Oh, fuck."

"Exactly." Kurt looked grim as he tore down the crime scene tape. "Wish we could call Sawyer. He hasn't released the scene back to me yet."

"If he charges me, he charges me. If I'm right about the danger, he won't give a damn."

"Why do you think you didn't break the spell?" Dave demanded. "I felt it go down."

"Give me a minute." Genevieve walked over to the patch of sand still dark with Fred's dried blood. She knelt there, resting a palm on the ground and closing her eyes as if questing with magical senses. "Maybe I'm just being paranoid. I hope that's all it is."

Kurt moved around in front of her until he could see her face. A frown line formed between her red eyebrows. Magic rolled out from her in waves he could almost see.

He'd felt the magic surge through him when she'd drawn those sigils in the garden, lifting every hair on his body. The sense of her magic now wasn't quite that strong. He closed his own eyes and looked, trying to see what she saw.

There was nothing.

When he opened them again, she still knelt, both hands flat on the sand, frowning deeply.

Her eyes flew wide as she recoiled, scrambling to her feet. "Fuck. Oh, Fuck!" She strode to the outer perimeter of the enclosure where he'd first seen the sigils of the terrorist spell. Kneeling, she again put one hand on the ground. Her expression hardened, going grim as she muttered a curse, stood and walked a few feet further, then repeated the procedure. "The death spell's still here."

"What?" Dave's ears flattened. "I thought you said you broke it."

"I thought I had too." A muscle flexed in the fragile line of her jaw. "Unfortunately, it seems all I did was douse the fuse. The barrel of gunpowder is still here."

"What in the hell does that mean?"

She rose to her feet again, dusting her hands off on her shorts. "I broke the spell's connection to Fred's life force. Without the sacrifice to power it, the spell should have simply melted like a bar of soap in a shower. But she apparently bound the sigils to the Earth's magical field, so the spell didn't wear away. It's still here. If she killed someone with Talent inside the spell, it would reactivate and go off." She drew in a deep breath and met Kurt's luminescent gaze. "Somebody like you or Dave."

Chapter Seventeen

"Why me?" Kurt demanded. "Is it because I'm Fred's son, or what?"

Genevieve shook her head. "No, it doesn't have to be you, but it does have to be a Feral. Look, think of it like a thermonuclear bomb. You need a hell of a lot of heat to fuse hydrogen, which you're not exactly going to get from fuel oil and fertilizer…"

"And a good thing, too," Dave muttered.

"So a thermo-nuke has three stages: a conventional explosive to trigger the initial fission explosion, which in turn generates so much heat it triggers hydrogen fusion."

"And *BOOOM*." The sound effect was so startlingly realistic, Gen jumped.

"Don't *do* that."

Dave flicked an ear. "Sorry."

"Yeah, not buying it. Point is, killing more than five hundred people takes a hell of a lot of magic, so all seven sacrifices must be as powerful as possible. Ferals like you two have far more magic than an Arc like me. Otherwise you'd never be able to generate a manifestation the size of a tiger."

"Which is why they didn't try to sacrifice you in Faraday Square."

"Exactly. I would've been much easier to kill than you, but they needed a Feral to power the spell. That's why they targeted your dad and all the other victims…"

Kurt frowned. "Now that you mention it, my AAFR contact said all of the others were melded Ferals."

"So I'm going to tell you what you told me. It's time to get the hell out of town."

He knew she was right, but fury rolled over him at the thought. Half of it came from Stoli -- tigers were territorial as hell -- but the rest of it was his. "What are my animals supposed to do while I go hide?"

"It's not permanent, just until we catch these bastards. Or until we figure out a way to break this thing."

"How long will that take? And how do you know you *can* break it? You were wrong before."

"There are thousands of Arcanists in this country. If enough of us gang up on the spell, we can tear it down."

"The Feds tried that. They still haven't pulled it off."

"Well, we can't just give up. The lives of the president of United States and the entire legislative branch are at risk. Yeah, a lot of them are assholes, but the stability of this country is on the line. You can't let them kill you and wipe everybody else out in the process."

"They are *not* going to drive me away."

"Kurt, be reasonable. We could take Dave and go on a cruise. How long has it been since you had an actual vacation?"

He forced himself to start combat breathing and fight his territorial rage. It took far more work than it should have. "Dad and I used to take turns taking a few days off while the other one ran BFS."

"So leave your volunteer coordinator…"

"Karla Morgen."

"Right, Karla. Leave Karla in charge for a while. Can she handle the job?"

"Yeah, I'm sure she'd be willing to pick up the slack, but that still doesn't solve the problem. We need to catch these guys."

"According to CNN, it sounds like everybody is getting as far away from DC -- and each other -- as possible," Dave pointed out. "Even if that spell blows up the White House and the Capital building, it's not going to kill the Commander-in-Chief and the entire legislative branch."

"You're assuming they have to be in one place to die. Considering how complex this spell is and how many moving parts Indigo scattered all over the country, it could easily be designed to kill the targets no matter where they are. In fact, it would have to be designed that way. The Fords have no way of knowing where their targets are at any given time. If I were Indigo, I wouldn't have targeted buildings."

Kurt frowned and raked his hands through his hair. "To cast a spell keyed on individuals, wouldn't you need samples of their DNA? Blood, hair, something like that. That's why the Secret Service treats every cell of the president's body like nuclear waste. They burn the hair from his hairbrush and every paper cup he drinks from."

Dave nodded his big striped head. "They've been paranoid about that kind of shit ever since JFK." His voice dropped to a rumbling growl. "Fuckin' Soviet Arcs."

"Yeah, but the Fords have Spook Suits. How hard would it be for an invisible man to get into the White House?"

"Pretty damned hard. That place has more wards than metal detectors. Same with the Capital building."

Gen shook her head. "Okay, yeah. But we're talking about politicians. They still go out in public to give speeches and campaign. Think of all the hands they shake. There's any number of ways you could get hair and skin samples. And it doesn't take much."

Dave grunted. "Whatever the technical issues are, the Fords must have overcome them, or the bastards wouldn't have killed all these people to begin with."

"My thoughts exactly." She huffed out a breath and rubbed her shoulders. "I've got to get Sawyer to call that FBI Special Agent and tell her what's going on."

"Wait a minute." He touched her arm. "The Fords know that spell is still here, right?"

"Oh, yes," a female voice purred from the darkness. "I am well aware the spell was just waiting for the right sacrifice to bring it back to life." A slim woman dressed in a formfitting white bodysuit stepped out of thin air, a rifle in her hands. A white mask covered her face except for a slit across her eyes. "And look -- here you are!"

"Fuck!" he spat, and reached for his magic.

Before he could manifest, a blur of snarling orange shot past. Dave cleared twenty feet in that single leap. For a heartbeat he seemed to hang in the air, huge paws lifted.

The bear blazed out of nowhere and slammed into him like a defensive lineman sacking a quarterback. The two tumbled across the arena, a clawing, biting ball of roaring fury.

"Shit!" Gen spun toward them instinctively. It was a fatal distraction.

Indigo pounced on Genevieve from behind, whipping her left arm around her neck and jamming the point of a knife against her throat. Fisting her left hand in her hair, the Arcanist hauled her backward across the bloody sand.

"Indigo, let her go!" Sparks exploded as Kurt manifested his tiger and sprang after them. "Or I'll rip your fucking heart out!"

Snarls and roars thundered behind him from Dave's battle with the bear, but he didn't dare take his eyes off the terrorist and her captive.

Indigo sneered. "Try it and she dies."

Genevieve's desperate blue gaze met his. A trail of blood rolled down the pale column of her throat, shining wet in the moonlight.

Stoli roared in the depths of Kurt's mind, his magic vibrating the surrounding air in a rolling wave. He wanted to crush her skull with one bite.

She'd slit Gen's throat before we had time to take her down. Our only chance is to stall, play for time, look for an opportunity to take her off balance.

"Years!" Indigo screamed at him over the roars of the battling Ferals. "Do you know how many years we worked to bring off that spell? Slipping into politicians' homes in Spook Suits, searching for hair or half-eaten food -- anything we could get DNA from... And you and this cunt tried to fuck it all up!" She shook Genevieve's head by the hair, sending another bead of blood rolling from her knife.

"You can't kill the President and the entire Congress!" Gen gritted, despite the blade pricking her skin.

"Shut up, Gen!" In his fury and desperation, Kurt's magic amplified his voice until it rolled over the arena far louder than he'd intended.

"Yeah, shut up," Indigo snarled, digging the knife a little deeper as she hauled Gen backward another pace, trying to put distance between herself and Kurt's blazing tiger.

Where the hell are the cops and FBI agents who are supposed to be guarding BFS? Have these psychos killed them all? Hell, considering the number of cops they killed yesterday, why not? They'd already bought themselves the death penalty. They couldn't be executed twice.

"Your precious President campaigned on stripping Talents of our rights!" Indigo snarled. "NTRA's just the first step of tracking us so we can be rounded up and forced into internment camps -- even killed whenever the hell they want. Those bastards are doing everything possible to punish us for crimes we might commit! Not *have*, *might*! We have to get them before they get us."

"Which will legitimize their bigotry and turn them into martyrs!"

"Better them than us." She thrust the knife harder into Genevieve's throat.

Gen went rigid, throwing her chin up to avoid the vicious point. Grabbing the other woman's wrist in both hands, she fought to haul her captor's arm back, angling her head into the crook of Indigo's elbow, trying to get room enough to breathe.

Twisting her fist in Gen's hair, Indigo cranked backward, hauling the shorter woman onto her toes. "Quit fighting me, or your boyfriend is going to watch you die just like Daddy."

Kurt met Gen's eyes and gave his head a tiny shake. *Don't fight, let me handle her.* If he could just distract the little psycho... "Indigo, NTRA is unconstitutional and everybody knows it. We've got a chance in the next election. But if you assassinate five hundred people, they're going to crack down even harder on us."

"They've got it coming," the witch snarled. "Ford and I served for three decades in hellholes you've never even heard of. I was captured by Al Qaeda four years ago, and they *tortured* me. Your precious Bigot-in-Chief said they wouldn't negotiate with terrorists. Virgil had to disobey orders to rescue me. Hell, he had to kill his own Familiar or he…"

"*What*?" It was the worst betrayal a Feral could commit against his Familiar. *Then again, they've been making human sacrifices…*

"Don't judge us, you sanctimonious prick! They wouldn't let him transport Nanuq. They had to meld, so Virgil shot him. It was quick. Before Virgil got me out of there, those bastards raped me. Over. And over. And *over*. No one gave a shit because I'm just a Talent."

Her husband killed his bear to save her. No wonder she's batshit.

"Fighting for them and bleeding for them means nothing. Entitles us to nothing. They savor their smug, comfortable careers while we give up our lives, our sanity, our humanity for them, and I'm sick of it!" Her lip curled into a snarl. "They need to die. And so do you."

* * *

Dave caught a flicker out of the corner of one eye, and dared a glance. *Oh shit*! The female terrorist had grabbed Genevieve and was pulling her away from Kurt, a knife at her throat. Before he could even think about trying to help, the bear charged him. He twisted aside, avoiding the snap of huge jaws by a whisker.

God, the son of a bitch is huge! And he glowed like a torch, radiating so much power the fur on Dave's spine rose in reaction. Gen was right -- Indigo must have been strengthening him with part of those human sacrifices.

The bear reared, towering even higher as he struck out with huge forepaws. Dave threw himself into a backward leap, avoiding the swipe.

The bear was fast, but he was faster.

Ford might not be as agile as Dave, but he was bigger and more powerful. To make matters worse, Virgil's manifestation protected the man beneath from Dave's claws and teeth, but all Dave had was flesh and blood. The Feral would rip him up before he had time to crack the bastard's shell. And his own manifestation was human, with weaker muscles that would do no good at all against this bastard.

"You know you have no chance," the bear growled, mocking and vicious. "I'm going to tear out your guts and eat them!"

"Big talk, Nanook of the North."

"It's more than talk." He dropped to all fours, massive haunches bunching in preparation for an attack.

Landing on the terrorist, Dave grabbed the great barrel in his forepaws and dove for the back of the bear's neck, right behind the glowing skull. Ford roared in rage as three-inch canines sank deep.

Magic exploded against Dave's teeth in stinging slaps of pain, but he held on, digging deeper and wrenching his head, trying to break the manifestation's shell. If he could just punch through...

The bear roared, flinging himself up and up and up, onto his back legs. Dave tightened his grip and clamped down even harder on the thing's neck.

Ford shook his huge body, throwing himself from side to side. Dave started to fall and scrabbled for a better grip, but his claws raked nothing but sparks. He fell. As he tried to leap away, a glowing paw slammed into his ribs.

The impact felt like the concussion of an IED.

He hit the arena sand in a rolling tumble. Light flared in his skull, so bright he couldn't see anything at all. Ford landed on him like an anvil falling from the sky. The manifestation should not weigh any more than the man who occupied it, but magic is force, and the Feral directed all that force right down on to him.

"I'm gonna tear your throat out and complete the sacrifice." Gold eyes blazed in the creature's skull as glowing lips drew back from dagger teeth. "It'll be over before the bitch witch and Briggs even know they lost. And then I'm going to help my wife gut them both!"

Fanged jaws opened, diving toward his face.

Dave acted on sheer instinct. The manifestation flared around him, blazing with the magical energy of his raw terror. *My human manifestation's too weak to last. The bear'll rip it apart.* But it was something.

Dave swung a paw at Ford's descending muzzle with all his strength, knocking the terrorist's head back. He didn't dare let the opportunity go. He grabbed the bear around the barrel and ripped at him, hind legs raking Ford's belly from beneath.

"Motherfucker!" With a howl, the bear sprang away from him. Dave flipped onto his feet and circled away, not daring to turn his back.

Ford's voice rang with contempt. "Don't think that trick's going to save you. It won't last." Automatically following the bear's gaze, Dave realized what he meant. *My paws are glowing.* He hadn't created a human manifestation after all. He'd created the shell of a tiger -- *over his flesh and blood tiger*.

He'd never done that before. Hell, to his knowledge, nobody had done it before. *God bless adrenaline. Better make the best of it while I can.*

Dave charged, rearing to swing both clawed forepaws. The blow glanced off Ford's manifestation in a shower of sparks. The terrorist lunged, swinging at his head.

Dave ducked and sank his jaws into the bear's foreleg. He bit down, grinding his teeth, fighting to punch through. If he could just crack the shell...

"Bastard!" Ford hit him in the head in an explosion of magical sparks. "You won't be able to keep that up for long," the bear sneered. "You're only putting off the inevitable. You're going to die and your death will fuel the spell."

"In case it's escaped your attention, Nanook, I ain't Fred Briggs."

The bear laughed, a grating, alien sound. "You don't have to be. All the spell needs is a melded Feral's death." Glowing things flashed. "Which means you don't dare kill me, because my death would power the spell too. I don't care who dies, as long as those Humanist fuckers do!"

"Oh, bullshit!" Dave snarled. "The bitch shot Stoli and that didn't activate the spell!"

"The spell needs a melded Feral to work," Ford taunted. "And right now there are three of us inside the circle."

* * *

Genevieve stared into Kurt's face over Indigo's arm, fighting to breathe. She'd truly fucked this one up. Panic and rage burned in his glowing eyes, the terrible knowledge that they were both about to die. She'd failed him. It was her job to deal with the witch, to keep them from falling into traps like this one, but she'd let herself get distracted. Let them get trapped.

Now her mistake was going to cost Kurt's life -- not to mention the president's and those of the entire Congress. She'd be responsible for plunging the entire country into chaos.

No! Goddamnit, no! There had to be something

she could do.

She met Kurt's gaze, trying to talk to him with her eyes, trying to reach out to him. *Jump her, Kurt! Don't worry about me!*

A massive glowing shape rolled into her peripheral vision, blazing magic. The bear and Dave clawed at one another, power snapping around them like the electrical discharge around a live wire.

"Shit," Indigo snarled and jerked her aside, trying to avoid the battling predators, probably worried that Dave's six hundred pounds were going to land on her. Even Kurt sidestepped, looking toward his friend and the bear.

Hauling Genevieve, she backed away. "Damn it, Virgil, kill him! Finish that cat off and come help me!"

This is my chance. Now, while the witch is distracted. Gen reached out with her aura, groping until her mind brushed Kurt's. The spell they'd cast when they made love snapped into place. It probably wouldn't have worked with anyone but a melded Feral with the Talent to bind mind to mind.

She couldn't so much read his thoughts as see flashes of images, feel his emotions -- and his cat's, and their joined magic, roiling against her senses.

An idea hit her. *No way in hell. My magic doesn't even work that way…*

But his does. She concentrated, imagined it until she could see it in her mind.

And sent it to him.

Kurt's eyes went wide. She felt his incredulity, his instant rejection of the image.

But Stoli -- *Stoli wants to do it. Now, now* before the witch sensed what they planned and cut Genevieve's throat. *Now,* while Indigo was so fatally distracted by her husband's battle with Dave.

Genevieve dropped every mental shield she had, knowing she was leaving herself completely vulnerable to the witch's magic.

But that was the only way it could work.

She felt the shadow of Kurt's fear through their fragile link, the terror that this impossible chance would fail and destroy her, that her body wouldn't be able to channel so much magic, that it would fry her like an egg.

They did it anyway.

Now! Kurt and Stoli surged through their bound auras and into Genevieve's.

And into her mind.

Alien images, alien thoughts, raw emotions she never felt before flooded her consciousness. It wasn't her magic -- her brain wasn't even capable of using that kind of power.

But she'd made herself into a conduit anyway, and Kurt and Stoli used it. Together they seized her aura, and through it her body. Together, Kurt and Stoli drove Genevieve's elbow into the witch's ribs with all the tiger's raw power.

Something crunched as pain exploded through her upper arm, but it was nothing next to the sheer alien burn that was Stoli.

With a howl of agony and surprise, Indigo flew backward as if hit with a giant baseball bat. Genevieve whirled and leaped for the witch, Kurt's tiger blazing around her. It felt as if someone had poured gasoline over her brain and tossed a lit match through her eye sockets. She shrieked at the pain even as the witch went down under Stoli's charge. Indigo screamed and slashed at her with the knife. Sparks flew, but the blade didn't penetrate the manifestation. Stoli's jaws closed over the Arc's skull, and she screeched, voice spiraling high with stark terror.

Bone crunched. The scream cut off.

Indigo went limp, magic draining away as the life fled her body. Genevieve could barely feel it for the searing pain of using a Talent her brain wasn't designed for. "Get out!" she screamed. "Get out of my head!"

And the tiger fled, flowing out through her aura and back to Kurt's.

The minute he was gone, she fell on her face, curling into a helpless ball, her arms wrapping around her skull. She'd never felt such pain -- as if at any moment, her head would detonate and blow chunks of bone and brain all over the arena.

Am I having a stroke? It was possible. Kurt and Stoli had hit her like a lightning bolt frying a computer. She could almost smell burning hair.

Kurt. Where's Kurt? Despite her pain, she managed to turn her closed eyes toward her lover. His manifestation blazed as he raced toward the knot of glowing fury that was Dave and Ford.

She wanted to watch, to make sure they didn't need her, but blackness rolled over her consciousness. The last thing she saw was Kurt's tiger flying through the air in a magnificent, impossible leap.

Chapter Eighteen

Rage burned through Kurt, blinding and vicious.

Ford had Dave down on the ground, ripping at him. He could see the weaknesses Dave had raked in the bear manifestation, the dimmer tracks of slashes and puncture wounds from teeth and claws.

Kurt landed on Ford's back like a Bengal tiger on a water buffalo. Roaring, the bear reared, attempting to throw Kurt off. Sinking all four sets of claws deep, Kurt held on, his own roars shaking the air.

There! Four dim puncture wounds at the base of the bear's glowing skull. Dave had damn near punched right through the creature's manifestation to the man beneath.

Now it was Kurt's turn.

As Dave gripped the bear from beneath, Kurt dug his claws deep and bit into those punctures. His teeth sank in -- and stopped, not quite breaking through. Focusing his magic, focusing his rage and Stoli's, blind with frenzy, he sank his teeth and claws deeper. His enemy's magic burned and popped against his, but he ignored the pain. Digging deeper, deeper... Magic flared, burning his senses, but he ignored the pain, ignored it just as Genevieve had. They had to kill this fucker. *Now.*

Die, you bastard. Die for Dad. Die for Gen!

Ford strained against him, magic blazing around them in a rain of Fourth of July sparks as the three men's auras clashed. Kurt crunched down harder, harder, ignoring the pain...

"Die!" he howled from his human mouth, as Ford cursed him viciously.

BOOM! CRACK!

With a sound like a lightning bolt hitting right in

front of his face, the bear vanished. Kurt dropped. He landed on something soft, heard a pained human grunt -- Ford's voice, un-amplified by magic.

Kurt and Dave had drained him so badly he could no longer hold the manifestation.

"Shit!" Dave gasped, and flung all four limbs wide to release the unshielded man, who still lay sprawled across his furred chest. His tiger manifestation vanished, leaving only the flesh and blood cat.

He's going to let me have the kill! Still manifested, Kurt reared over his foe, lifting a clawed paw, ready to rip the bastard's head off his shoulders.

"No!" Dave roared. "Don't kill him! You'll set off the fucking spell!"

Kurt barely heard him, aware of nothing but his rage, his bloodlust. Fred had died just a few feet away. Indigo had almost killed Gen, and Virgil had just tried to kill his best friend.

No, he wouldn't use his claws. He'd bite the fucker's head off. Kurt opened his jaws wide…

Ford's eyes blazed Feral gold, his face twisted in terror, rage and anguish. "Do it!"

Dave's paw slapped Kurt hard across his manifestation's muzzle. His claws were retracted, but it was still a stunning blow, with all the tiger's great power behind it. Had it not been for Kurt's shell, it would have broken his neck.

"Don't kill him, Goddamnit!" Dave snapped. "Ford's death would activate the fucking spell! It's what they want! Do you want to kill us all?"

Kurt recoiled. *Oh, hell, he's right.* But Stoli didn't care. He wanted to watch his enemy die -- die for killing Fred, die for threatening Gen and Dave, die for all the men he'd killed.

"Your daddy begged me like a pussy for his life," Ford sneered, his face white. "He was gutless. He wasn't even a fit sacrifice!"

Kurt screamed in rage, and the sound emerged as a shattering roar. In the back of his mind, the voice of sanity cried, *I can't! I'll kill us all...*

But the rage did not give a shit.

Kurt started to fall on Ford...

And his father's voice spoke. Not a memory, not a voice in Kurt's head, but his *voice*, as if Fred was standing right beside him. "You know how to control your cat. Don't let this bastard win!"

The sheer shock of it jarred him back to sanity like a bucket of cold water in the face. Swallowing, Kurt closed his eyes, wrestling with Stoli's fury. The tiger fought him, wild with rage and bloodlust.

If we kill him, Genevieve will be the one to suffer. Her life will be destroyed. She's our mate. She's part of us. We have to protect her. Stoli's rage began to drain.

Rolling to his feet, Dave sank his jaws into Virgil's shoulder and dragged him back, ignoring the killer's shout of pain. The man kicked and fought and bellowed as the tiger hauled him toward the arena's open gate.

Kurt looked around, instinctively seeking his father's ghost. "Dad?"

There was no answer.

Of course not, idiot. That was Dave. It had been one of those magical vocal tricks the furry smartass loved. *And it's a damn good thing he suckered me, or I would've killed us all.*

As Dave dragged Virgil past Genevieve and Indigo's body, the assassin got a look at his wife and howled like a banshee. "Indy! Indigo!" He began to fight in earnest despite the pain, thrashing savagely as he struggled to wrench free of Dave's grip. His yells of grief and fury became a screech of agony again as Dave clamped down harder. Kurt heard a crunch. Ford went limp as the tiger dragged him from the circle.

Safely beyond it, Dave pinned the killer down with one big paw, opened his massive jaws, and enclosed Ford's head in his teeth.

For a moment Kurt thought he was going to bite down, but then Dave's voice sounded. "Try to manifest, motherfucker, and I'm going to find out how your brain tastes."

Kurt dropped his head and stood still, concentrating on controlling his anger. *That was way, way too close.*

When he was confident he wouldn't lose it again, his gaze sought Genevieve. He froze.

She lay limp in the circle in a pitiful heap, not far from Indigo's bloody corpse. It was a damn good thing the Arc terrorist's magic wasn't great enough to power the spell, or they would've been fucked.

"Genevieve," he said, and started toward her. She didn't move. Terror stabbed his heart, and he broke into a run. Falling to his knees beside her, Kurt pressed two fingers against her throat.

To feel her pulse throb beneath his fingers.

Alive. He sagged in relief. *She's still alive, but she needs an ambulance. And I need a cell phone.* Kurt patted his back pocket, but it was empty -- his cell probably still lay on the blanket where they'd made love. He patted Gen down, but she didn't have one either.

Grimacing in distaste, he moved to Indigo's body and searched it despite the blood and gore that covered her. Stoli had done quite a job on her head.

It turned out she did have a cell phone. It was locked, of course, but he thumbed the word "emergency" on the lock screen and listened to the beeps dialing 911.

Crisply, Kurt filled in the county dispatcher, who told him to hang tight while she sent ambulance and county units. He hung up and returned his attention to the woman he loved.

Gently Kurt stroked Genevieve's cheek, then ran his fingers through the tangled red riot of her hair. *She's still alive.* He could feel the heat of her magic against his skin, faint, far fainter than it should be, but it was there. "Gen, wake up. Let me see those pretty eyes." His voice cracked, and he fought to control it. *Oh God, let her be all right!*

Her eyes flickered beneath closed lids, then finally opened. "Kurt?" She blinked as if she couldn't quite focus.

Relief rolled through his chest. "Yeah, baby, it's me. How are you feeling?"

"Don't talk... so loud." Genevieve closed her eyes and licked her lips. "My head feels like it's... going to split open."

"I'm not surprised. That was a hell of a chance we took."

"The spell!" Her eyes flew wide and she tried to sit up, then sucked in a gasp of pain. Tenderly, he pushed her back down as she clutched at him. "Did they set off the..."

"No. We stopped it. Indigo's dead. Ford's still alive -- barely. Dave dragged him outside the circle." Kurt smiled grimly. "Broke the bastard's shoulder, judging by the crunch."

She went back down with a groan of relief. "I'm surprised you let him live."

"Believe me, I was tempted." He grimaced. "Dave told me that if I killed the fucker, it would activate the spell."

Genevieve's eyes flew wide in horror. "What?"

"Yeah. Evidently you were right -- it just required that a melded Feral die. Anybody would have done -- me, Dave or Ford." He picked up her hand, small and cool within his, with barely any magic to it at all. He was pretty sure the magic would come back, but he had no idea how long it would take. "And I wanted to kill him anyway. Not just for Dad or those cops, but for what they tried to do to you." He bent over her and kissed her with exquisite care, just a brush of his lips on hers, afraid to cause her any more pain.

Gen made a little sobbing sound against his mouth, and he started to pull away. Her hand caught the back of his head. "No," she breathed. "No, kiss me."

So he did, savoring the taste of her mouth, the petal soft texture of her lips. Worry nudged him into breaking off the kiss to look down at her. "Other than your head, are you hurting anywhere else?"

Genevieve swallowed, drawing his attention to the dried blood on her slender throat. "Scratches here and there. Nothing bad." Her eyes slipped close. "But I wouldn't turn down a couple of Excedrin."

In the distance, his tiger hearing detected the wail of approaching sirens. "Sounds like your Excedrin is on the way."

She stirred, but he held her down gently. "Speaking of cops, where are the guys who were supposed to be guarding BFS?"

"I have no idea. But it's not a good sign that none of them put in an appearance during the fight. I'm sure people heard the roaring for miles around, much less inside the park."

Genevieve looked sick. "The terrorists killed them."

Kurt was very much afraid they had. "Let's hope not." His instincts demanded he stay with Genevieve, but he was fairly sure she was all right. He was less sure about the cops. "I'd better go check. Will you be all right?"

"I'm fine, just a headache." She grimaced. "A really bad, bad headache. But the terrorists are down, so we should be safe."

Kurt nodded and rose to his feet to head for the gate, where Dave sat patiently. He had one paw planted on the terrorist's chest, but he no longer clamped Ford's head in his jaws. "How's the prisoner?"

"Unconscious." Dave sounded more than a little smug.

"Couldn't happen to a nicer asshole. You'd probably better get off him. We don't want to set off the cops."

"Good point. How's Gen?"

"Nursing a headache, and damn lucky she didn't get her throat cut."

"I noticed." He flicked an ear. "The po-po are pulling into the drive. Come to think of it, you'd probably better stay put. If you go wandering around in the dark, somebody might shoot you."

That, too, was a damn good point. He turned around and headed back to Genevieve. He couldn't help those poor cops faster than the EMTs anyway.

Assuming they could be helped.

* * *

As they'd suspected, the cop and the two FBI agents assigned to guard BFS were dead. They'd had their throats slit or their necks broken. Their bodies were still warm, as if they'd been eliminated just before the terrorists had shown up in the arena.

Genevieve went to the hospital with Kurt to be checked out, but it turned out neither of them had sustained any serious injuries that couldn't be taken care of with a few stitches.

Kurt drove them home a couple of hours later, his hands light on the wheel.

Genevieve eyed him and felt some of her lingering tension drain. Grief still hung over him -- and probably would for a while -- but the anxiety caused by the terrorists' threats had lifted.

She felt considerably lighter herself. "The good news is, with Indigo dead, her spells will be easier to break."

He flicked a glance at her as he stopped at a red light, concern in his glowing eyes. "I thought it was drawing its power from the earth's magic. Are you sure it's going be that easy?"

Genevieve shook her head. "I just used those same sigils myself, remember? They draw part of their energy from their caster, which means Indigo's death should create a weakness I'll be able to use to dismantle it. I won't know for sure until I give it a shot tomorrow. I'd like to try now, but I really need to recharge first."

Kurt flashed her a wicked grin. "I'll be happy to help."

"I'm sure you would. And I'm looking forward to it."

His smile faded. "What about the other spells? Will you have to travel around the country to take all of them down?"

"I sent the sigils to our FBI contact, along with an explanation of what they do. I don't think the Fed

Arcanists will have a problem. Hell, they'll probably be able to take them down faster than I will."

"Yeah, but some of those spells have been around for months, getting stronger the whole time."

"Could be. It may take several Arcs working together to dismantle the older ones. Still, I won't be surprised if they're not all down by this time tomorrow." She shrugged. "Though I thought that the last time, and it turned out I was wrong. I'll do my best to dispel the arena casting before the funeral."

Kurt grimaced. "Speaking of the funeral, that's going to be a madhouse. The reporters will be all over us. I'm going to have to give a press conference, but I'm damned if I'm going to do it tomorrow." He curled his handsome upper lip. "The vultures can wait a day. It wouldn't hurt them to show Dad a little respect."

As if on cue, his cell phone rang from the cup holder. "See who that is, would you?"

Gen picked it up and checked the display. "It's that guy from the *Laurelton Leaf.*"

"He must have contacts on the force."

"Want me to answer?" she asked over the shrilling ring tone.

"Hell no." He hesitated a long moment before shooting her glance. "I realize I have no right to ask you this, considering the amount of time you've already spent away from your house and business, but would you consider staying a couple more days?"

Gen flashed him a deliberately light grin. "Would I? I'd be downright grateful. If I try to go home, I'll be swarmed with reporters without BFS's gates to keep them away." A new thought struck her, and she frowned. "How's Dave?" She knew the tiger had used the house phone to call Kurt while they were in the ER.

"He's got some nasty bites and punctures. One of the EMTs bandaged them up until he could get hold of the vet." Correctly interpreting her frown, he added, "A human doctor isn't licensed to treat tigers."

"I should be able to do something for him once my magic recovers. Hopefully tomorrow -- or should I say today, given it's 2 AM."

"We have got to start getting more sleep," Kurt said.

Genevieve took note of that "we" and smiled a little.

Evidently reading that smile, Kurt asked quietly, "Is there a 'we'?"

"Do you want there to be?"

"I asked you first."

"You're the one who doesn't believe romances with non-Ferals can work."

"That was what Dad thought."

"Given his wife, I don't blame him."

Kurt hesitated. "I'll admit, a couple of weeks ago I wouldn't have been able to imagine a relationship with a witch. But you've taught me that just because my mother was a manipulative bitch doesn't mean all Arcs are."

She smiled, and her heart lifted. Maybe they did have a chance after all.

Maybe.

* * *

They got home to find BFS swarming with cops yet again. They'd already answered questions from a detective back at the hospital -- evidently Sawyer was busy interrogating Ford -- so they left the deputies to do their jobs and headed for the house.

They found Dave curled up asleep in the living room, his massive red-gold body covered in bandages.

Evidently the vet had made an emergency house call, stitched up his cuts and left.

He jerked awake when they came in. "Oh, there you are. Good." Dave searched Genevieve's tired face with concern. "Are you okay, kid?"

She dropped to her knees beside him and sighed. "I'm fine. Just some bruises and a couple of interesting cuts. I wasn't the one fighting the polar bear. How are you?"

The tiger grimaced, revealing impressive canines. "I have stitches. Lots and lots of stitches."

Genevieve nodded. "Yeah, I gathered that from all the bandages. I'll heal you up in the morning, or the afternoon, or whenever I get enough juice to do it."

He nodded. "I'd appreciate that."

"You need any water or anything?" Kurt asked.

"Nah, the vet hooked me up. Phone's been ringing off the hook with calls from reporters ever since you left." He grinned. "You should've seen that FBI agent try to interrogate me. I've never seen somebody try to be a hard ass while looking so thoroughly spooked. It was funny as hell."

"You're a scary, scary guy. You also saved my ass today, buddy. If you hadn't been there…"

"Well, if you're feeling grateful, you could always find me a melded girl, and we'll be even." He pricked his ears forward with a sly grin. "I'm craving pussy like you would not believe."

Kurt shot Genevieve a look. "I feel your pain."

Dave laughed and slanted Gen a look, flipping his tail. "No, you don't. You've got a girl."

When they finally headed to bed, it wasn't to make love. They were both too battered, too drained magically and emotionally.

Instead, they curled up together, face to face.

Genevieve stared into the deep gold of Kurt's eyes. Extending her aura, she touched him even as his fingers slid up and down her arm in feathering caresses. The touch felt so good, she closed her eyes, to see Stoli lying next to her in the darkness, gold eyes on her. He made that funny huffing little sound tigers use for a greeting, the one Kurt called a chuff.

Last week, she probably would've jumped right out of bed at the sight. Today she just stroked her aura over his as if it were a hand.

She opened her eyes just as Kurt leaned forward and took her mouth. The kiss was slow and gentle, a lush exploration of lips and tongue.

Powerful arms wrapped around her, and she moved into them with a sound somewhere between a sigh and a moan. He rolled onto his back, pulling her on top of him. She listened to his heart thump against her ear, slow and strong. Her hands tightened where she gripped his arm. His biceps felt like silk-covered steel. "I came so close to losing you," she said, her voice sounded ragged in her own ears.

His arms tightened around her, hard and warm and strong. "But you didn't."

A peaceful silence fell between them. Kurt began to comb his fingers through her curls in gentle tugs. "I love your hair."

She smiled, and slid her hand down to the center of his chest to tangle in the soft curls there. "I love yours, too."

"You sure you don't want me to shave?"

"Nah. Tigers are supposed to be a little fuzzy."

"Well, I am that." Stroking her shoulders in slow caresses, he relaxed under her. Smiling, she let the sound of his heartbeat lull her to sleep.

* * *

The funeral two days later was as painful as Kurt had known it would be -- though at least nobody was trying to kill them.

The church was standing room only. It looked as if the entire town had turned out, including everybody who'd ever volunteered at BFS, along with a large contingent of grieving cops who faced painful funerals of their own over the next few days.

Kurt managed to get through the eulogy without breaking down, mostly using the iron self-control his father taught him.

At the internment, he accepted the folded flag from Fred's coffin with steady hands. He even managed to endure "Taps," -- played by a bugler rather than Dave this time -- though his eyes stung.

It helped that Genevieve wrapped her fingers around his hand and held on tight, giving him her silent support. He wished Fred had had an opportunity to get to know her better. Had a chance to see that it was possible to love without being used.

Kurt's mother, fortunately, was conspicuous by her absence. It seemed she'd taken his threat seriously.

As if reaction to the anger that ran through him at that thought, Genevieve's magic brushed against his own, cool, calming, offering comfort. He looked down at her lovely profile -- at the straight line of her nose, the curve of the soft lips he'd tasted the night before. She looked up at him, and he saw the shimmer of tears in her eyes. Her hand tightened on his in a supporting squeeze, and he felt the grip of grief ease.

A little.

* * *

Following the service, the house filled up with people who came to offer their respects.

Dave hadn't been able to attend the funeral, of

course, though Kurt had offered to take him anyway. The tiger turned him down, reasoning the public was understandably twitchy around Ferals right now.

He made up for it as the usual throng of volunteers surrounded him. Though Dave seemed his usual joking, laughing self, Kurt knew it was an act. Tigers couldn't cry, but there was grief in the droop of his whiskers and the set of his ears, and his tail lay still on the floor without its usual energetic flips and twitches.

"There you are." Sawyer walked up to Kurt, as he stood next to Genevieve. The detective looked tired, as if he hadn't slept in days -- and he probably hadn't. Still, he wore a suit and tie and looked freshly shaved, and his grip as he shook Kurt's hand was warm. "I managed to question Ford before the FBI took him away from me. He admitted they planned to lure you into the arena, but you showed up before they had a chance. Bastard said they figured even if he lost the fight with you, the spell would still go off."

"Asshole." He shook his head, then met Sawyer's gaze. "I'm so sorry about your officers. I wish we could have prevented it."

The cop shook his head. "There was no way you could have known. They killed our guys fast and silently -- took them only about five minutes -- right before they headed to the arena. Ford said they figured they had only fifteen or twenty minutes at most before dispatch would realize the deputy and feds hadn't checked in and send someone to investigate. Just to make sure, Indigo cast a spell to block cell transmission to keep you from calling out."

"So that's why I couldn't get through to you," Gen said. "I wondered about that at the time, but I figured we had to check the arena anyway."

"Good thing you did." The grim look in his eyes lightened a little. "You three saved a hell of a lot of lives last night. Bad as it is now, it could have been much, much worse if not for you."

Feeling uncomfortable, Kurt shrugged. "Thanks, but I came a little too close to blowing it all to hell myself."

"But you didn't. You're a hero, son, and I can't tell you how delighted I am. Not least because Ford is so pissed about it. That's the whole reason they staged that attack on the town square, by the way. They'd hoped to kill you, but even if they didn't, the witch added that spell trap as much to destroy your reputation as to kill Gen. They'd been worried that you'd be painted as the hero of the piece, and neither one of them could stand that idea."

"What's going to happen to Ford?" Gen asked.

Sawyer shrugged. "The Feds have charged him with five-hundred-plus counts of attempted magical assassination, plus fourteen counts of magical terrorism resulting in death. They've got him in a warded cell that will keep him from being able to manifest his bear. If he's convicted, he'll be executed."

"Good. Fry him."

"We're going to try." The FBI Arcanist Katilia Doran stepped out of the press of people. Elegant and tall, she wore a simple black sheath dress and pearls. "I wanted to tell you again how sorry I am about your father. The more I hear about him, the more I regret I didn't get a chance to meet him."

Kurt smiled. "So am I. He would have liked you. He always appreciated people with a low BQ." When she lifted a brow, he explained, "Bullshit quotient."

"Ahh." She smiled, then hesitated a moment before sighing. "I realize this is probably not a particularly good time, but I'm giving a press conference and I want you to be there. You're the hero of the hour." Her gaze flicked to Genevieve, and then Dave, who had wandered over to listen. "You and Ms. Reyes. And Dave, of course."

Kurt frowned. "I have no interest in…"

"Yeah, I realize it probably goes against the grain. But we need you front and center, reminding people that though there are evil assholes who are Talents, most of us aren't like that."

Genevieve slanted her a look. "Especially given NTRA."

"Exactly."

"So even though we saved their lives, those ungrateful bastards are still going to try to strip us of our rights?"

The FBI agent shrugged. "I'm sure they do feel grateful, but the president made the registration act the centerpiece of his campaign. He's not going to forget it just because you almost died trying to keep him alive."

Dave's tail whipped. "He'll say it proves his point that Talents need to be tracked like sex offenders."

"Probably. But if we play this right, we can make them all look like ungrateful bigots."

"Which is pretty much exactly what they are," Genevieve said tartly.

Kurt sighed. "Fine. I'll do the press conference."

"Good. I'd like to hold it in front of the arena with you, Genevieve, that Feral cop…"

"Jake Nolan," Kurt supplied.

"Yeah, Jake." She looked down at the tiger. "… And Dave and all his many bandages."

Chapter Nineteen

The next day, Kurt found himself enduring a press conference after Gen and Agent Doran took down the arena spell.

He listened, uncomfortable, as Agent Doran described the fight and lauded their heroism in terms that glowed brighter than Stoli's manifestation.

The reporter from CNN held up a hand. When Doran called on him, he directed the question to Kurt. "The Humanists are trying to push through NTRA, which will force Talents like you to register. Why did you risk your life to save people who seem to view you as an enemy?"

Kurt had been expecting the question, so he didn't let it throw him. "I'm an Arcane Corps combat veteran. I took an oath to defend the United States Constitution. Whether I agree with the President's politics or not is beside the point. I'm not going to let five hundred people be murdered if I can help it."

Another reporter directed a question to Gen. "Ms. Reyes, you're not a vet, yet you risked your life too. That bear could have ripped you apart, and the female terrorist attempted to cut your throat."

Genevieve shrugged. "I just did what generations of Talents have done. We could've stayed in the shadows during World War II, let the Nazis and their Talents win. Instead we came out of the closet and fought for our country. Just as we have in every war the US has ever fought, even when you didn't know we were there."

One of the bloggers glowered. "But doesn't this prove the Humanists are right? How long are we going to let these... people run around killing normal Americans?"

Gen's cool mask didn't even crack. "Yes, Indigo and Virgil Ford were terrorists. And yes, they were Talents. But that doesn't make us all criminals. There are at least three million Talents in this country. If even a tenth of us were killers, you'd have even more death and destruction than these two managed to commit. Instead we do everything in our power to keep the public safe. But if the Humanists make us second-class citizens, you'll be providing mentally ill fanatics with a justification for their crimes. Indigo Ford cited NTRA as the reason they decided to do all this…"

"So are you saying you think that was justified?"

"No, what I'm saying is the vast majority of serial killers, sex offenders, terrorists, and murderers are men, but we haven't made men second-class citizens. This is no different."

"But one man can't kill as many people as a witch!" the blogger spat.

In the depths of Kurt's mind, Stoli growled. Kurt took a slow, deep breath, working to contain his growing anger.

Genevieve's aura brushed against his like the stroke of a hand over his skin. He looked down at her and smiled in gratitude. He hadn't really been in danger of losing control, but that one touch made it easier to focus.

Looking up into his eyes, Gen smiled, and he smiled back. They'd get through this together.

"By the way," Dave said into the jumble of questions, his magic giving his voice a booming amplification that startled everyone into silence. "If there are any melded Feral tigresses out there, I enjoy long swims, playing Call of Duty, and turkey dinners." He gave them an enormous, toothy grin. "And I'm looking for love. Call me." He held up one paw against an ear as if miming a phone.

The reporters laughed and the ugly tension eased.

Kurt blew out a breath. Trust Dave and his wicked sense of humor to save the day again.

* * *

After the press conference, Dave asked Gen to come to his tree house and work a healing now. "I'd like to get to know you a little better," he told her, giving her a tiger sort of smile. "Since it seems we're going to be spending a lot of time together."

"Oh, God. I can almost hear the rimshots now." She gathered her supplies and headed over to the tree house with him. Jake, newly released from the hospital, joined them. The two ragged on each other until she finally had to tell them to shut up so she could concentrate on the spell.

Fortunately, the vet had done a good job on Dave's wounds, so the casting wasn't as difficult as it could have been. Gen felt pretty good when she headed back to the house as the sun began to set.

As she approached the house, she saw a plume of smoke roll up from the back yard, accompanied by the mouthwatering scent of roasting meat. Kurt must have something on the grill.

She walked around to the back yard and opened the gate in the privacy fence.

He looked up from the big brick outdoor grill. "How do you like your steaks?"

"Medium rare. What's all this?" A sweet, nervous anticipation tensed her muscles as she noticed he'd again spread the BFS blanket they'd used before on the grass, piled with an inviting collection of pillows.

Off to one side, the picnic table stood covered in

a white tablecloth and gently steaming plates of food. Champagne chilled in a bucket near a spray of bright orange blooms.

Walking over to the grill, she found a pair of thick ribeyes smoking over the coals. Kurt flipped them with a graceful gesture of one big hand.

The light dawned. "I wondered why Dave wanted me to do the healing at his house."

"Dave always was a great wingman." He looked up from the steaks and grinned, but there was a shadow of something in the back of his eyes. Nervousness? "I just wanted to thank you for everything you've done. I'd probably be in jail and a lot of people would be dead if not for you."

Gen leaned in for a kiss, opening her lips to sink into it, drinking his mouth, savoring the taste. She caught his lower lip between her teeth and gave it a gentle tug before easing back. "I'd say the rescue was mutual."

Male heat flared in his eyes, and his smile turned hungry. He lifted a hand and cupped her cheek. "Either way, thank you."

His hand felt warm and calloused against her skin as power flared in his eyes. For a dizzy moment, it seemed she was falling into that golden glow.

Something brushed against her aura, and she heard a rumble in the depths of her mind: Stoli. There was something distinctly satisfied in the sound of the tiger's voice, almost a purr.

Genevieve's heart began to hammer in her chest, and she had to work to steady her voice. "If you don't turn those steaks, they're going to end up charred."

"Damn!" He jerked around and flipped them over.

A ripe silence fell between them, sensual as the

fragrant smoke. Standing so close, she could feel the magic of his aura, thrumming with his desire -- and a trace of uncharacteristic nerves.

She dropped her gaze, and her eyes widened as they fell on his zipper. *Yep, he's definitely turned on.* That was a very formidable erection forming a thick ridge behind the fabric of his jeans. Her nipples tightened as her pussy clenched.

Gen's eyes flicked up to meet the bright glow of his. He jerked his eyes away and flipped the steaks neatly onto a plate. "Come on. Let's find out if I can cook."

Genevieve followed him. "Somehow, the way you put that doesn't exactly fill me with confidence."

"Don't worry, I started learning my way around the kitchen when I was six. Mom wasn't exactly Betty Crocker, so it was that or starve."

Genevieve sat down on one bench, eying the china, silver and crystal champagne flutes. Besides grilled ears of corn and fresh vegetables, there was a broccoli casserole, macaroni salad, and a gorgeous strawberry cake she knew volunteers had dropped off that afternoon. An arrangement of fiery orange blooms with dark speckles stood in a crystal vase.

She smiled up at him. "Tiger lilies? Cute."

"I thought so." He picked up a bottle of champagne, aiming it away from them both. He sent the cork flying with a flick of his thumb as easily as if she could've popped the tab on the can of Coke. The champagne foamed up, and he poured it skillfully into the tall crystal glasses.

Genevieve eyed the label. She'd drunk more than her share of expensive booze in the course of rubbing elbows with the rich, and her eyebrows flew up. "That is not cheap champagne."

"You're worth it." He raised the glass to her. "To the bravest woman I've ever known."

Genevieve's cheeks heated. "You're not so bad yourself."

The champagne was crisp and light. When she lowered her glass, she found Kurt watching her, obviously waiting for the verdict. "It's delicious. But then it better be, for what you paid for it."

He shrugged. "It's a celebration."

She gestured toward the pallet with her fork. "I think it's a little bit more than that. Are we planning to cast another spell?"

"The first one is still there, right? It's permanent." The way his voice dropped on that last word gave it a lot of significance. More lightly, he continued. "I thought we'd recharge your magical batteries again, what with healing Dave and breaking that spell."

She gave him a wicked little grin. "Well, I'd never turn down a… charge."

He laughed.

The steak was every bit as good as it looked. He'd marinated it in some combination of wine and spices. The corn had a perfect crunch and the potatoes steamed, soft and delicious.

At last she sat back with a sated moan. "If I eat any more, I'm going to be too full to recharge." She grinned wickedly on the last word.

Kurt's eyes flashed gold. "I guess we'll save the cake for later." Rising, he moved around the table to take her hand and tug her to her feet and into his arms.

The kiss was deep and slow and tasted of champagne and hickory smoke. She sighed into his mouth. At last he drew back to give her a little smile. Taking her hand, he led her toward the pallet.

Kurt turned to face her, grabbed the hem of his shirt and pulled it off. Genevieve's eyes widened. He reached for the snap of his jeans then paused. "Unless I'm jumping the gun?"

"No," she said hoarsely. "You're not."

She watched, mouth dry, as he stripped off his jeans and toed out of his boots. Deliberately, he folded his clothing and put it aside, muscles flexing with every move.

It made for a hell of a nice view -- the width of his shoulders, the power of his arms, the length of those long, hard thighs and powerful calves. Some well-built men tended to look short-legged, but his were in proportion to his considerable height.

His thick shaft bobbed over tight, firm balls fuzzed with soft hair. She watched, heart hammering with anticipation.

This is going to be good.

Kurt straightened and faced her, stepping in close. His fingers found the buttons of her blouse, flicking them open one by one. Genevieve felt acutely conscious of the swell of her breasts as he revealed them. She'd worn a pretty bra, all peach lace and satin from Victoria's Secret.

She'd never been more thankful to have expensive taste in underwear.

"I promise not to destroy this one." Kurt flashed her a boy's smile, all mischief and amusement. Then he looked down at her breasts, and suddenly there was nothing of the boy in that smile at all.

Genevieve lowered her arms and shrugged her shirt off her shoulders, letting it fall in a soft pile at her feet. But before she could pick up the shirt and fold it, he stepped full against her. His cock nudged her belly, and she licked her lips, staring up into his eyes. Again, she had that sense of Stoli sharing his gaze.

His mouth swooped to cover hers in another of those impossibly sweet kisses. She rose on her toes and wrapped her arms around his neck, kissing him back, drinking in the taste and heat of his mouth.

For a moment she felt the brush of fur against her ass. Stoli again, playing with her aura. It was disconcerting, but she found she wasn't at all frightened. She'd stopped being afraid of Stoli after they'd melded in the arena.

Kurt pulled away, his fingers brushing up over her shoulders. Satin slid over her skin as he pulled her bra off. She hadn't even noticed him unfastening it in the depths of that kiss. "You are good."

"Why, thank you, ma'am." He flashed the smile again. His gaze flicked to the tips of her breasts, drawn into peaks. There was no humor at all in his gaze, only raw need.

Bending, he cupped her soft flesh in both hands. His mouth covered her nipple in a hot delicious kiss, deep and suckling, that made her breath catch as he lifted her off her feet.

Kurt held her easily, tugging the other nipple as he nibbled ever so gently. She shivered at the hot sensation, shivered again as his magic surged against hers. She could feel the heat of his need, could sense how much he loved her.

Genevieve hooked her legs around his waist as his tongue tip drew wet designs over her breasts. Teeth closed ever so gently over the tip, tightening in a tiny bite, then tugging backward.

He released her for another licking swirl, feeding at her lazily, until her eyes rolled back at the stark pleasure. She wrapped her arms around his head and rested her chin on top of his head.

His tongue licked and swirled over her nipple, each sensation as delicate as a brush of a butterfly's wing, yet sweetly piercing and intense. Her breathing roughened as she dreamily stroked his brawny shoulders.

God, she craved this. Craved him. She hadn't realized just how alone she'd been until she'd found him. The only contact she'd had in far too long had been the brush of her magic against someone else's aura.

As satisfying as that could be, what she'd really wanted was this -- this perfect blend of physical touch, emotional closeness and the roil of his magic.

No man had ever touched her like this -- not just her heart, not just her body or her magic, but all the way down to the soul.

His hands tightened on her ass as he held her so effortlessly, making her feel like a featherweight in his arms.

Safe.

But she wanted to touch him, kiss him, run her tongue over all that smooth skin, flexing muscle and soft hair.

She rolled her hips against him, loving the thick promise of his erection butting against her belly.

"Put me down," Genevieve breathed. "I want to touch you."

He made a low growling sound and dropped to his knees. Her arms tightened convulsively, but where any other man might have had to put her down, Kurt was so strong, he balanced her weight easily.

God, he makes me feel… safe. Cherished.

Kurt spilled her onto her back. She lay looking up at him as he rocked back on his heels, his eyes dwelling possessively on her breasts. Her nipples ached, flushed and hard from his attentions. One corner of his mouth curled up in a wicked little smile.

He reached for the snap of her jeans. Gen canted her hips up, helping him slide them off. Catching her panties and waistband, Kurt tugged both down with one long pull. His gaze heated with hunger as he glimpsed the copper threads of her bush, intent eyes narrowing. His pupils expanded in the glowing rings of his irises.

Pausing, Kurt wrestled her shoes off with an impatient growl that made her smile. He pulled her jeans the rest of the way off, then put them aside with his own clothing.

For a moment they just stared at one another. Genevieve could feel her heart pounding so hard, her breasts juddered with the beat.

Gold glowing eyes scanned down her body, pausing at nipples and pussy while she admired the muscular width of his shoulders and the elegant jut of his cock.

Kurt looked up and met her gaze, and it seemed the world fell away under his demanding, possessive gaze.

Yet there was tenderness in it, a need for more than just sex. Looking in those eyes, Gen knew she was more than just pussy to him. More than just magic or skill or art.

He wanted her, just her. All of her.

And she wanted him right back. Not just the physical power of the magic, or the wit and intelligence, but Kurt. Just Kurt. All of Kurt.

She felt the brush of fur against her chest again, and knew Stoli wasn't just a dangerous complication or a possible threat, but as much a part of him as that intelligence and courage. A part that made him even more than he would've been otherwise. He and his tiger formed a whole greater than either of them was separately.

Just as she and Kurt were more together.

He lowered himself over her, bracing on hands and knees, those broad shoulders and glowing eyes filling her vision.

She reached down his body, stroking along his ribs with one hand, and down his back with the other. Kurt's eyes slid closed, and he chuffed -- that warm tiger sound of greeting and affection.

He bent down to kiss her again, magic and tongue swirling, until Genevieve felt like a leaf floating on currents of pleasure. His cock pressed against her, and she rolled her hips against him, caressing it with her body.

The air rumbled: Stoli again. Kurt started nibbling his way down the length of her jaw as his big hands cupped her breasts.

"Let me be on top!" she gasped. "I want to play too…"

He laughed, the rolling chuckle vibrating against her chest. "If you insist."

Kurt rolled over onto his back as Gen sat up with a wicked surge of anticipation. She swung a leg over his hips and settled down on top of him, trapping his thick cock under her ass. She grinned down at him, savoring the moment.

Deliberately, he slid both big hands under his head, making impressive biceps bunch. Noticing the direction of her fascinated gaze, he flexed first one arm and then the other, then gave her a wicked waggle of the eyebrows. "Like what you see?"

Genevieve sat back on her heels, and rolled her shoulders back to thrust out her breasts. "Do you?"

His gaze locked on the soft globes and darkened until there was only a thin ring of gold around each pupil. "Oh, baby, do I."

* * *

Kurt caught his breath at the sensual anticipation in her smile. "Good." She raised herself off his aching cock and began to work her way downward. Her slick little pussy slid down his length. He grew even harder, something he wouldn't have even thought possible.

As she moved downward, she braced her weight on her elbows. Lowering her head, she extended her tongue to give herself room to paint elegant little sigils over his skin. Each one seemed to stroke over his magic as much as his body, and he caught his breath.

A week ago, he would never have allowed a witch to work magic on him in any way, shape or form. Especially here, where the spell she'd already laid made her magic even stronger.

This wasn't something they had to do to stop terrorists and save lives. This was all for his pleasure -- and hers. And that was all.

He knew Genevieve now, every bit as well as he knew Stoli or the men he'd fought and bled with in the wars.

And he knew that he loved her.

So now he lay under her as she worked her magic with tiny licks and swirls of her tongue, her hair tumbling over his body in cool copper curls that rolled over him like foam. He stroked one hand through those curls, feeling them spring and coil as he pulled at them gently.

With the other hand, Kurt traced the surprisingly strong muscle of her narrow shoulders. His gaze slid up to her ass, its sweet double curve thrust in the air by her kneeling position, pale in the light of the moon.

In the depths of his mind, Stoli growled possessive satisfaction. The tiger wanted to mount her, wanted to drive his cock into her.

And fuck and fuck and fuck.

Humans like to take their time, he told the tiger. *Make it last.*

Stoli's reply was an impatient growl.

Then Gen stopped to bite his belly button with her sharp little teeth, not quite hard enough to sting. She raked her nails up the line of his ribs, and the ticklish sensation made him twist and growl. "Watch it, woman!"

Blue eyes flashed up at him, glowing with her magic. "Well," she purred, "Is the big bad Feral ticklish?"

He narrowed his eyes at her in a mock glare. "Are you?"

She pretended to pout. "You're no fun." Then she turned her head and closed her mouth over the head of his cock.

He gasped. "You are."

She pulled that talented mouth off of him. Blue flashed at him as she smiled. "I live to serve." Her tongue did something to the curve of his dick, just a tiny little design, something intricate and swirling.

It grabbed him by the magic and reached all the way down into his balls.

He threw back his head with a gasp. "Don't… Do that! Or this is going to take… A lot less time than either of us wants!"

"Wouldn't want that." She released him, and he damn near moaned in loss.

Until she blew a little puff of breath across the head of his cock and the cool sensation made his cock throb all over again. One small hand closed around his balls, caressing gently.

He waited, breath caught, for her to do that thing she did with her tongue again. Instead she turned her head and pressed a gentle bite to one of the tight tendons of his leg. Slowly, she licked another little symbol and he gasped.

Okay, he understood why the one on his cock felt like that. But that was his thigh.

Gen drew another design further down his leg, then switched to the other to nibble and taste and draw spells.

Kurt's spine bowed and sweat broke out across his forehead. He clenched his fists in the thick fabric of the blanket they lay on, fighting desperately to hang on. She switched her attention to his cock again, licking those intricate designs. And with each one, the connection between her magic and his intensified.

Stoli yowled. An image flashed through his head -- tigers coupling, the male gripping the back of the female's neck tenderly in his jaws like a tigress carrying a cub.

Not yet. His knuckles grew white as his grip tightened on the blanket.

* * *

Genevieve felt Kurt's big body strain upward under hers. She could sense his desperate struggle to control his need. The air rumbled around them, and she suspected he didn't even realize he was doing it.

Then again, he probably wasn't. *I seem to be in a ménage à trois with a tiger.* Which was something no sane woman would really want to do; tiger dicks were barbed.

And yet she wasn't worried in the least. She was too damn busy enjoying herself. Loving the sensation of power and pleasure she felt from having such powerful creatures so thoroughly in her control. It was wicked and kinky, and she adored every minute.

Closing her eyes, Gen contemplated the spell she was working. Glowing shapes revolved just over Kurt's body. Sigils not to control him, not to force anything on him that he didn't want, but to let their pleasure intensify each other's.

Hers had always been a solitary magic, but it wasn't now. Now the pleasure she gave him was hers too.

But the spell needed something else. Genevieve studied the glow through her closed lids, conscious of the magic rolling around them, of tiger eyes watching her.

She balanced over him, took his big shaft in hand, and positioned him against her pussy. Then slowly, carefully, Gen sank down, impaling herself by delicious fractions.

Kurt arched his hips, thrusting upward, deepening the penetration. The spell she'd cast sprang to life, lighting up every sigil she'd painted on his body. The glow rolled over him in a rainbow wave that spread into her hands, her pussy, radiating up her body, glowing brighter and brighter. Until... Magic detonated through them in a blinding explosion of light and life. Genevieve scented something wild and dark, heard Kurt's bellow as his golden eyes blazed up into hers.

Feeling his love for her, she showed him hers in all of its delicious intensity. Soul fused with soul, fused with soul, in a three-part chain reaction even more intense than their bond. The climax hit her hard, a furious surge of energy and magic. The orgasm shuddered through every fiber, shaking her until she lost it and screamed. And screamed, the sound blending with Kurt's bellow and Stoli's roar.

All around them, it seemed every cat in the park roared, screamed, screeched, a shattering feline chorus.

For a moment they both went blind, senses lost in whiteout, two humans and a tiger fused into one mind, one soul.

She collapsed over him, and they curled their arms around each other, sweating, hearts hammering in unison. They said the words in chorus: "Marry me."

And in chorus, "Yes!"

Kurt laughed and hugged her close. "You know, we can't keep doing the tandem thing. People are going to be creeped out."

"Screw them. Let them get their own tiger."

They clung to one another while their breathing eased.

At last Kurt murmured, "I'm going to have my hands full reorganizing BFS without Dad." Genevieve knew he still had grieving to do.

Listening to his heartbeat, she smiled, slow and peaceful. "I'll help."

He turned his head to study her. "But you've got your art."

"I can do both. After what we've done, we can handle anything." She cuddled closer to him.

Which was when a snippet of a familiar song floated over the fence. "*Tale as old as time, Song as old as rhyme, Beauty aaaand the Beeeast…*"

Kurt lifted his head. "Dave, damn it!"

A rimshot sounded, followed by chuffing tiger laughter.

Angela Knight

New York Times best-selling author Angela Knight has written and published more than sixty novels, novellas, and ebooks, including the Mageverse and Merlin's Legacy series. With a career spanning more than two decades, Romantic Times Bookclub Magazine has awarded her their Career Achievement award in Paranormal Romance, as well as two Reviewers' Choice awards for Best Erotic Romance and Best Werewolf Romance.

Angela is currently a writer, editor, and cover artist for Changeling Press LLC. She also teaches online writing courses. Besides her fiction work, Angela's writing career includes a decade as an award-winning South Carolina newspaper reporter. She lives in South Carolina with her husband, Michael, a thirty-year police veteran and detective with a local police department.

Angela at Changeling: changelingpress.com/angela-knight-a-26

Changeling Press E-Books

More Sci-Fi, Fantasy, Paranormal, and BDSM adventures available in e-book format for immediate download at ChangelingPress.com -- Werewolves, Vampires, Dragons, Shapeshifters and more -- Erotic Tales from the edge of your imagination.

What are E-Books?

E-books, or electronic books, are books designed to be read in digital format -- on your desktop or laptop computer, notebook, tablet, Smart Phone, or any electronic e-book reader.

Where can I get Changeling Press E-Books?

Changeling Press e-books are available at ChangelingPress.com, Amazon, Apple Books, Barnes & Noble, and Kobo/Walmart.

Changeling Press, LLC

ChangelingPress.com